Praise for

JUDY BAER

and her novels

"[A] cute continuation of Baer's *The Whitney Chronicles*
revisits Whitney and her husband, Chase."
—*Romantic Times BOOKreviews* on *The Baby Chronicles*

"Fans of Baer's *The Whitney Chronicles* will enjoy
this lighthearted Christian romance."
—*Publishers Weekly* on *Norah's Ark*

"*Million Dollar Dilemma* is sophisticated in
structure and story, but sweet and accessible."
—NBC10.com

"Just like Bridget [Jones]...chick-lit readers will appreciate
all the components of a girl-friendly fantasy read.
Quirky characters...flashes of genuine humor keep even
the poignant segments...from becoming too heavy.
The results are genuinely enjoyable."
—*Publishers Weekly* on *The Whitney Chronicles*

"Baer has created fascinating characters with real-life
problems and triumphs that show readers the details of
living out faith daily. Full of humor and infused with God's
truths, this book will allow readers to come away with a happy
heart and incre___ __ __th."
—*Romantic Times*
The Whitney

Books by Judy Baer

Steeple Hill

The Whitney Chronicles
Million Dollar Dilemma
Norah's Ark
The Baby Chronicles
Oh, Baby!

Love Inspired

Be My Neat-Heart #347
Mirror, Mirror #399
Sleeping Beauty #415

OH, BABY!

JUDY BAER

Steeple
Hill
Café™

Published by Steeple Hill Books™

STEEPLE HILL BOOKS

ISBN-13: 978-0-373-78619-0
ISBN-10:   0-373-78619-0

OH, BABY!

Copyright © 2008 by Judy Duenow

All rights reserved. Except for use in any review, the reproduction
or utilization of this work in whole or in part in any form by any
electronic, mechanical or other means, now known or hereafter
invented, including xerography, photocopying and recording, or in
any information storage or retrieval system, is forbidden without
the written permission of the editorial office, Steeple Hill Books,
233 Broadway, New York, NY 10279 U.S.A.

This is a work of fiction. Names, characters, places, and incidents are
either the product of the author's imagination or are used fictitiously,
and any resemblance to actual persons, living or dead, business
establishments, events, or locales is entirely coincidental.

This edition published by arrangement with Steeple Hill Books.

® and TM are trademarks of Steeple Hill Books, used under license.
Trademarks indicated with ® are registered in the United States Patent
and Trademark Office, the Canadian Trade Marks Office and in other
countries.

www.SteepleHill.com

Printed in U.S.A.

For Connie G. and Nancy L., because you're special.

Acknowledgment

· Thanks to doula Tracy Repasky for her input.

Jesus called a small child over to him and put the child among them. Then he said, I assure you, unless you turn from your sins and become as little children, you will never get into the kingdom of heaven. Therefore, anyone who becomes as humble as this little child is the greatest in the kingdom of heaven.

—*Matthew* 18:2-4

BIRTH PLAN, *Couple #1—*

This birth plan is intended to make known our preferences and desires for and during the birth of our child as long as it is a normal, uncomplicated birth.

- I want to move around and change position during labor.

- I prefer dim lights and soft, calming music.

- I prefer intermittent fetal monitoring to continuous monitoring.

- Offer medication only if I am uncomfortable.

- I want my baby placed on my stomach immediately after delivery.

- I would like my husband to cut the cord.

- I want to breast-feed in the recovery room. Do not offer my baby a bottle, even of glucose water.

- Do not offer the baby a pacifier.

- I want a video recording of labor and birth.

- I want my husband and doula present during labor and delivery.

BIRTH PLAN, *Couple #2*—

Assuming that we will have a normal, uncomplicated birth, this plan is intended to make our wishes known for and during the birth of our child.

- I want to be unconscious as much of the time as I can.

- Rap music. Definitely rap.

- Medication—as much and as fast as possible.

- And massage. I love massage.

- No interns, residents or other Lookie Lous.

- If my husband tries to use his video camera, I want him kicked out of the room.

- Don't offer my baby a pacifier to suck on. That's what thumbs are for.

- I want my husband and doula to be present during labor and delivery.

Chapter One

❧

"Be careful, Molly. Dr. Reynolds's bite is worse than his bark."

I spun around to see my friend Lissy Franklin hurry past me pushing a med cart. "Tiptoe softly," Lissy mouthed before turning into one of the birthing rooms on the third floor of the Bradshaw Medical Center.

I took a deep breath and recalled all I'd heard about Dr. Reynolds in the few short weeks he's been at Bradshaw General. It isn't pretty, at least not from my professional perspective.

He's a great ob-gyn physician, no doubt about that. His reputation preceded him from his former position at a large hospital in California. He's only been practicing medicine in the Twin Cities of Minneapolis-St. Paul for three months and already women are booked weeks in advance to be his patients. I, however, hadn't had a client who was his patient until today.

He's cute, too. Gorgeous, actually, with dark hair, impossibly blue eyes and a trim physique that, it's rumored, comes from running and working out two hours a day. Where a doctor gets time like that, I don't know, but maybe it helps take the edge off his temper. It's his personality that gets low points from all the nurses. He demands perfection and settles for nothing less. Felicity, or Lissy as I usually call her, says he can make them cry with a look.

Maybe not all the rumors are true. Fortunately, at least one of my personal experiences with him has belied that opinion.

"I'm so glad you agreed to come to this visit with me," new mother Tiffany Franks had told me several weeks ago as we sat together in the waiting room of her pediatrician's office. "I didn't want to go to the baby's first doctor visit alone. My husband said he couldn't take time away from work and no one else was available. I'm still so nervous with the baby." The baby in question was a solid sleepy lump in my lap, hardly a reason for Tiffany's anxiety.

A week or two of experience would resolve that. "The doctor will tell you little Max looks great and you will feel a hundred percent better in no time."

We were examining Max's chins—all four of them—when a man strode into the office and up to the receptionist's desk. "Is Dr. Harley in?"

The receptionist looked up at him and her eyelashes began to flutter like hummingbird wings. "Why…uh…who?"

"Dr. Harley," the insanely handsome Dr. Reynolds said. "Your boss?"

"Oh, yes." She blushed. "Do you have an appointment?"

"Do I look like I should?" he snapped impatiently as he opened his hands to show that there was no baby in them.

His legs, however, told a different story. A blond toddler with lemonade curls and sapphire-blue eyes had glommed onto his left leg. She held her teddy bear in one hand and clung to his calf with the other. On his right leg, a little boy proceeded to run a Matchbox car up and down as if his expensive trousers were a vertical racetrack. Two or three other children were creeping closer to get a good look at the man.

"I've never seen anything like it!" Tiffany whispered. "He's like the Pied Piper. The children don't seem to have any fear of him at all."

He appeared accustomed to being a human jungle gym.

"I'm Dr. Reynolds," he told the starstruck receptionist. "We'll be working closely since I deliver babies and he picks up where I leave off. I need to talk with him." His words were clipped.

"Of course. I'll just…" The woman's voice trailed off. She seemed to have lost track of her job description under his expectant and impatient gaze.

"Now."

That woke her up. She jumped to her feet and trotted toward the examining rooms.

As she did so, Dr. Reynolds picked up the blond cherub. "Hi, baby girl. How are you?"

The child gurgled gleefully and patted his cheeks with her little palms. "Where's your mommy?"

A young woman in jeans stood up and came forward.

"She's beautiful," he said as he handed her the child.

The woman flushed with pleasure. Dr. Reynolds might have said more, but the little boy with the toy car held his arms out to be picked up.

"He's a kid magnet," Tiffany whispered. "They aren't the least bit afraid of approaching him even though he snapped at the receptionist. Remarkable."

I'd thought of the incident several times since. Dr. Reynolds has subsequently put a number of Bradshaw employees in their places for minor infractions and he has the personnel tiptoeing on eggshells. What did little kids know about him that the staff didn't?

As I pondered the question, a nurse's aide walked by. Her eyes were wide.

I caught her arm. "What's going on?"

"Dr. Reynolds, that's what. He just kicked everybody out of the birthing room because they were in the way. He said no one but the baby's father could stay. The family is up in arms, and he won't budge. He's stubborn, that one."

She looked at me appraisingly. "All I can say is that I'm glad I'm not you. When you come in with one of your clients, he's going to chew you up and spit you out."

That's not a rosy prospect. The kid thing at the pediatrician's office must have been an anomaly. Too bad.

What is a driven man like that going to do with me, an innocent doula, whose client unfortunately insists her baby be born at this hospital, with this attending physician? Bradford is a private hospital that hasn't experienced a lot of birthing coaches in the past, and from what I've heard of Dr. Reynolds, that pattern won't be changing anytime soon. I'm not too eager to be the bomb-sniffing dog who is first to go in and check for booby traps.

So far I've chalked his negativism toward my profession up to lack of sleep, pressure and the fact that he's not yet settled into the routine at the hospital, but those justifications are wearing thin.

I walked into my client's room. Brenda Halbert's face cleared and her shoulders relaxed, but she still kept her telephone to her ear. She patted her belly, which looked like a gigantic haystack hovering under the bedding.

"You have *got* to cover for me on the Smyth case. We were supposed to meet today at three, and there's no way I'll make it." She scowled at the response from the other end of the line. "I'm having a baby, not getting my hair done! It's not as if you can expect me to drop by the hospital and then hurry back to work. Besides, you'll do a great job. It's just a deposition, after all, but we can't take any chances...."

She gestured at me to sit down and mouthed, "I'll be off in a minute."

I see more and more women already in the hospital tying up loose ends so they can have a baby without worrying their cell phones might ring during delivery. Well, maybe it's not *that* bad, but it is getting ridiculous. More than once in my acquaintance with Brenda, I've feared she'd bring a briefcase to the delivery. Then I glanced around the room and spotted a suspicious looking attaché case in the corner. Oh, my.

"There you are, Molly Cassidy." She greeted me as if I were the one who'd been on the phone. "I don't want to do this without you, you know."

The room was sunny and welcoming. The necessary medical equipment for a healthy birth was still stashed away behind closed doors. The room looked more like a comfortable efficiency apartment than the delivery room it would become. Bradshaw is known for its upscale amenities. I vaguely wished my own house looked this good.

"No need to worry about that." I plumped the pillows behind her back and handed her fresh ice chips. I felt honored to be trusted by a woman who, in her ordinary, everyday life is a highly capable trial attorney. "I'm stuck to you like glue unless you tell me otherwise."

She smiled beatifically at me and leaned back against the pillows. That lasted for only a moment before she began chuffing and huffing like the Little Engine That Could.

"Another contraction?" I moved closer to put a comforting hand on her arm. "Focus, just focus."

She glared at the gigantic orange lollipop I'd taped to the wall on the other side of the room, concentrating so deeply on the brightly colored sucker that nothing else mattered but her breath and the baby preparing to be born.

I love my job. Being a professional labor assistant is the greatest occupation in the world. Better even than my former occupation as a preschool teacher, which was a pretty exciting and entertaining job. Talk about never knowing what will happen next! I always kept a change of clothes in my car while I was teaching because I never knew when I was going to be splatter painted, thrown up on or hugged repeatedly by little ones with sticky hands.

As a doula I provide emotional support, loving touch and comfort to a woman in childbirth. It is the best of both worlds. Not only do I get to soothe and cheer for the mom, I am present for the miracle of birth. I'm useful, too. Having a doula present at birth tends to result in shorter labors, fewer complications and less requests by the mother for pain medications.

That's why it puzzles me that Dr. Reynolds is rumored to be so against doulas and barely tolerates medical midwives. Gossip has it that he came to this post saying he wanted as few people as possible involved with his patients' births and has so far discouraged clients from hiring the likes of me. Most doctors don't pay much attention to who is there to support the mothers as long as they aren't causing trouble. Reynolds, however, appears ready to campaign actively against my profession.

It's no wonder I'm nervous. In such a state, Lissy's warning did not help one bit.

He can't do much about it if a mother requests a doula in her birth plan, but he certainly doesn't encourage anyone to do so. A birth plan is devised by a mom and her husband to let their preferences for their labor and delivery be known in order to make it the experience they want. It's not guaranteed to work out exactly as planned—babies choose to come when and where they want and come in very small and very large sizes, both of which may change the birth plan in a heartbeat. Still, it allows the people supporting the parents to know their ideal and to strive for it.

It also makes the new parents feel heard. I insist on having scrambled eggs when I eat breakfast in a café, not over easy, not poached. If I'm that careful to express my needs about something as simple as eggs, surely I should get some input on one of the most momentous days of my life.

My own grandmother thinks it's ridiculous, but she's of the "just wake me up when it's over" school. To each her own.

His "bite is worse than his bark." That doesn't bode well for me or my dream of introducing an actual doula-and-parent-education program into Bradshaw General. Obviously his bark is plenty nasty unless one is under four years old. Then he's putty in your hands.

"Is Dr. Reynolds here?" Brenda wondered impatiently. "I thought he would have been in to check on me by now." Ever the professional, she had no doubt worked out a schedule of her own. I just hope she hasn't made any appointments for tomorrow.

"He's in the building."

"Don't you just love him?" she asked as another contraction subsided. "He is so adorable."

"Adorable?" I'd never heard him described like that. Abhor-able, maybe, or just plain horrible. Never adorable.

"Actually, I've never worked with him before. Bradshaw General hasn't seen as many doulas as some of the other hospitals." Although Bradshaw is one of the smaller private hospitals in the city, it is also one of the best. "Usually Dr. Reynolds doesn't recommend doulas to his patients."

Brenda waved a dismissive hand. "That's only because he's so protective of us. He says he doesn't want anyone around who might disrupt the labor and delivery. My friend Sheila had a baby here last month, and she couldn't say enough good things about him. He's a bit of a fanatic about it, but I told him that there'd be *no* labor and delivery at this hospital for me if I couldn't have you, so he gave in."

So that's how I'd gotten here. It wouldn't make me any more welcome in Dr. Reynolds's eyes, I'm afraid. I might as well add to my business card

Molly Cassidy, Certified Doula,
Nuisance, Troublemaker and
Unwelcome Guest.

Oh, well, women have crossed picket lines, gone to the North Pole in dogsleds, climbed Mount Everest and flown into outer space. I can certainly attempt to convince Dr. Reynolds that he is mistaken not to welcome doulas. Of course, heroic things always come at a cost.

Feeling very much like Amelia Earhart leading the way for other women and well aware I might crash and burn for the sake of those who followed, I offered Brenda a massage and hoped this baby would be born so smoothly and quickly that Dr. Reynolds didn't have time to notice me.

That was, of course, not to be.

At 2:00 p.m. Brenda's husband, Grant, arrived from the airport. He'd taken the first plane he could catch from Madrid where he'd been shepherding a group of students from a local Spanish immersion school. He came in looking tired but excited.

"Did I make it?"

His wife gave him a don't-you-ever-speak-to-me-again look and started her choo-choo-train imitation again.

"Just in time. Her contractions are coming close together."

He flopped onto the chair. "We were scheduled to leave Madrid tomorrow but I was lucky to catch an early plane back."

His wife was mumbling under her breath. I didn't tell him that she was muttering things like "should have stayed in Spain" and "you'll never touch me again." That's another wonderful thing about childbirth. It's energetic, strenuous, exhausting, painful—and completely forgettable once you have a baby in your arms. He would be back in her good graces again when they heard that first beautiful cry.

Within moments of Brenda's husband's appearance and her wishing a plague upon his head—which many women seem to do in the last stages of birth—Dr. Reynolds arrived.

He entered so regally and with so much confidence that I almost stood up and saluted.

I've always thought a doctor in a tie and lab coat is attractive, and Dr. Reynolds is no exception. In fact, he may be the standard to which other docs should aspire. His tailored trousers were navy, his shirt white, crisply starched. His dark hair has a natural curl but was combed into submission except for a naughty cowlick at the crown of his head. His eyes are a deep, devastating blue and fringed with short black lashes. A charming smile, too. It's no wonder women drive many miles to his office. The scenery alone is worth the trip.

Then my attention fell on his tie. I blinked twice, thinking my eyes were deceiving me. But no, there *was* actually a sea of little faces staring back at me.

Brenda noticed, too. "Your tie, it's…full of babies."

He glanced down at his chest. "My former nurse made it. She used to give me one for Christmas every year. It's a collage of pictures of babies I've delivered. She had the photos transferred onto fabric."

Aww… How can I be upset with a man who loves babies enough to wear a tie like that?

"I see things are progressing nicely."

Brenda stared fixedly at the lollipop and panted heavily. "Nicely for who?" she muttered through gritted teeth. I turned away to hide the grin teasing the corners of my mouth.

Grant reached out to pat his wife's hand. Her eyes widened. "Don't touch me," she snapped. "Only Molly touches me." It wasn't so much a statement as a snarl.

I winced as everyone's attention turned to me. So much for staying in the background and not causing trouble.

Those blue eyes were suddenly cold as the polar ice cap.

"So this is the doula." Dr. Reynolds's voice was flat and hostile. He might as well have said, "So this is the virus you've been talking about."

"Ms…." He waited for me to fill in the blank.

Our previous encounters hadn't even registered with him. Maybe I *can* dislike a guy secure enough to wear babies on his tie.

"Cassidy, Molly Cassidy. How do you do, Dr. Reynolds. It's a pleasure to meet you."

"Yes, I suppose it is." He looked at me frostily. "Well, just as long as you stay out of the way." Then he dismissed me completely despite the fact that Brenda was hanging on to my hand for dear life.

That went swimmingly, I thought, and turned back to Brenda, praying that not only would this birth be smooth and successful, but also that the chilly Dr. Reynolds wouldn't toss me out on my ear.

"Why is this taking so long?" Brenda whined a half hour later. Everything seemed to have ground to a halt laborwise. "Doesn't this child have any sense of time?"

"They usually don't come out with a degree in time management," Dr. Reynolds said calmly. "Or even a wristwatch." He'd remained surprisingly close to the labor room, even staying to talk football with Grant and baby names with Brenda.

"Make something happen, will you?" Brenda, like many lawyers, was not accustomed to letting nature takes its course.

"It is happening," Reynolds said with composure as he studied the printout from the fetal monitor. "Just more slowly than you'd like." His unruffled presence spoke volumes. Even though he didn't want me here, I felt better knowing that Brenda was in his hands. He is an approach/avoidance kind of guy—babies on his tie and fire in his eyes.

She cast her gaze around the room and it landed on me. "Then *you* do something, Molly."

"I can read to you."

Brenda's expression grew peevish. "Sing."

"You have got to be kidding!" her husband, Grant, bleated, but she stared him down.

Dr. Reynolds turned away and I could see the smirk on his otherwise gorgeous features.

"Show tunes."

My mouth worked but nothing came out.

"Brenda," I finally managed, "I don't know any show tunes."

"You're a doula," Dr. Reynolds interrupted. "I thought you do 'anything' for a client."

"That's not what I meant…."

They both stared at me. Brenda looked expectant; Reynolds, maddeningly amused.

If I did it, I'd make a fool of myself. If I didn't, well, Brenda would be unhappy and Reynolds would have more fuel for the fire.

Never let it be said I don't stand up to a challenge. Unfortunately I've never been one to actually memorize all the words to any song except for a couple, and they weren't show tunes.

"'The farmer in the dell, the farmer in the dell, hi-ho, the dairy-o…'"

Later, Lissy and I recapped the delivery.

"You mean he actually said that? 'Stay out of the way?' What did your client think of that?" Lissy slathered peanut butter onto a stack of buttery crackers and ate them one by one.

"She had a lot more to worry about than my feelings. She was the star of the show and performed heroically. Anyone who gives birth to a ten-pound, one-ounce baby boy rocks in my book."

"Still, 'Stay out of the way,' just like that? What a—"

"Don't say it," I warned. "Just because Reynolds doesn't like doulas, it doesn't mean he isn't a good doctor. Frankly, after watching him in action, I think he's a great doctor. He has so much compassion for his patients that it practically oozes out of every pore. He was gentle, kind, patient, encouraging and supportive, all necessary things when a mother is giving birth to a baby the size of my bowling ball."

"You're defending him?"

"He didn't kick me out of the hospital."

"I've heard he's campaigning with the hospital board to limit the number of people in a birthing room. Everyone reads that to mean that he doesn't want birthing coaches or anyone but spouses or the very closest family involved."

"Maybe I showed him that it can be a good thing." I cleared my throat. "Unless he didn't like my singing."

"Your singing? I thought you were at a birth, not the opera."

"It was totally embarrassing," I admitted, "but Brenda heard me humming once and told me I had a pretty voice. I never dreamed she'd demand that I *sing* to her during delivery."

"No kidding? You *sang* this baby into the world?"

"If I'd been that baby, I would have hung on to my mother's rib cage and refused to come out after listening to me for five minutes. My repertoire is limited. My mind went blank, and all I could remember was the theme song from *The Brady Bunch,* 'Farmer in the Dell,' 'Jesus Loves Me' and 'How Great Thou Art.' Brenda enjoyed it, but Dr. Reynolds's jaw was twitching by the fourth or fifth time through 'and the mouse took the cheese.'" I shrugged. "But whatever a client wants, including distraction, she gets."

"When I have a baby I want you to be my doula," Lissy said. "And I want you to start learning words to new songs right away. I would not deliver a baby to the theme song from *The Brady Bunch.* Do something more contemporary, will you? Or show tunes like the soundtrack from *Les Mis* or *Phantom.*"

Lissy washed down her peanut butter crackers with milk from my refrigerator and started to dig in my cupboards for candy. She's as comfortable here as she is in her own home. Lissy and I have known each other for years. We met in an exercise class and bonded because we were the only two that had actually come to exercise and not to meet men. She and I in our ponytails and sweats had stood out in a room full of beautiful women in Danskin with full face makeup and hairdos sprayed so as not to move even during tae bo. After class, while all the others mobbed the instructor, a hunky guy with protruding veins and bulging muscles, to ask questions and to get a closer look, Lissy and I went to the juice bar and drowned our sorrows in chocolate-banana smoothies. We've been friends ever since.

Lissy is a nurse at Bradford Medical Center and the one who actually told me what a doula was and suggested that I should become one.

"What do you think makes him that way?" I asked.

"Dr. Reynolds, you mean? I don't know. It's his particular hangup, I guess, the nobody-but-medical-people-present-during-birth thing. Too bad you're on the opposing team. I guess he can be really nice when he wants to be."

"Tell me about him." I didn't really care, but I didn't want Lissy to go home, either.

Two months ago I broke up with a fellow I'd been dating from church. To be truthful, the relationship was more serious on his side than it was on mine, but I do miss his company. Nights are longer without him to talk to on the phone or drop by.

It was for the best. Hank Marcus has a plan for his life. It includes a wife, which could have been me had I said yes, and a fast track in his business. He'd begged me to marry him and come with him to Mississippi where his company is opening a new plant. That was a huge part of the problem. My life plan does not currently include marriage or Mississippi. Although I miss Hank, I'm not devastated without him, either. When I marry, it will have to be to a man I refuse to live without. And that, I'm learning, may take some time to find. The prospects are dim right now, but I'm so busy it doesn't really matter.

"I don't know much about him. No one does. He keeps to himself. He's well respected in the medical community and when he speaks, people listen. The board is giddy with joy at having him here, of course. His patients love him and the nurses are scared of him because he is so meticulous and exacting. He spends almost no time in small talk with anyone. He leaves immediately after his work is complete and doesn't ever tell anyone where he is going or what he is doing. I've heard he has a child, a little boy. He's great with kids. I've seen him with the brothers and sisters of new babies. I've never heard anything about a wife, but who knows? He's certainly not telling."

"For not knowing anything about him, you seem to have quite a bit of information," I observed. I dug into the bag of chocolate chips Lissy brought to the table.

"People talk, I listen." Then she grew serious. "Listen, Molly, I really think that since you are the first doula ever to darken Dr. Reynolds's doorstep, so to speak, you should tread very carefully if you want him to give you his stamp of approval. He's got a lot of influence in this hospital."

"How did he get so powerful, anyway?"

Lissy looked at me, shocked. "You don't know?"

"Know what?"

"Bradshaw Medical Center. Dr. Everett Bradshaw?"

"Sure. He funded the hospital forty years ago. He was a relatively young man at the time. His picture is hanging in the front lobby where no one can miss it."

"Exactly. Dr. Reynolds is Clay *Bradshaw* Reynolds. His grandfather funded this hospital. If it weren't for the Bradshaw family, this facility wouldn't exist. When he moved here to be on staff, the buzz was that when he spoke, everyone was to listen."

My heart sank. He really could put the kibosh on my idea for a fledgling doula program at this hospital.

"He hasn't been as demanding as everyone expected," Lissy continued, "but he is fanatical about what happens to what he calls 'his' mothers. All I can say is, watch your step."

His mothers? And all along I'd thought they were *my* mothers.

Chapter Two

"How's my favorite Irish lassie?" Tony DeMatteo grinned at me and dangled a Snickers bar in front of my nose. "Want to share?"

"Of course I do, but only if you promise to quit calling me a lassie. I feel like you're talking to a dog every time you say it." I took a swipe at the candy bar, and he pulled it neatly away.

"That's the last thing you are, Molly." His dark brown eyes twinkled with warmth. "But a rose by any other name would smell as sweet."

Tony is the only male nurse on the ob-gyn floor, a Shakespeare buff and an incorrigible romantic. Combine that with his unquenchable enthusiasm for living, passion for good food and lots of fun and Tony is virtually irresistible. All the single women in the hospital are, or have been at one time or another, madly in love with Tony. He has a knack of dating and breaking up with women and leaving

them still loving him. He is a professional bachelor
and masterful at it. At one end of the spectrum,
Tony is the ultimate charmer. Dr. Reynolds, according to the hospital rumor mill, is the other. The men
at Bradford Medical Center run the gamut.

I love Tony, too, but as a friend. I might have succumbed to his charms myself if I hadn't watched
him sweep woman after woman off her feet and
then, after a few weeks or months, let her down
gently. It was easier, I decided, to go directly to
friendship with Tony. I'm glad I did. He might have
been harder to resist than Hank had he decided to
propose to me and move to Mississippi.

"I have Almond Joys in my locker," he whispered seductively. "An entire unopened bag of mini-
atures. Want to go to the cafeteria with me and eat
them with whole milk?"

"What are you trying to do, make me fat?" It's a
joke around the hospital that Tony can eat anything
and not gain an ounce. That's another reason I've
avoided a romance with Tony. The women who date
him usually gain ten to fifteen pounds during their
relationship.

"Why don't you ever fall subject to my charms?"
he asked conversationally as we walked toward the
lunch room.

"You're a slippery slope, Tony. I just don't get too
close to the edge."

He looked at me thoughtfully. "But you could be
coaxed a little nearer, couldn't you?"

I glared at him. "Don't get any ideas in your head about romancing me, big guy. I've got your number. You love women and you love dating. You just hate committing."

"Commitment. Such a problematic word." He sounded put-upon just saying it.

We entered the cafeteria and picked out our lunch. Cottage cheese and a pear for me, three slices of pizza, a strawberry shake and a Dove bar for Tony. Oh yes, and several Almond Joys—with milk.

"I just haven't found the right one yet, that's all. Once I do…" He gazed thoughtfully toward the large aviary outside the cafeteria's glassed windows. "'Journeys end in lovers meeting, every wise man's son doth know.'"

"What's the Shakespeare stuff, anyway? Why do you always quote it?"

He grinned. "I figured out by the time I was fifteen that girls love romantic junk, poetry, flowers, candy. I could get 'older' women, the seventeen- and eighteen-year-olds, to date me with that stuff."

It probably didn't hurt that you looked like a young Adonis, either, I thought.

"The unexpected part was that, while I was re- searching good pickup lines, I discovered I liked it—Shakespeare, Byron, Keats, Shelly." His eyes twinkled again. "Better yet, I found I couldn't go wrong with those guys."

"You are an incorrigible, totally irredeemable, unmitigated flirt."

He leaned back to look at me and put his hands behind his head. The fabric of his white uniform stretched tight over a great set of pectorals. "I know. Ain't it grand?"

Tony's gaze flickered from me to something just over my shoulder. I turned to see what had attracted his attention.

It was what—or rather, who—was attracting everyone's attention these days. Dr. Clay Reynolds.

"Have you worked with him yet?" I asked.

"He's a perfectionist," Tony said, "and a control freak during delivery."

"I just had my first experience with him."

"How'd it go?"

"I didn't feel very welcome. It probably didn't help that my client kept telling Dr. Reynolds that she wouldn't have been able to get through the delivery without me. She didn't exactly praise him for his part in it all. In fact, I think she included him with all the other men in the world who should be shot by a firing squad. You know how touchy these mothers get when they're dilated to nine. The birth went well, though."

"Maybe you'll grow on him," Tony said encouragingly. "You help with Lamaze classes here all the time, and the volunteer program at the free clinic would fall apart without you. He'll get used to you."

I could hardly disagree with Tony. He's fought some uphill battles himself as a male nurse in the utterly feminine obstetrics ward. His competence and professionalism ultimately win people over. I had to do the same.

Of course I'm hopeful for a little more than that, like a good working relationship and a shot at starting an agency and clearing house for doulas right here at Bradshaw General.

It was late by the time I got home. My German shepherd, Hildy, was standing, legs crossed, by the front door dying to get out. We took a quick run through the streets of my neighborhood, a quiet little area that is slowly and inexorably being absorbed into the city. It is still, however, a quaint and quiet haven for me to retreat to and regroup after a long, intense labor with one of my moms.

I live life simply. Home, family, friends and faith are what is important to me. Someday I want a family of my own, but until that happens, I live vicariously through my clients bringing new life into the world. Oh, yes, and animals. I adore animals.

Hildegard, Hildy for short, led me on a circuitous route through the neighborhood to sniff at fire hydrants, shrubs and a popular squirrel hangout before bringing me back to my front door. I put out her dog food and fresh water and walked through the house to my bedroom.

Knowing I wasn't alone in the house, I went looking for my other roommate. Geri usually hangs out in the sunroom when I'm not home. I found her there, looking out the window, dressed in her glitzy denim jacket studded with rhinestones.

"Bedtime, Geri."

She moved away from me.

"Come on, Geri, don't give me any trouble tonight. I'll help you take your jacket off." Feeling bone weary and ready for bed, I wasn't ready for an argument. Geri is a bit of a night owl. "You aren't going to a fashion show, you know."

She grunted in protest and planted her hefty backside on a floor pillow as if to say, "Make me."

"Let's take off the jacket."

Geri looked at me as if to say, "Who, *moi?*"

She can be so willful and obstinate sometimes—especially when I'm already exhausted. "Okay, you stubborn, vain, egotistical sow, I'll teach you!" And I lunged for her thinking I could wrestle her to the ground, but Geri squealed and escaped like the proverbial greased pig. She ran into the bathroom and skidded into the side of the bathtub.

Geranium is never very good on tile. Her little hooves just can't get a grip.

It's not every woman who owns a pig—or wants to—but I've never considered myself an ordinary woman.

Geranium was, for a time, a preschool mascot at the private school at which I taught. When I announced my resignation, the staff and children voted that Geranium should come with me, a bit of tender pork by which to remember them. This was much to the relief of the administration, who had been wondering how to break it to the kids that Geri's feed bill had been cut out of the budget.

Although my mother did become hysterical for a while upon learning her first grandchild was actually a potbelly pig, she's come to appreciate Geranium. Pigs are very smart. Geranium is capable of similar reasoning and mischief making to that of a four- or five-year-old child. She needs me. Having been a kindergarten teacher, I'm able to stay one step ahead of her most of the time.

I wrestled her out of her little denim jean jacket with the industrial snaps on the arms. Geranium loves her jacket. She's very vain and self-important for a pig.

Once she realized I wasn't going to back down, she willingly let me unsnap the jacket, and trotted outside through the pet door that leads to her sandbox-size litter box and her bed. Geranium is small, which is fortunate for me. She weighs about sixty-five pounds and stands just over a foot tall and approximately two feet long. Pigs are very compact and have hard bodies, so Geri actually takes up very little space—not much more than a large footstool. She's at least twenty pounds lighter than Hildy and has no tail to sweep everything off coffee tables. In truth, she's a lot easier to handle than Hildy, who, when I enter the front door, sometimes jumps up and puts her paws on my shoulders to lick my face.

That was another thing about Hank that made me know we'd never work out as a couple. He thought pigs belonged in pigpens in the state of Iowa and nowhere else on the planet. He's going to have a bad shock when he sees his first pig farm in Mississippi.

He also bought into all the clichés and fallacious stigmas about pigs, and wouldn't be convinced that the term "dirty as a pig" is pure falsehood. Pigs are very clean animals if not forced to live in untended stys. In fact, even under those conditions, a pig will use only one corner of the pigpen as a toilet. It's where they're forced to live, not the pigs themselves, that is to blame for the phrase "stink like a pig."

Pigs have no odor. I tried to make Hank smell Geranium once to find that out for himself, but he refused. Yet another chink in our relationship.

The other public relations problem pigs have is that they like to roll in the mud. They don't like being warm and can actually get sunburned if they're exposed too much. Therefore they roll in the mud to cool off and keep the sun off their skin. Does anyone criticize a woman for using sunblock? I think not.

The telephone rang just as Hildy and I were settling in for the night. It was Mandie, a young single mother whose parents had just hired me to be her doula. She was crying.

"Molly?"

"What is it, honey?"

"I'm so scared. I went to the doctor today, and he says that I could give birth any time now. I don't want to give birth, Molly." She hiccuped tearfully. "I want it to stop!"

It's a little late for that now. Tactfully I didn't point that out.

"Things are going to be fine," I assured her. "You're a healthy young woman. You have a wonderful doctor to care for you, and I'm here for you, too."

"I'm not a woman, I'm just a kid!"

Truer words were never spoken. Babies having babies. I see far too much of it and it breaks my heart. But it's not my place to judge. I'm called to be salt and light to these girls, Jesus embodied in me.

"How do you feel?" I asked. "Are you having pain?"

"No. I just keep thinking…"

"How about if I talk you through some deep-breathing exercises? It might be time to give your brain a rest."

I stayed on the line until Mandie was calmer and ready to sleep.

Hildy snuffled wetly and shifted so that her legs were rigid, managing to take up two-thirds of the mattress. I could hear Geranium rooting around in her pen for nonexistent truffles and the tick of my grandparents' old clock in the living room. All was right with the world.

The telephone rang at 8:00 a.m. I tried to ignore it and let my answering machine pick up, but then I remembered Mandie. She might be in labor.

"Hullo?" I snuffled into the phone, my voice scratchy from disuse.

"Wake up, sleepyhead! It's play day!" Lissy sounded annoyingly chipper.

Saturdays are always play days for Lissy. She tries to pack an entire week's worth of fun into eight or ten hours and always wants company doing it—me.

"I might have a baby coming today."

"Then we should go soon so we can get a few hours in before you have to be at work."

"I need to do laundry," I reminded her. "I've had a busy week."

"Nonsense. We'll just buy you new clothes. If you can't go two or three weeks without washing, you're definitely short."

"I thought we were going to a museum one day."

"Fine, be cerebral and dull. How about the Science Museum? That's my speed. They've got lots of dinosaurs."

"Do we need to borrow a child to go there?"

"Nah. We'll just pretend ours are already there, running around. That place is always stuffed with kids. You shop with me, I'll go to the museum with you. Deal?"

Why fight it? Lissy is a lot like Geranium and Hildy. It rarely pays to argue with hardheaded females.

Chapter Three

Of course Lissy had her way and I didn't. We went shopping.

Lissy pulled a navy-blue suit off the rack and waved it under my nose. "How about this? This would be great for church and it would subdue that red hair of yours."

"Why on earth would I want to do that?" I held up a broomstick skirt in all the colors of the rainbow. "What do you think of this?"

"It's a bad accident in the crayon factory. Too many colors."

I held it up and looked at myself in the mirror. My red hair was fighting against the bond of the braid I'd woven, and so a wild cloud of rusty red framed my face. The bright teal shirt I wore accented the giddy colors in the skirt.

"If that skirt could talk, it would say—" Lissy covered her ears "—too loud, turn down the volume!"

That helped me to make up my mind. I handed it to a hovering clerk. "I'll take it."

"She's a free spirit," Lissy muttered grimly, as if in apology for my fashion blunder. "I've been trying to tame her but it is like domesticating the wind."

"I think it's lovely," the clerk assured me. "Distinctive."

"See?" I hissed when the woman moved away. "Distinctive. Like me."

"I can't shop with you any longer," Lissy announced. "I'm having a color overload. Let's get something to eat."

That was fine with me. I'd rather eat than shop any day.

After we ordered lunch, Lissy sat back into the padded booth and studied me.

"How's The Project going?"

The Project. My big idea, my dream.

Maybe it has something to do with the fact that as a kindergarten teacher I used to like things orderly in my classroom. Everything had a place and that's where we kept it. Although I actually thrive in chaos at home—my arty side coming out, I suppose—I was very different at school, the only teacher at school who had a Rolodex and a tickle file to remind me of upcoming events. Things make sense to me when they're organized into groups. Snow pants go in closets, blocks go with blocks and crayons go into the crayon bins.

And doulas, I think, would fit nicely into an

agency where they are available and easy to find. When patients start asking questions about birthing assistants or coaches, I believe a doctor should be able to hand them a business card with the name of my big idea—Birthing Buddies—as I fondly refer to it, and allow women to research dozens of doulas before they pick the one best suited for them.

My biggest hurdle and one of the most important parts of the dream is to be an independent agency that has office space and headquarters within the facility. Just being under the Bradshaw Medical roof would be an amazing way to let people know we exist. They rent space to the people with coffee and snack carts on the main floor. Why not me?

Why they should oppose it, I can't imagine. Labors are shorter by twenty-five percent, and the use of C-sections, epidurals, forceps and medication drop significantly when doulas are involved. We also help the bonding process between mother and baby. When a laboring mother has someone mothering *her,* things simply go more smoothly.

"It's going to be an uphill climb. Worse, now that Dr. Reynolds is at the hospital. I suspect he will be opposed to a doula program, especially one offered in conjunction with the birthing classes with which I'm involved."

"Why Bradshaw General? Why not an independent office somewhere?"

"Because a gift was left to the hospital for the

express benefit of encouraging them to enhance a doula and midwife program."

"I heard something about that. Why? What happened?"

"Some wealthy grandparents watched their daughter breeze through her labor and delivery and credited it all to her doula."

"And that would be you?" Lissy asked suspiciously. "Why didn't you tell me until now? That's a huge affirmation to doulas everywhere."

"I was just doing my job. Apparently the woman had been very difficult prior to hiring me, that's all."

"You do much more than that," Lissy said. "I've had patients tell me that if they could have *one* person with them through labor and delivery, they'd pick their doula over their spouses, even over the doctor."

She eyed me thoughtfully. "So that buzz about the hospital getting some sort of gift *was* because of you. Impressive."

"It's not that big a deal." There's been more than one time in my life—and less stressful ones than giving birth—that I would have liked someone to watch over me, give me ice chips, rub my back and turn up the aromatherapy. "A doctor I met at another hospital while his own wife was giving birth encouraged me to pursue it. Dr. Chase Andrews seemed to think it would work."

"Then why don't you go to *his* hospital and ask if you can coordinate Doula Central there?"

"Bradshaw is the hospital that received the

money. I'd like to see it here. It's a five-minute drive from my house. I help Tony with classes here at Bradshaw and—" I hung my head, ashamed to admit I'd been snooping in the nooks and crannies of the hospital "—they have a couple of unused rooms right now. It would be easy to have something up and running there in no time."

"Bradshaw is a pretty staid private hospital," Lissy pointed out. "But it seems that agreeing to spend money already specified for a doula program wouldn't be that difficult. What is standing in your way now?"

"The new wrinkle is Dr. Clay Reynolds. Everyone defers to him, and I know he's opposed. He steamrolled right over me and my client. His form of medicine is 'my way or the highway.' There's no way he'll encourage this."

"Just the kind of guy that bothers you most." Lissy looked concerned. "Don't stir up any trouble, Molly. People love you and you have a great reputation, but if Bradshaw has to choose between you and their new golden-boy doctor, you know they won't choose you."

I know that all too well. It's just that I care so much about seeing this happen and I believe so completely in what doulas do. We make a difference.

"I've already spent way too much time trying to figure out what Clay Reynolds's problem is. It's getting boring."

"Yeah. What's not to like about birthing coaches? You'd think he'd like the idea of having someone in the room calming nervous mothers before they give birth. You'll just have to prove to him how indispensable you are."

"I'm as 'indispensable' as tissue paper as far as Reynolds is concerned. It's written all over his face."

"His very handsome face," Lissy corrected.

"When he looks at me it's as if he smells bad cheese or sour milk."

"Don't you think you're exaggerating just a little?"

I thought about my encounter with Dr. Reynolds on my way out of the hospital after Brenda's delivery. I was carrying my inflated exercise ball and CD player, equipment I use for my clients during labor. If I'd had a dirty pitchfork over my shoulder and the fragrance of eau de cow barn as my perfume, he wouldn't have looked any more distressed to see me. Surely my Birkenstocks hadn't been what pushed him over the edge.

"Don't worry. He'll loosen up."

"I'm not so sure. He's a throwback to the 1950s, as far as I'm concerned."

"What a shame. He's probably one of the best-looking men I've ever met." Then Lissy shrugged her shoulders and held out her hands, palms up. "But pretty is as pretty does, and this whole thing doesn't look all that attractive."

My cell phone rang and Lissy groaned. "Don't tell me our shopping trip is over."

I flipped open the phone. "Hello...."

"Hey, beautiful. Did you forget our date?"

"Tony? What are you talking about…?" I glanced at my wristwatch. "I'm sorry, I completely forgot. I'll be there as soon as I can."

"I'll hold the fort, but they will be wanting you."

I closed my phone. "Sorry, Lissy, I have to go. Tony's waiting for me at the free clinic. We volunteered to do a class for expectant moms today. I can't believe I forgot."

"It was that dumb skirt you bought," I heard Lissy mumble behind me. "All those colors made you go insane."

The free clinic is not much to look at but it serves the purpose. Built in the seventies, the rooms are small and sterile-looking with ugly tan-and-brown tile and white cinderblock walls. Still, it's clean, and the volunteers have hung brightly colored pictures on all the walls. In the pediatric area, there are bright, childlike drawings everywhere. The room in which Tony and I do our Lamaze classes has posters of babies in utero, showing the amazing growth from a few cells to a fully formed infant.

Tony had already set up the room for class and was standing, legs spread, knees locked and arms crossed over his chest, with his back to the room, staring out the window onto the street. He dipped his head in recognition as I moved to stand beside him but he didn't turn to look at me.

"You believe in God, right, Molly?"

"Of course. So do you."

Tony is from a large, boisterous family with a strong background of faith. That is one of the things that I enjoy most about him, his openness to conversation about faith. "Why would you ask?"

"Do you doubt Him sometimes?"

I took a sip from the cup of muddy coffee I'd poured upon entering. "I'm human, if that's what you mean. Sure I doubt…and question…and wonder… but I always come to the same conclusion."

"And that is?"

"That He's up there and I'm down here and He knows best."

"Yeah, that's what I think, too, but…"

"Did something happen to put you in this mood?"

"My older sister called this morning. She and her husband have been trying to get pregnant for nearly five years and they've finally decided to pursue adoption." His gaze locked on a boarded-up storefront across the street. "Why do some families get to experience a pregnancy and bring home a baby and others don't?"

"You know the scientific answers better than I do."

He looked at me despairingly.

"'Hope deferred makes the heart sick, but when dreams come true, there is life and joy,'" I murmured. "Proverbs 13:12."

"My sister and her husband are heartsick right now, that's for sure."

It's easy to move from optimistic and expectant

to despondent and give up hope when we don't get what we want. I have traveled that path plenty and I've only figured out one solution.

"I like to remind myself that hope is *deferred*. It's delayed, not *canceled* or *destroyed*."

"So you think that just because you don't get something right away, that doesn't mean you will never get it?"

"I may not get it in the form I expected, but I have to trust I'll get something better."

"When does 'life and joy' come, then?"

"The Old Testament saints waited a long time for Christ to come. That's what that verse talks about."

"My sister hasn't got that long."

"Sometimes God gives us something even better than what we think we want."

Tony looked irritated. "What's better than a baby?"

"You've got me there." I put my hand on his arm. "I don't know the answers, Tony. I doubt I even know the questions. Sometimes I just have to trust that things will work out. That's what God asks of us, after all."

I recalled a verse from Luke that I'd learned in Sunday School. "'Don't be afraid, little flock. For it gives your Father great happiness to give you the kingdom.'"

"I just wish He'd hurry up. My sister is going nuts."

"I can't do anything else but I can pray," I offered. "That's one thing I've had a lot of practice at."

A smile broke through, and the sparkle came back

into his eyes. "You're something else, Molly. I'm crazy about you." He wrapped his arms around my waist and swung me in a big circle. "If I ever *were* to settle down, it would be with someone like you."

That statement didn't even make me think twice. Tony will never be ready to settle down. He'll be flirting his way through the nursing home, making every woman there, no matter her age, wish they had a Tony in their life.

Chapter Four

"Now tell me exactly what a doula does."

Emily Hancock, a painfully well-dressed, worried-looking creature stared at me intently, as if I were planning to extract a wisdom tooth, not aid her in guiding a new child into the world. We sat in the highly polished stainless-steel kitchen of her three-story Tudor, looking out over gardens and grass manicured within an inch of its life.

"I know very little about this. Midwives, I'm familiar with, but doulas… They're new, aren't they?"

New? As in something developed recently to maintain new technology such as the latest generation of cell phones or MP3 players? Hardly. "A doula is actually a very old concept.

"*Doula* is a Greek word meaning a woman who serves other women." I tried to smile encouragingly at the nervous woman. "We use massage, aromatherapy, positioning and reflexology to make our clients comfortable during birth."

"I had no idea," Emily murmured approvingly.

"A doula's function is to be there for a mother in labor in any way she can, from ice chips to foot rubs, reading aloud to singing lullabies. During labor, your wish is my command."

"Nothing medical?"

I held up a hand as if to ward off a bad idea. "I always defer to medical personnel. I know how to stay out of the way when necessary. Women have even hired me to be in charge of their husbands so that they won't have to worry about them fainting during labor."

"There's no worry about that with my husband," she said wistfully. "He won't faint. If he's even there, that is. He's taking part in a mission trip to Guatemala about the time the baby is to be born. The trip has been in the works much longer than the baby, and he's been instrumental in the planning, so he's hoping to go and still get back in time for the birth."

Finally her shell cracked and tears sprang into her eyes. "What made me think it would be a good idea to have a baby when I'm well over forty? I should have known better."

"You aren't the first forty-year-old mother and you won't be the last. You are in wonderful shape, healthy and you've had an easy pregnancy so far. My mother had her last child at forty-two and she's absolutely fantastic. She took up golf last summer."

"Really?" Emily looked hopeful.

"I'm from a family of nine. My mother had a baby every two years for eighteen years. Her 'caboose' baby was born at forty-two." Poor little Kevin, I thought. Mother, when she called him the little caboose on a very long train, had never meant for the name to stick. At twenty, his nickname is still "Caboose." I know very few people outside our family who actually realize his name is Kevin. His girlfriend calls him Coby so maybe the next generation will eventually forget the nickname.

"Nine? Imagine." Emily appeared unable to grasp the concept.

"We did come one at a time, and we were small to begin with. Fortunately, my dad said that our house was made of rubber and that the walls could stretch to accommodate any number of children. Somehow he was right."

"No wonder you are in this business. You love children, don't you?"

"I do. I taught both preschool and kindergarten before becoming a doula. I can't get away from people under six years of age—or their mothers."

Emily looked at me thoughtfully. "Frankly, when I asked you here today to interview you, I really didn't plan to hire you. It was more to salve my curiosity, to leave 'no stone unturned' concerning my pregnancy. My doctor didn't recommend having a doula. In fact, he discouraged it rather vehemently."

I felt a knowing chill run through me.

"But I've changed my mind. I like you, Molly, and I like what you say a doula is and does." She gave a small, wry laugh. "And at my age, I need all the help I can get."

I drained my teacup before speaking. "Your physician wouldn't happen to be Dr. Clay Reynolds at Bradshaw Medical Center, would he?"

Emily looked surprised. "Yes, it is. How did you know?"

"I didn't. I just know that he's not a fan of having doulas—or anyone but medical personnel—around during a delivery. Lucky guess." *Or very unlucky.*

"He's a wonderful doctor," Emily said. "So compassionate and thorough. I know he is a bit old-fashioned when it comes to his mothers, but he'd do anything in his power to protect a woman or a child. A lot of women trust him implicitly."

There it was again, *his* mothers. I'm not sure I like anyone as proprietary about mothers as he is. Until he came along, they were mine, all mine.

"I had high hopes for Bradshaw," I admitted, "but now I think I'll have to turn my sights elsewhere."

Emily stood up to refill my teacup. Her body profile was slender but for the "baby bump" around her middle. She wore a black sleeveless knit top, trim khaki pants, casually expensive black heels and diamonds that would make the queen wince. She could have been taken for twenty-five instead of forty. "What do you mean?"

"Never mind, I shouldn't have said anything. Just a pipe dream."

"It's too late now. You've already started." She also refilled the plate of tender date cookies and rich macaroons.

"I have this vision," I admitted reluctantly, "of creating an agency through which mothers and doulas can connect. Somewhere an expectant mother can go to discover if a doula is right for her. Currently moms are referred to us by health nurses, nurse practitioners, doctors or by word of mouth from friends who've used a doula. Some doulas have formed small group associations in order to promote their practices, but I envision something more."

I was on a roll now, excited, like I am every time I think of what I'd like to have happen. "I want everyone to know what a doula is and how to hire one. I'd like to create an agency that not only has a roster of doulas but also educational programs and support groups about all things concerning mother and baby."

"It sounds like a wonderful idea. Why would you give that up?" Emily sat down, kicked off one shoe and tucked her foot beneath her leg.

"I'm not giving it up entirely, but I may have to give up on creating it at Bradshaw Medical Center. I'd love to start the program through a hospital. Because of Bradshaw's size, it would be a good place to begin a pilot program. They already have a free clinic in one of the more depressed neighborhoods so it would be a simple matter to add an agency like this. But now that Dr. Reynolds is head of the obstetrics department…"

Emily had an odd expression on her face as she patted my hand. "Don't worry about the hospital or Dr. Reynolds right now, my dear. That can be worked out. You did, after all, sell *me* on the value of a doula."

For no good reason that I could discern, Emily's words comforted me greatly.

After I left the Hancock home, I drove my red Volkswagen convertible to the Yarn Shack to buy what was, for me, almost better than chocolate or sleeping in late—baby yarn.

"Back already?" Matilda, a robust woman in her sixties, said when she saw me enter. "You knit faster than anyone else I know."

"Not really. I just buy yarn faster than anyone else you know." I headed straight for the soft pinks, blues, yellows and greens. "I want enough to knit a couple of baby hats."

"I've got something you'll like even better." Matilda dug beneath the counter and came up with a pattern book. "New hats. Look."

She opened the book to reveal a massively colorful jester's hat with six points and silver bells on the tip of each point. There was also a knitted stovepipe hat reinforced with a cardboard liner that looked like something the Mad Hatter might wear, and an alligator hat with its jaws open at the back of the wearer's head. "Anyone you know need a new hat?"

My weakness is hats, the louder and more garish the better. I make them for everyone I know. What's more, I insist they wear them. Poor Caboose, er, Kevin. Because he was the youngest, he got more of my hats than my other siblings. The boy wore my knitted hats in the shapes of animals or vegetables until junior high when I made him a hat that tied beneath his chin and had an elephant face and trunk on the back.

I gave up pressing him about it when he said he'd fear for his life in the boys' dressing room if he wore the hat to school. I gave it to my oldest brother, Mike's, son. He was three at the time and had less violent friends.

Crazy hats strike me as funny and lift my spirits. If everyone in the world wore a zany hat, we wouldn't take ourselves so seriously and news programs and political debates on television would be much more fun.

After purchasing the pattern book and yarn I needed, I drove toward Bradshaw Medical to meet Lissy and Tony and for lunch.

Everything about Bradshaw Medical is picturesque. The hospital sits on top of an undulating hill with a gradual slope. It was built by Everett Bradshaw in the sixties. Bradshaw had made his wealth early as a reconstructive cosmetic surgeon, and rumor has it that he'd felt compelled to "give back" to the community. Not a big hospital in size but very impressive in reputation, the facility has long since been a place where very public personalities go for treatment away from prying eyes. It had also been at Everett Bradshaw's suggestion that the free clinic had come into being. Other than Everett's grumpy grandson, a lot of good things are happening at Bradshaw Medical.

And not only that, they have a great cafeteria.

Lissy and Tony were already waiting for me.

"Where's your nurse's uniform?" I asked as I joined Lissy at a small round table.

"I'm already off for the day. I came in early to cover for someone. I changed out of my uniform so I'd be ready to rumble when you got here."

"I'm hardly in a 'rumbling' mood. I have chores to do at home."

"I know, I know, feed the livestock, slop the hogs…"

"I do not give Geranium 'slop' as you so crassly call it!"

"…paint a picture, knit a hat, live a horribly boring life…."

"Molly's not boring. She's the least boring person I know." Tony, looking dashing in pure white, leered at me. "Beautiful, too."

He put a tray on the table and began to unload it. "I though I'd get my food right away."

"Turkey sandwich, potato chips, chili, nachos and cheese, French silk pie and ice cream? Tony, there's enough food there to feed my entire family!" And that's saying a lot.

He put his hands protectively over the pie. "It's barely enough to keep me alive. Get your own."

Lissy eyed his trim waist and washboard abs beneath his shirt. "Life is not fair. I'm going to gain weight just sitting at the same table with all that food."

Tony dragged a big chip through the warm orange cheese and popped it into his mouth. "Mmm. Fresh chips. You'll have to get some."

Shaking our heads, Lissy and I went through the cafeteria line and each picked up a salad and, as a wildly extravagant gesture, decided to split a piece of fresh strawberry pie.

When we returned to the table, Tony shook his head sorrowfully.

"We can't help it if our metabolisms can't keep up with yours," Lissy said as he stared at the food on our plates.

"'My salad days, when I was green in judgment.'"

Lissy and I stared at Tony.

"That's what Cleopatra says at the end of Act One of *Anthony and Cleopatra*," Tony informed us.

"You mean she was on a diet, too? I hope she didn't get as sick of lettuce as I have." Lissy stared down at her plate. "It's been going on a long time, then. Dieting, I mean."

Tony rolled his eyes. "'Salad days' doesn't mean she's on a diet. Cleopatra regretted her youthful inexperience and indiscretions. She meant that when she was young she was, like, well, green." He looked at Lissy's confused expression. "You know, like the tender shoots in spring—new."

"Young and dumb," I provided.

"What does this have to do with anything?" Lissy demanded.

"Nothing," Tony said. "I looked at the salad on your plate and thought of Shakespeare, that's all."

"If there's a woman out there for you, she's going to be a strange one, Tony. If my salad reminds you of Shakespeare, what does my—" Lissy picked up a piece of cutlery "—my *fork* make you think of?"

Tony opened his mouth but I shut it for him with my finger. "Stop right there. I'm not up to a Shakespeare discussion right now."

Then I turned to Lissy. "Don't encourage him."

"Tony, you're too bright and too handsome for your own good," Lissy pointed out. "You're going to have a hard time meeting your match."

He shuttered his eyes to half-mast and looked at me. "I've already met her. She just won't have anything to do with me. Right, Molly?"

Lissy mimed sticking her finger down her throat and gagging at that.

I quickly changed the subject. "Are either of you going to volunteer at the free clinic this month? The new schedule comes out soon."

"I can't. I'm scheduled to work most of the days the clinic is open."

"Me, too," Tony said. "But I'm planning to be with you the nights we teach Lamaze classes."

"I said I'd fill in at the reception desk when I can, although it won't be enough," I said. "The clinic is growing by leaps and bounds."

"It seems odd to me that a medical facility like Bradshaw opened a *free* branch," Lissy commented as she ate most of the strawberries off our slice of pie.

"The people they treat have to be low income and have no medical insurance," Tony pointed out. "These people might not even seek medical help otherwise."

"Whoever thought up that idea was very forward thinking," Lissy commented.

Everett Bradshaw, I thought. It was odd how cutting-edge he'd been—and how his grandson was now retreating to the "old" forties ways.

"Want to go sailing with us this afternoon?" Tony asked. "The weather is perfect for it."

Tony, among his other manly, girl-attracting attributes, owns a sailboat. I don't think he's a very good sailor, but he loves to see his dates in bathing suits. That's his best and only reason for keeping the boat. He prefers a snowmobile. Unfortunately his dates then have to dress up in snowsuits so fluffy they look like the Michelin Man.

"I can't. Hildy and I have an appointment today at three. We're visiting the nursing home. I have to run home to get her after I eat and bring her back."

"You're no fun." Lissy pouted. "Dates with dogs, knitting weird hats, rubbing pregnant ladies' backs… You've got to get some new hobbies."

Tony's eyelids drooped seductively, and he put his hand over mine as it lay on the table. "How about me? I've been told I'm entertaining."

"You certainly are, but I don't have enough time for a high-maintenance hobby like you."

"You need romance in your life, Molly. I could provide it."

He looked so hopeful that I had to let him down easy—again. I disengaged my hand, put it on his cheek and stared into his eyes. "Listen to me, Tony. I refuse to ruin a good friendship by dating you. Sooner or later you'll have to quit asking me."

He cradled my hand in both of his. "I choose later. I'm not a quitter and I'm not ready to give up yet."

"I'll go out with you as a friend anytime, you know that."

"Small comfort," he retorted cheerfully. "Do you want a bite of my pie?"

Dates with Tony, I'll refuse. Pie? No way. I opened my mouth and he popped a bite of the French silk, the prime piece—the little tip at the end—into my mouth.

Just then a tray clattered onto the table next to us with more force than usual. I looked over to see Dr. Clay Reynolds throw himself onto a chair and scowl at the food before him. What *was* the chip on this man's shoulder?

He bent forward, hovering over his tray and yet not seeming to see it. His gaze was fixed inwardly, seeing something invisible to the rest of us. What was he seeing? Who or what was he remembering?

We finished up quickly and, with a nod to Dr. Reynolds, scurried out of the cafeteria.

"I've seen grizzly bears protecting their cubs that look more cheerful than Dr. Reynolds did just now," Lissy commented.

We both looked to Tony, who, because of his many connections, always knew all the hospital gossip.

"He blew up during a delivery today. Apparently a nurse hadn't called him until the baby was almost here. He was furious. He's the only doctor I know who prefers to be called off a golf course early to be with a woman in labor."

"Is she in big trouble? He's got a lot of influence around here," I whispered, acrobats in my stomach doing handstands and flip-flops.

"Who knows? He kept it together until the baby was born, but several people heard him chastising her later. He's got a lot of influence around here. She's a good nurse. Too bad she crossed him."

That dream about having a doula program at Bradshaw? Like a helium balloon released into the atmosphere, it drifted higher and farther away with each passing moment.

Chapter Five

"Come on, Hildy, time to go!"

Hildegard opened her eyes but didn't lift her head from her paws. She gave me a cold, disinterested glare from her new doggie bed. Ever since I'd brought it home, the cedar chips still fresh and fragrant inside, Hildy had refused to budge. Even Geranium rooting in her dog dish had not prompted her to rise. That usually started a pig-dog skirmish worthy of the evening news.

I went for the big guns. I reached into the closet and pulled out a scrap of red fabric with writing on it and dangled Hildy's therapy-dog identification cape in front of her nose. She sighed, one of those deep, heartfelt, comes-from-the-gut sighs, that told me this was the most difficult decision of her life.

Bed or nursing home? Bed or nursing home? Which will it be? I could practically hear the struggle in her thoughts. Still, all the creature comforts in the world couldn't keep her from the job she loves. Finally she rose and trotted to me to put on the uniform that displayed her official designation as a therapy dog.

"Come on, sweetheart, we don't want to be late. Mrs. Olson will be waiting for you with doggie treats burning a hole in her pocket."

River's View Estates is only minutes away from Bradshaw Medical Center and overlooks the Minnesota River. Mrs. Mattie B. Olson had been new to River's View when Hildy and I first came to visit the residents three years ago. They'd forged a bond that had helped the elderly woman "over the hump," as it were, of loneliness and homesickness, while she adjusted to her new place. They've been friends ever since. When Hildy sees Mrs. Olson, she trots to her and lays her furry head in the old woman's lap. She will stay that way indefinitely as Mrs. Olson strokes the soft silky top of Hildy's head.

Some of the people at River's View do not have family nearby so affectionate hugging or touching of another living being rarely occurs. The tactile experience of petting a dog provides immeasurable pleasure and connection. I should know. Hildy comforted me many times after I broke up with Hank. Frankly, as time passes and my vision clears, I see how mismatched Hank and I were. It's apparent to me now that whoever I marry will have to share all my passions—including my life as a doula. If I can't find that, other than for an occasional whiff of sour doggie breath, Hildy is a mighty fine companion.

"Hello, darling," Mrs. Olson said. Only then did she look up at me. "And hello to you, too, Molly."

"How's your cold?"

"Much better, thank you." She peered at me, a pretty lady, even at this age. She must have been stunning as a young woman. Her intelligent deep blue eyes were sharp and clear. "You look tired. Have you been up all night delivering babies?"

"I don't deliver them," I reminded her. "I just cheer them on as they come into the world."

"When I had my children, I was alone except for the doctor. My husband, poor soul, didn't have much of a stomach for medical things. He passed out on the floor on the other side of the door every time I gave birth. Once he hit his head on the corner of a table and got a concussion. We always joked that that was the most difficult birth I ever had—I ended up caring for both him and an infant. I could have used you back then."

"How many children do you have?"

"Four. All doctors, if you can believe it. There are several generations of them. We tease each other about being related to Luke of the gospel. He was a physician, too, you know. A family tradition, I guess, including several pediatricians. The men in my family are all good with children. Most of my family is in the medical profession. My husband was an accountant, however, and the closest he came to the medical field was doing my siblings' taxes."

She patted Hildy on the head. "As much as I love talking with the two of you, I think you should visit room 209 today. There's a gentlemen who recently moved in, and I think he's feeling rather blue."

I bent down to give Mattie a hug. "You're always taking care of someone, aren't you?"

"Like I said, I'm from a family of healers and nurturers." She held tightly to my hand. Even in her late eighties, she was still strong. "Besides, you nurture me. You have no idea how much I enjoy your visits."

"We'll be back." Of all the people we visit at River's View, Mattie is my favorite. If we'd been contemporaries, I believe we would have been best friends.

"We'll stop to see you again before we leave," I assured her.

As we walked away, Hildy looked back longingly at her friend.

The gentleman in 209 was, indeed, lonesome, but after a long chat about dogs from his past, he was considerably cheered. It didn't hurt that Hildy gently licked his hand as we were about to leave.

It was nearly six o'clock by the time we'd made our rounds, visited again with Mrs. Olson and found our way back to the nurses' station near the front door. I was surprised to see a familiar masculine figure bending over the desk, reading a chart. What was Dr. Reynolds doing here, the place that represented the other end of life's spectrum from the delivery room?

He glanced up, saw me and did a double take. He must have thought the same thing about me.

"What are you doing here? And what's that?" He pointed to Hildy.

"We work here, thank you very much. This is my dog, Hildegard, and she's a therapy dog. We hang out at River's View quite a bit. The better question is this—what are *you* doing here? Surely not delivering babies?"

A faint smile quirked his lips and hinted at what it might be like to see the man actually smile. Dazzling, I surmised.

"I have friends, too, you know. Maybe I'm visiting someone."

"You just moved here."

"Perhaps I bond quickly with people."

I'd opened my mouth to tell him that that was as unlikely as snow in August before I realized he was actually teasing me.

I, who can babble like a brook, suddenly couldn't think of anything to say. The man's presence was intimidating, not only because he had influence over my welcome at Bradshaw, but because he gave off an impressive aura—solid, impenetrable and capable of harboring secrets like Fort Knox shelters gold. I shuffled a little and Hildy looked at me inquiringly. "I guess we'd better get going. Nice to see you, Dr. Reynolds."

He nodded curtly and returned to reading the chart, as if Hildy and I no longer existed.

We were almost home before I realized that I still didn't know why Dr. Reynolds had been at the nursing home. It was curious, really. He'd just moved to the Cities, after all. How many people could he know here? He really was a man of mystery. Too bad he was also in the role of dream squasher for me. Otherwise I might have been intrigued, very intrigued.

When we got home, Lissy, Geranium and Tony were watching television in my living room. There were empty tortilla chip bags, soda cans, a carton of guacamole and a nearly depleted bag of red licorice twists on my coffee table. Geranium had her nose in one of the bags of chips, and Tony was eating a bowl of ice cream smothered in butterscotch topping and walnuts.

Hildy trotted immediately to the table to see what she could lick clean. Geranium gave a squeal of protest when the dog nosed her out of the way but toddled off when Hildy wouldn't back down.

"I leave this house for a couple hours and it's vandalized. I'm going to have to move to a better neighborhood."

"That's the thanks we get for keeping Geri company?" Tony looked genuinely hurt, as if his eating all the groceries I'd purchased yesterday were no big deal.

"Oh, sorry. Thank you. I think."

"You're most welcome."

"His date stood him up," Lissy said, her eyes never moving from the television screen where some wannabe singer was auditioning for a panel of judges.

"She had appendicitis," Tony corrected. "That's not exactly being 'stood up.'"

"Why aren't you at her bedside making points and ensuring your place in history as the world's most romantic male nurse?"

"That would be too pushy. I don't want to scare her off."

"When did this cautiousness come about?" Lissy inquired.

"I'm still waiting for Molly to admit she's in love with me. I don't want anyone else to get too crazy about me in the meantime."

"Right," I said with a laugh. "Have you seen anyone about your delusions? They have medication for that, you know."

"'Let me not to the marriage of true minds admit impediments.'"

Tony grinned at me and went back to his butterscotch-walnut sundae.

Lissy, who had coaxed Geranium to her with a potato chip and was using her as a footstool, inquired, "Why do people always name pigs after flowers? Geranium, Petunia…" She took a swig of her soda.

"Don't forget about Miss Piggy," Tony pointed out. "She's no flower."

"Geranium was named before I got her. If I'd

purchased her as a piglet, I would have named her something else."

"Like what?" Lissy leaned forward and scratched Geri behind the ear, and Geri grunted in appreciation.

"Piggy Sue."

"I know what I would have named her," Tony said dreamily.

We both eyed him warily.

"Spamela Anderson."

A gusher of soda erupted from Lissy's mouth and she started to cough. Tony helpfully slammed her on the back a few times.

Fortunately the phone rang, and I was able to leave the Two Stooges to clean up after themselves.

"Molly? It's me, Mandie."

"Are you…"

"In labor? No, but the baby is kicking up a storm. I just needed someone to talk to. My roommate is out on a date, and my mom's not home."

"I'm here for you."

"I know." There was a catch in her voice. "I don't know what I'd do without you."

Sadly, the father of Mandie's child, the one who should have been present for her, was a sore subject. He was, unfortunately, long gone. She didn't even know how to reach him. God knew what He was doing when He instructed His children to wait for marriage to be intimate. Mandie is the perfect example of how things can go wrong when kids do it the other way around.

"What's been going on?"

"I can feel the baby's position in my belly. It's weird to think of this little person inside me."

"It shouldn't be long now," I said. "Have you got a bag packed?"

"Everything on the list you gave me. Are you sure you'll be here in time?"

"Call me as soon as you notice anything different and I'll be there."

I often start with the mother at home and travel with her and her husband to the hospital. That leaves a nervous father to pay attention to traffic rather than be distracted by the huffing and puffing in the passenger seat.

"I feel better now," Mandie said. "I just needed to hear your voice."

"Anytime."

"If you ever want me to give you a recommendation or anything, I'll give you the best one ever."

"You haven't even had the baby yet," I reminded her.

"I don't care. You've already saved my sanity."

As I returned to the living room, I thought about Dr. Reynolds. If only *he* would talk to Mandie, maybe he'd change his mind about my profession. Then I recalled the look on his face when he'd first seen me in Brenda's birthing room. Or maybe not.

Tony must have read my mind, because as soon as he saw me he said, "I got some scuttlebutt on Dr. Reynolds today."

"The Mount Rushmore of doctors?" Lissy sat up a little straighter and Geri trotted off. "Old stone face?"

"He does have a child, a little boy. The rumor mill was right."

"When did he take time off to have a child?"

I poked Lissy with my finger. "Be nice."

"He's not nice." She pouted. "Why should I be? I heard him order a midwife to get out of the room when she crossed him today. Fortunately he allowed her back in later, but…"

There was one lone chip left in the bottom of the bag on the coffee table. I shook it into my hand. "Maybe I could get a loan from the donated money to start a doula center somewhere else if Reynolds nixes it at Bradshaw. That wouldn't be so bad. I probably wouldn't need much out of pocket."

"Put your own finances into a concept that would be perfect at Bradshaw? I don't think so. They need you. It's a wonderful, woman-friendly idea."

"We're covering the same territory again," I reminded Lissy wearily, tired of talking and getting nowhere.

I turned to Tony. "A son, huh?"

"He's about six years old and his name is Noah. That's all I know. Apparently Dr. Reynolds is close-mouthed about him, too. I wouldn't even know this but his receptionist let it slip."

"Aren't you dating his receptionist—among others?"

Tony shrugged helplessly, as if he had no control over his bountiful love life.

Lissy sighed. "It's just not fair. All I want is one good man, just one, and Tony has a whole field of flowers to pick from."

"'Love sought is good, but given unsought is better.' That's from *Twelfth Night.*"

"Maybe *I* should start quoting poetry. Right now the only way to describe my dating status is 'This little piggy went to market, this little piggy stayed home.' Men! Bah, pigs!"

Geranium, seeming to recognize her species, raised her head and grunted.

"Sorry, Geri, I didn't mean to insult you." Lissy tugged at her hair. "I've been stood up twice this week—and not because anyone had a good excuse. I'd break up with the guy, but I feel like I should do it in person and he never shows!"

Lissy's love life is the opposite of Tony's. All the men she meets have issues of one kind or another. Watching Tony and Lissy navigate the dating world is reason enough for me to decide it's not worth it. Come to think of it, I'm thankful Hank moved to Mississippi. If he hadn't, we might have drifted into a longer, going-nowhere relationship before we decided we weren't right for each other.

"I'd better leave," Tony said. "Your food is gone, and I have to get up early tomorrow."

"Me, too." Lissy jumped to her feet and gave me a hug. "You're a peach, Molly."

I didn't say anything, but the way I allow these two to run roughshod over me, I don't think I'm a fruit at all. I'm a nut.

Lissy paused at the gigantic bulletin board I keep by my front door. It's filled with baby pictures my clients have sent me. "Is there anything cuter than this?" She pointed to a chubby baby with three extra chins. "Or this?" Her finger landed on a pair of twins in pink ruffles that threatened to engulf them.

"You've got a great job and a wonderful service to offer," Tony said as he opened the front door. "We have to figure out a way to execute your idea."

Execute. Right. And Dr. Clay Reynolds is running the guillotine.

Chapter Six

If there were an Oscar for Performance by the Most Nervous Husband of the Year, Randall Summers would win hands down.

The man, all six feet, two inches, 165 pounds of him, quaked like an aspen leaf as he watched his wife, all five feet, no inches, 165 pounds of her, pant like a polar bear in Alabama in July. They reminded me of the "Jack Sprat could eat no fat" rhyme of my childhood. Honest to goodness, I heard his bones rattling inside his skin. He has no body fat to cushion his knees and they clattered like castanets.

Worse yet, Randall is detail oriented, and his wife, Ellen, in a momentary lapse of judgment, had handed him a copy of the birth plan we'd devised for her. He clutched it tightly, determined that it be carried out to the letter. Sir Randall, Knight Protector of the Birth Plan, was on the job.

"Is the room the right temperature? It says right here that my wife doesn't want to be too warm."

I checked the thermostat. "Just right." The room, decorated in pale green and soft pink, was soothing, but it didn't seem to do much for Randall. A small table with two chairs waited in the corner for the celebratory dinner the Summerses could share after the baby was born. If Randall made it that far.

"It says here that Ellen has requested that she be allowed to keep her long-wearing contact lenses on during the birth. Only if there is a serious emergency are you to consider asking her to put on her glasses." He peered down at her through serious pop-bottle lenses of his own. "I told you that you should have picked out new frames. What if you need a Cesarean?"

"Be quiet, Randall." Ellen, looking both pale and annoyed, glared at him malevolently. She'd been tolerant of him the first hours of her labor, but it was obvious he was wearing on her. If dripping water can erode stone, then Randall was an incessant river running over all our patience. Soon there would be nothing left.

"She doesn't like how she looks in glasses," he explained to me, still blissfully unaware that his wife would happily have done mayhem to his person if she weren't so busy giving birth. "Frankly, I think women look very intelligent when they wear glasses. Sophia Loren designs and sells frames, did you know that?"

"Be *very* quiet, Randall."

Fortunately, at that moment a nurse bustled in and announced cheerily, "Dr. Reynolds is here, Ellen. He'll be in to see you any moment so rest assured…"

My stomach took a roller-coaster dip. "Ellen, I thought your physician was Dr. Lannard." I kept the panic I felt out of my voice. Was Dr. Reynolds stalking me, or what? I hadn't mentally prepared for this.

"Dr. Lannard broke his leg earlier today," the nurse informed me. "He fell off the roof of his garage while cleaning his gutters. Dr. Reynolds is filling in."

"They say he's very good," Ellen informed me. "Isn't he?" She suddenly looked worried.

"He's fabulous," I assured her. Fabulous for women giving birth to babies, yes. Those attempting to give birth to a doula program inside these hospital walls? Not so much.

"Her birth plan says she wants to be able to walk around during labor," Randall read from the plan. "Shouldn't you have her up and walking?"

"I changed my mind," Ellen said. "I don't want to walk."

"And she specifically has requested no pain medications. She wants to savor the entire experience, don't you, dear?"

"Not anymore, Randall."

"But you said right here…" He waved the paper under her nose.

I put my hand on his arm. "Women in labor often change their minds about things. The plan isn't etched in stone. The mom is always in charge."

"Then why do we have it?" Nervous Father morphed into Crotchety One. "What do we need a doctor for," Randall yelped, "if she's already making all the decisions?"

"Anything medically necessary will override a birth plan. This is just a guide, a map, to let everyone know how she'd like things to proceed."

"Too messy. Much too messy," he muttered. "I thought things would be much more organized than this."

"Don't worry, things are remarkably well organized."

I spun around at the sound of Dr. Reynolds's voice. At least I thought it was his voice. Chipper, cheerful, encouraging—all the things he never is when he talks to me.

He walked into the room with the easy, confident gait of an athlete. He would no doubt get a haircut in a week or so but I preferred the gentle curl currently threatening his dark hair. It made him softer and more accessible.

He bent over Ellen like a tender father consoling a child. I couldn't hear what he said, but I watched the tension bleed from her body as he spoke. Oh, he is good, very good.

Then Randall flung himself toward Dr. Reynolds waving the troublesome plan. "What kind of monitoring is she having? Intermittent or continuous? It says here…"

I saw Ellen stiffen. Not good. Giving birth was job enough without contemplating how to fling one's husband through an open window to the pavement three stories below. I went to my bag and pulled out a candle with the promising moniker Serenity. We could use a little of that right now. The scents of chamomile and lavender usually do the trick. I'm not sure how much good any of this does, but anything that makes a mother more comfortable and content works for me. Then I recalled a new candle I'd just purchased. It's called Stressless and promises to relieve stress with a mixture of lavender, lemon and sage. I glanced at Randall as he hovered over Ellen's bed, bouncing slightly on his toes.

Stressless it is, then.

I lit the candle, and a delicious scent slowly began to waft its way through the room. Now things were moving in a direction I liked. The calmer the mom, the better.

Suddenly a volcanic-size eruption came from the foot of Ellen's bed.

"Aaaaaachooooooo! Ah…ah…ah…chooooooo!" Randall dived for the box of tissues on Ellen's bedside table. His eyes were streaming. "What is that? Oo hab to bow it owdt!"

I and Dr. Reynolds stared at the man as he snuffled into a wad of damp tissue. "Aaachooo!"

"He said 'You have to blow it out.' There's sage in that candle," Ellen explained calmly, as if she were vaguely glad that her husband was suddenly occupied elsewhere. "Randall is allergic to sage."

"I'll put it right out."

Before I could even turn around, Ellen added hopefully, "Or maybe Randall should leave?"

"I don wanna leab you!" He snuffled.

"Just for a few minutes, perhaps," I said.

Ellen squeezed my hand in agreement.

"I'll open a window. The sage scent will be gone shortly and you can come back."

He gave his wife a watery glance and she nodded encouragingly. Apparently even for her, a little of Randall goes a long way. It wasn't my best moment, but I was beginning to wish—as were, I sensed, his wife and Dr. Reynolds—that Summers would go away…far, far away.

No such luck. Instead he hovered outside the door like a vulture over carrion, waiting for the sage to dissipate so he could land again.

"Thank you," Ellen whispered, "but maybe you could burn the candle just a little longer?"

Dr. Reynolds turned aside, but I could see him fighting a grin.

I went into the hall to shepherd Randall, but it didn't take long for him to insist on returning to the room—and the birth plan.

"Ellen, it says here than you want the baby to have a pacifier!" Mr. Summers sounded appalled, as if he were discovering this for the very first time. Maybe he was the type of guy who never really did believe his wife was going to give birth, that somehow the child would magically appear in the hospital nursery via UPS—Unusually Prolific Stork—like a package of Omaha Steaks or an order from the JCPenney catalog. "Did you read the material I gave you? Do you know how much dental work costs?"

"The baby won't be using a pacifier forever," Ellen said sharply. "It will be done with the pacifier before it has teeth!" Beads of sweat broke out on her brow and I, working around Randall, sponged her forehead with a cool towel.

"Just stay calm," Dr. Reynolds said. "We don't want your blood pressure to jump. It won't be long now...."

Randall started flapping his arms in excitement. He resembled a greater sandhill crane, a bird with a seven-foot wingspan, trying to take off.

A tic started along the imperturbable Dr. Reynolds's jaw. Randall was even getting to him.

Ellen stared at me as if an idea were coming to her.

"Molly," she whispered so only I and her doctor could hear. "Would you mind if I fired you, then rehired you for my husband instead? I've got Dr. Reynolds. Randall doesn't have anyone and... Oh!" She grimaced at a contraction. "And he's driving me nuts."

Welcome to the crowd.

"It's no problem for me but what about him?"

"Leave us alone for a moment, will you? I'll talk to him."

Dr. Reynolds and I looked at each other and nodded. Finally, something about which we were agreed. Together we backed toward the door to the hallway.

"Where are you going?" Randall's nose twitched as if he smelled a conspiracy in the air. He looked up from the birth plan he held as we headed for the door. The fresh breeze had already helped his sneezing. "Aren't you supposed to be here for my wife? You aren't going to let any interns or residents in here, are you? This specifically states that no unnecessary personnel be present."

"Here." Ellen pointed to a spot on the floor beside her. "Now."

We made our escape to stand by a wall of charts near the nurses' desk. I shifted from one foot to the other, unable to think of a thing to say. The doctor is spectacular at a distance but standing this close to him was downright unnerving. Even his earlobes are good-looking.

"I've seen a lot," Dr. Reynolds muttered, "but this takes the cake."

"I've worked with Mr. and Mrs. Summers for some time. I didn't suspect we'd have any issues. Of course, Mr. Summers never appeared to be paying attention but…"

He looked at me intently, his mesmerizing eyes

boring into mine. "You don't mind working with him? He's a case."

"I'm all about whatever the mother needs. If she needs someone to babysit her husband, so be it." I felt a little short of breath in close proximity with this man. Maybe I'm allergic to him, I thought wildly. I hope that's it.

"Maybe there *is* one decent reason to have a doula in a birthing room," he commented under his breath, a statement obviously not meant for my ears.

I suppose I should have been happy that he'd found anything good at all about my profession, but it was the most backhanded compliment I've ever heard.

"Do you think she's had time to convince him?" I glanced at my watch.

"She'd better have. That baby isn't going to wait for her husband to make up his mind." He squared his shoulders. "Neither am I."

One would have thought it was Randall who was about to give birth. By the time we returned to the room, he'd opened the collar of his shirt and was holding a plastic glass full of ice chips to his forehead. The ice chips did nothing to help the fact that he was hyperventilating and his eyes were beginning to bulge.

I dove for my canvas shoulder bag and took out a small paper bag. "Here, blow into this." I opened the bag and helped Mr. Summers put it over his nose and mouth. Gradually, as carbon dioxide returned to his system, his breathing slowed.

His eyes grew wide over the paper bag. "It works," he mumbled and the paper bag crinkled. His knees buckled and he grabbed my arm to steady himself.

"Why don't you and I sit down over here, out of the doctor's way?" I nudged him gently toward a large leather recliner. "You need to rest. You've been under a lot of strain."

"I have been, haven't I?" He melted like chocolate in my palm.

"You'll be a new father soon. You need to be calm and strong for Ellen and the baby."

"Calm and strong…" As the wind came out of his sails, the skittish blowhard disappeared and his more vulnerable side emerged. The poor man was a mass of twitching nerves.

"Focus on your breathing. Inhale…exhale… That's right…."

Ellen gave me a thumbs-up.

From the corner of my eye I saw Dr. Reynolds look at me with a mixture of relief and disbelief before he turned back to his patient. For an instant I felt an unsaintly smugness. There are horse whisperers, and there is a reason Tony calls me a "father whisperer" in the birthing room.

"That's right, Mr. Summers. Just let your eyes focus on something on the other side of the room and concentrate on your breath…."

There is nothing, absolutely nothing, like being a part of escorting a new soul into the world. In this case it was Marie Constance Summers, named after her two grandmothers and the apple of her parents' eyes before she'd even emerged.

I stayed with Ellen and Randall until they had counted Marie's fingers and toes, decided she had Randall's ears and Ellen's lips. When Ellen was ready for me to leave, I stowed my things in the back of my car and headed for the hospital cafeteria where Tony was waiting for me.

He had a piece of strawberry shortcake, a pork chop and a pile of sauerkraut on the plate in front of him.

"Why are you eating?" I dropped into the seat beside his.

"I couldn't very well sit in the cafeteria and not eat, could I? It's impolite."

"Tell that to everyone in here who is just drinking coffee."

"Someone has to support this hospital. This is my small way of keeping Bradshaw solvent."

"You're a saint, Tony."

"Thank you." He dug into his sauerkraut. "How was the birth?"

"At the last moment Dr. Reynolds stepped in for Dr. Lannard."

His dark eyebrows shot up toward his hairline. "How'd it go?"

"Could have been worse." I picked up the spoon on his tray. "Can I have a piece of that shortcake?"

"I thought we were going out to eat."

"You're eating an entire meal. How can you go out for dinner?"

"I'll use one of my other stomachs."

"When did you become a ruminant?"

"Okay, I'll get a to-go box. This will be my midnight snack." Tony jumped to his feet and trotted toward the counter. Narrow hipped and broad shouldered, he was oblivious to the three women staring at him with yearning in their eyes. If he could ever figure out how to bottle his charisma, the man would be a millionaire. Women would pour it into their husbands' breakfast cereal by the gallon.

He returned with two small boxes, loaded them with cake, pork and sauerkraut and stacked them one on top of the other.

"Maybe I should put this in the refrigerator in the staff room. I can have it for a snack tomorrow," he suggested. "Let's run upstairs right now."

I trailed behind him as Tony led the way, greeting every single person on the staff by name.

"You are a social butterfly," I commented. I can be exceptionally outgoing, but next to Tony, I'm a hermit.

"Actually, I'm more of a social hummingbird," he corrected as we entered the break room. "I like to take pleasure in a flower and move on." His white grin flashed in his sun-bronzed face.

"And I'm the flower of the moment? What? A dandelion?"

He touched my red hair. "A tiger lily, red, fierce and beautiful."

He opened the refrigerator door and stashed his food in a corner. Then he turned around and put his hands on my shoulders. "For you, Molly, instead of being a hummingbird, I might consider becoming a parakeet in a gilded cage."

"Caged? Is that your euphemism for marriage?"

"What do you think?"

"I think, Tony DeMatteo, that you are so full of blarney it's a shame you aren't Irish. I also think that the only reason you say these things to me is because you know perfectly well I'm not going to fall for them. You use me to practice your new pickup lines and sweet talk. And you are hoping to soften me up so much that I'll offer to buy you dinner. Well, here's the news flash. We'll each pay our own way because you eat too much and I can't afford you. I'm completely impervious to your flattery because I grew up with a bunch of Irishmen who have the patent on smooth-talking blather like this. And you know you're safe with me because I'm not going to run out and subscribe to a bunch of bridal magazines and insist you go shopping with me for a white dress."

"You look lovely in white," Tony teased. "Almost as good as you look in green."

"I'm onto you, Tony."

He looked at me pensively. "What if I'm telling the truth?" He took my hand, trying to lure me in. "'Truth is truth to the end of reckoning.'"

"Then I still wouldn't believe you."

"You see my problem, then, don't you? If I do decide I want to marry you, you'll just laugh me off."

"Because it will be hilarious and you know it."

"It's why I love you, because you have a head as hard as a brick."

"And I don't let you get away with anything."

"That, too." Tony bent down and put a light kiss on my forehead.

Unfortunately Clay Reynolds chose that very moment to enter the staff room.

What my little tête-à-tête with Tony looked like to Clay, I had no idea, but I knew it couldn't be good. If he doesn't approve of doulas in the birthing rooms, he certainly doesn't put a stamp of approval on doulas committing hanky-panky—or what *looks* like hanky-panky—in the break room.

The storm-cloud expression on his features made Tony and me hurry out of the room and toward the balmier climes of the Polynesian restaurant just down the street.

Chapter Seven

Louie's Bamboo Hut isn't exactly a Polynesian paradise, but we managed to get into the spirit of the islands anyway. Tony ordered the fresh mahi-mahi, and I decided on my standby, pad Thai with chicken. Louie personally took our order and brought us our favorite drinks—diet cola with extra ice for Tony, iced tea with an umbrella in it for me.

Even though the Bamboo Hut is just a hole-in-the-wall restaurant, I feel special that someone takes my preferences into account. Remembering the penchants and favorites of others has served me well as a doula. Mothers love the fact that I know exactly what they want almost before they do—banana Popsicles, ginger ale, fizzy raspberry-flavored water or a massage.

My mother maintains that what I do requires a servant's heart. The more I think about it, the more I have to agree. The honor of being present at a child's birth—and providing for their mothers during the amazing process—is astounding to me. I have the opportunity to witness a miracle every time I go to work.

"What are you thinking about?" Tony waved a paper-wrapped straw in front of my face. "You're smiling like the *Mona Lisa*. Do you have a great secret you won't tell?"

"Just something my mother said." I told him about the servant's-heart comment.

"She's right." One of Tony's greatest charms is that he listens—really listens—to what I have to say. "You bring a nurturing touch to the birthing experience." Another one of his attributes—he's totally in touch with his sensitive side. "Everybody has gifts. This is one of yours." He grinned. "That and painting gigantic pictures and knitting ridiculous hats."

"What's your gift, Tony?" Our conversations often broach subjects like this. We both come from families that believe that dinner is a forum for both children and adults to share their thoughts and to fill minds as well as stomachs. Tony and I can't have food in front of us without solving a world problem or two.

He absently moved a big slice of pineapple off his salad as he considered the question. "I'm not sure. What do you think?"

"You are a peacemaker and a poet. I don't know anyone who is better at making and keeping connections between people than you are. Look at all the women you've dated and how much they all still love you."

"So I'm a lover, *not* a peacemaker?" A lock of black hair curled against his forehead and his eyes lit playfully at the thought.

"Your talent is keeping peace in difficult situations. I've never known anyone who could do it better," I assured him, thinking of all the women who were crazy about Tony even after he broke up with them.

"If that's the case," he responded with a mischievous glint in his eye, "let's see if I can keep the peace when Dr. Reynolds reads us the riot act about smooching in the break room."

"We weren't smooching. You kissed my forehead. You and I don't smooch."

"So sad," Tony said blithely. "One of my biggest regrets. I think we should remedy that, don't you?"

Before I could set him straight, Tony looked up and his gaze fixed on the front wall of the restaurant.

My back to the door, I couldn't see why Tony was staring toward the entrance.

"And look who just walked in," he commented. "The great Dr. Clay Reynolds, eating at Louie's Bamboo Hut? How the mighty have fallen. I didn't know you could eat at a place like this when you were born with a silver spoon in your mouth. Doesn't the acid in the pineapple tarnish the silver or something?"

"Be nice." I put a finger to my lip.

"He doesn't appreciate you," Tony pointed out. "Why should I be nice to him?"

"Because it's the right thing to do."

"You are the perfect example of living the 'turn the other cheek' philosophy."

"It's more than a philosophy, it's scriptural."

"See why we should be together? You keep me on the straight and narrow." He flashed another of those devastating smiles of his at me and wound his fingers around mine as my hand rested on the table.

"You are incorrigible. Now quit playing with my mind or I'll get my pad Thai to go."

"No, you won't. Things are just getting interesting." His dark eyes began to sparkle.

"What's that supposed to mean?"

"He's going to be seated next to us."

There goes the neighborhood.

Dr. Reynolds didn't look any happier to see us than I was to see him.

Tony, however, appeared delighted.

"Will this do?" Louie asked the doctor, gesturing toward a narrow table only three feet from ours.

Dr. Reynolds glanced around the room, searching for another empty spot, but the room was full to overflowing. "Sure. Fine."

The tables are so close that a private conversation is virtually impossible. Reynolds might as well be sitting at our table, I realized. Tony caught my eye and winked. My fingers twitched, aching to be around his neck, squeezing tightly.

Dr. Reynolds nodded briefly, acknowledging our presence. He'd likely just done rounds, and was dressed in camel trousers and a crisp navy jacket on which no lint would dare to land. His white shirt was heavy on starch and his tie a bit of silk art. Louie's Bamboo Hut didn't see much of this.

"Evening, sir," Tony said politely. "I'm Tony DeMatteo and this is Molly Cassidy…."

"Yes, I know." He smiled faintly, as if Tony should have expected that he'd have the names of everyone on staff memorized. The man oozed sophistication like Crest oozes toothpaste.

Fortunately, our meals arrived while the good doctor began to study his menu. As I observed him from the corner of my eye, an unexpected wave of sympathy washed over me. He looked not only out of his element, but very much alone.

Tony and I didn't say much as we ate. Our conversations were often hospital talk and that was precluded by Dr. Reynolds's presence. Finally, just to break the awkward silence, I leaned toward the other table. "The pad Thai is great. The chicken is excellent, but so is the shrimp."

Reynolds looked up, startled.

"The mahi-mahi is good, too. If you like fish, I'd have that or the yellowfin tuna," Tony added.

"Ah…thank you. I haven't tried this place before so recommendations help." Reynolds smiled briefly and his austere expression was replaced by something boyish and charming.

Tony caught it, too. Before I realized what he was doing, he added, "If you want to be alone, we understand, but if you'd like to join us, I'm sure Louie would shove our tables together. We come here a lot. It's a pretty casual place."

I could see Clay Reynolds muddling through the conundrum. To dine with his nemesis or ignore her and hope she'd go away? To consort with the help, like Tony? I don't know Dr. Reynolds's take on nurses. Some doctors have more respect for the profession than others. Tony had deftly managed to put him in an awkward position, and he'd done it on purpose, stinker that he is.

"Thank you. I'd be happy to join you." He stood up, shoved the small table closer and sat down again.

Louie came by, nodded approvingly at our seating arrangement and took his order.

"The yellowfin tuna, please. Mr. DeMatteo recommends it."

"Good choice." Louie beamed at both of them. "Tony is a regular customer of ours, a good eater, too. He knows what to recommend." Louie probably put one of his kids through college on Tony's meal tab alone.

"How do you like Minneapolis-St. Paul?" Tony asked. "Quite a change from… Where was it? California?"

"I like it." He relaxed against his chair and crossed his arms over his chest. "It's a good, wholesome place. I visited my grandparents here often while I was growing up."

"Are they still here?"

"They keep a home in the cities." A flicker of amusement tweaked his already pleasing features as memories came racing back to him. "My grandfather is a deep-sea fisherman so they spend a lot of time in Florida. They often come to Minnesota during the summer, however. My grandmother refuses to 'waste' a perfectly good summer anywhere but here." Reynolds turned intense blue eyes with long, dark lashes on Tony. "How about you? Where are you from?"

"I grew up in St. Paul. My family still lives there. My dad was a blue-collar worker and my mom did babysitting out of her home. I grew up playing hockey on a lumpy homemade rink in our backyard. Doesn't sound like much, but I still say I had a perfect childhood."

"Hockey? Interesting."

He turned to me and for the first time I felt the full brunt of his charm. With his complete attention on me, I felt like the only woman in the universe, his universe, at least. Charm, toughness, brilliance, passion, intensity and intelligence: this man had it all in spades. I felt myself being drawn into his orbit against my will.

"You like hockey?" Tony blurted. "Are you a Minnesota Wild fan? I heard…"

And Tony was lost to the world of pucks, sticks, icing and goalies. Reynolds went astray right along with him.

They'd covered every sport known to mankind

except curling, badminton and ice dancing by the time the waiter came by to take our dessert order. I, at least, had had time for a nice nap while the play-by-play sports commentary was going on. That, and the pleasure of watching the enthusiasm these two shared for anything involving a ball or a stick. It made Dr. Reynolds seem a little more human.

"Until I moved here, I've always coached a team," Reynolds said, a little wistfully. "I haven't even had time to look into it here."

"High school?"

Reynolds looked shocked. "Oh, no. I like the little guys, the beginners."

"That takes a lot of patience," Tony commented.

"I've got it—" Dr. Reynolds paused "—for them, at least."

Then Louie arrived at our table.

"Coconut pie." Tony ordered for both of us. "You'd better try it, Doc. It can't be beat."

So it was "Doc," not "Dr. Reynolds" now? When had that happened? Somewhere between the 1991 World Series and Wayne Gretzky's involvement with the Phoenix Coyotes, no doubt. At least, that's about the time I fell into REM sleep. I like sports, but I don't know when Gretzky played for the Kings or even the years Kirby Puckett spent with the Twins. At least Tony and Dr. Reynolds bonded. Maybe Tony could put in a good word for me next time I broached the doula question.

The pie and coffee came, and about the same

time the men remembered that I was present at the table. I hadn't minded much. I busied myself watching the play of expressions on Dr. Reynolds's face, something I might not have the opportunity to do again without being observed. What an incredible-looking man.

"Have we been boring you?" Dr. Reynolds inquired solicitously.

I started a bit, hoping he couldn't read minds. If he did, I should have been blushing.

"Did we talk too much about sports?" Tony asked. "Your eyes were glazing over. I'm sorry if we did. It's not very often I find someone who is as much a sports buff as I am. Which reminds me, Doc, do you follow NASCAR?"

"Not as much as I once did. I did see the race on Sunday, though…."

Gentlemen, start your engines. And they were off again.

To entertain myself, I studied Dr. Reynolds's tie. The tie with all the children's faces was absent, but he did have an interesting tie tack, which, until I studied it closely, I didn't realize was silver and made in the shape of a baby bottle. Another gift from his receptionist, perhaps? Curiouser and curiouser.

Dr. Reynolds glanced discreetly at his wrist-watch. "I lost track of time. If you'll excuse me…" He flashed a smile that might have graced a magazine cover.

Neither Tony nor I noticed that Clay asked for

our checks as well as his own until we went to the cash register to pay for our meals. Before we could thank him he'd managed to disappear.

On the way home Tony was elated. "He's really a cool guy, Molly. He was on a rowing team in college and even played polo! Do you know how athletic you have to be to do that?"

"Rich men's sports," I commented. "Did he ever play pickup basketball on a school playground?"

"Don't judge him too quickly. When you get to know him, maybe you'll like him."

That's also what my mother said about cabbage and brussels sprouts.

Tony dropped me off at my front door. I could hear Hildegard woofing a welcome. She knows the sound of my car, Tony's and Lissy's. She also knows the UPS truck—the driver carries treats—the FedEx man, who is scared stiff of her, and that of several members of my family. Everyone else sends the fur on her back straight into the air and puts her on guard-dog status. She's as good as a security alarm except she eats more and needs to be walked. And unlike Clay Reynolds, her bark is worse than her bite.

"Thanks for a great evening," Tony said, giving me a hug. "I had fun."

You and Dr. Reynolds had fun, I wanted to correct him, but I didn't. That would sound too much like sour grapes.

It wasn't until Tony had driven away, Hildy had laved my face with her tongue and I'd brushed my teeth and crawled into bed that I realized that even after an entire evening of listening to Dr. Reynolds converse with Tony, I had learned nothing about the man. Oh, the rowing and polo thing, I guess, but he'd managed to keep the conversation totally impersonal yet charm Tony's socks off while doing so.

Dr. Reynolds is smooth, that's for sure, and careful to divulge nothing of himself.

Chapter Eight

Lord, I ask for Your hand in this day. Bless my mothers and their babies. Make me Your servant and give me patience. Lots and lots of patience...

I put my Bible and devotional on the coffee table and stared out the window at the birds feeding on the deck. Some people watch the food channel to get recipes. Me? I watch nature programs in order to get my birds' diets just right. When I'm successful, I have a beautiful color show—the Ziegfeld Follies of birdies—right outside my window. I feed sunflower hearts and grape jelly for the orioles, meal worms for the indigo buntings, thistle for the goldfinches and suet for the red-bellied and pileated woodpeckers.

Bird brain that I am, lately I've been making my own suet with peanut butter, oatmeal, cornmeal, raisins, ground unsalted peanuts and, of course, lard which is rendered fat. Lissy says I could be making her chocolate-chip cookies with macadamia nuts for the cost of the suet ingredients. She, however, does not perch on the birdfeeder outside my window and look cute, so I've declined her request.

Hildy loves the birds, too. She and Geri sit in front of the picture window for hours, staring at their feathery antics. My brothers Hugh and Liam are birdwatchers, as well. I'm planning to give them each ten pounds of homemade suet for Christmas.

The Cassidys always make each other gifts at Christmas. My family thinks it is more personal and sentimental to give these kinds of gifts, and it is—if one gets choked up over lard, peanut butter and sunflower seeds, that is. Usually our gifts are a disaster, because I'm the only crafty one in the bunch. At least I can paint and knit. One year I got five pounds of inedible fudge, a Popsicle stick birdhouse and a collage made out of dryer lint and buttons. A coupon for an oil change from Hugh was the best gift I received that year. I've blocked the others from my memory as a survival mechanism. Otherwise it would be difficult to face another family Christmas.

Of course, what we lack in gift giving, we make up with food. As well as ham and turkey, there is always a Christmas goose and a steamed Irish pudding made with currants, raisins, dates, prunes, dried cherries and a hard sauce. Even my family refers to the pudding as a "gut bomb," but Mother makes it anyway and we all eat it, digestive issues or not.

I pulled my peripatetic mind back to the issues at hand.

I had two mothers "on deck," so to speak, in the final countdown to delivery. My young mom, Mandie, needs lots of TLC. That I can handle. The other mom, a woman named Hillary Perceval, is a bigger concern.

"I was forced to fire my previous doula," Hillary told me the first time we spoke.

"You *fired* her?"

"Insubordination," she said. "Very upsetting."

A noncompliant doula is an oxymoron in my book. Doulas do everything they can to ease a mom through childbirth.

Doulas Do. Maybe that should be my new slogan.

When I'd asked exactly what the problem with the former doula had been, the woman had broken into tears. She was desperate, she said, and I had come highly recommended. She planned to give birth at Bradshaw Medical Center and would I *please* take her on. Dr. Clay Reynolds was her physician.

If I'd had two brain cells to rub together, I would have said no immediately, but I hesitated for an instant and Hillary jumped on my uncertainty like a fox on a hen.

"You'll do it, then? I'm very busy, so we'll have to talk by phone. I don't have time to fit you in right now. I'd like to tell you what I expect...."

I hope she has time to fit the baby into that schedule.

By the time she was done with her list, I envied the fired doula. But perhaps I shouldn't be so negative. I went to bed visualizing a perfect—and short—labor and delivery for Hillary.

It was late afternoon when the telephone rang even before I'd made coffee—an inauspicious beginning to my day.

"Molly?" said a quavery voice on the other end of the line. "It's Hillary. We're on our way to the hospital."

The last night's staccato-sharp delivery of a woman accustomed to being in charge was gone. A stock broker, Hillary was singularly self-assured and very intimidating when she chose to be, but there was none of that in her voice now.

"I feel strange, Molly. This isn't like anything I've ever felt before. I'm dizzy and it came on so quickly…"

"I'll start out right now and meet you there."

"Something's not right, Molly. The baby and I are going to be okay, aren't we?"

"You've got one of the best doctors in the city," I told her. I didn't have to like Reynolds to respect him.

"I've got to go, Molly. I feel sick, my head aches…"

I'm no doctor, but I've been around enough pregnant women to wonder if Hillary was suffering from pregnancy-induced hypertension.

In a quick change of attitude, I breathed a prayer of thanks that Dr. Reynolds was Hillary's doctor.

Unfortunately, he tested that gratitude to its breaking point.

I arrived at the hospital at the same time as Hillary and her husband, Jim.

"I'm so glad you're here." Hillary was pale as the white sweater she was wearing and there was sweat on her brow. "Dr. Reynolds told Jim he suspects pre-eclampsia and wanted me here *now*." She looked imploringly at me. "What does that mean, exactly?"

Elevated blood pressure and excess protein in the urine. I bit my lip. "I'm sure Dr. Reynolds will be able to tell you."

I hiked my bag of tricks higher on my shoulder. "Push faster," I told the nurse guiding Hillary's wheelchair.

Dr. Reynolds was pacing the hallway when we got to the obstetrics floor. His face convulsed with concern, his own blood pressure obviously rising. To give him credit, when he saw us coming, it was as if he pulled a mask down over her face, a facade of smiling, relaxed features and a comforting smile.

With Hillary's wheelchair in the lead and Dr. Reynolds close behind, we walked into the birthing room. Or at least they did. Dr. Reynolds turned around and stopped me at the threshold. "You can't be here," he said icily. The statement brooked no discussion.

He lowered his voice so only I could hear. "This may not be a fluffy, feel-good delivery and I don't want you and your relaxation CDs and essential oils anywhere near this mother. Got it?"

Clear as a bell.

"I'll have to tell Hillary."

"I'll tell her." He walked inside, and the door closed in my face.

Inside the room, I heard a plaintive voice say, "I want Molly. Where's Molly?"

"Don't get upset, honey," Hillary's long-suffering husband said. "She'll be along. Won't she, Dr. Reynolds?"

The silence inside the room was deadly. I wanted to slink away and hide in a linen closet somewhere, but no such luck.

"I don't think we need Molly right now, Hillary. You have elevated blood pressure. We may have to consider…"

"I want Molly."

I'd known Hillary was going to cause trouble somehow. I was mightily relieved that it was Dr. Reynolds's trouble and not mine.

The nurse, an ex of Tony's—as most of the single nurses are—stuck her head out of the room and beckoned me in.

"He says to stay in the corner and keep out of the way. You aren't to move or to say a word." Her eyes were wide. "Sorry."

"It's not your fault." I was amazed to be brought inside the room at all.

I trailed into the room and saw a look of relief flood Hillary's features. The look on Reynolds's face, however, was its antithesis.

The next few minutes were a blur. I stood help-lessly by as Dr. Reynolds determined that an emer-gency C-section was required.

In the hallway, as Hillary was being taken to surgery, he spun to face me. "I don't want to see you here when Hillary gets out of the operating room. This is not the time or place for nonprofessionals. You are excess baggage and I'm just thankful you didn't cause any harm. I don't approve of your touchy-feely nonsense. It can be a detriment to the birthing process if not outright dangerous in cases like this."

Excess baggage? A detriment to the birthing process? Dangerous?

The kick I felt in my gut nearly sent me reeling. Clay had delivered it with black-belt precision and not looked back.

I wandered, stunned, to the nurses' desk where I was met with pitying looks.

"I heard he didn't like doulas, but I didn't realize he disliked you guys *that* much," Lissy murmured, her eyes wide. I hadn't even noticed her on duty when I'd arrived. "Sorry about that."

"He's right. This wasn't a circumstance in which a doula could help." I sat down on a hallway chair. "He just didn't have to be so…firm…about it."

"Firm? Don't you mean harsh?" Ellen, one of the older nurses, blustered. "The man is Jekyll and Hyde! He's amazing with his patients, but with everyone else…"

"His patients come first," I said weakly. My knees had begun to shake, and I yearned for a glass of water. "Maybe I'll go down to the cafeteria and get something to drink. I'd like to hang around to hear how Hillary does, so I'll come up later and speak with her husband." *After Clay Reynolds has gone home for the night.*

The room was empty and the only food to be had was from the row of vending machines along the wall. That suited me just fine. I had no desire to sit and chat with anyone. I get a coffee and a candy bar from the machines and retreated to a table in the far corner.

My shock at Reynolds's response to me was turning into rage. How dare he talk to me like that? *Excess baggage, a detriment, a danger to the birthing process?* Those were fighting words—unfortunately I don't have an ounce of fight left in me.

I put my head into my hands and closed my eyes, trying to lock out the look I'd seen in Clay Bradshaw Reynolds's eyes.

I must have fallen asleep because I awoke with a start. The only sound in the large room was the hum of the many vending machines and a rather annoying clock on the wall which read—was it possible?—midnight.

I sat up and was assailed by a pain in my neck and shoulder from sleeping too long in an awkward position. I groaned and wobbled my head from side to side. A series of cracks and pops emanated from the area and, although it felt like my head was about to roll off my neck and fall to the floor, it didn't. As I straightened, a small sound got my attention.

Across from me at the far end of the table was an exhausted-looking Dr. Reynolds. His usually perfectly combed hair was tousled, there were red rims around his eyes and a shadow of a beard was appearing on his chiseled jawline. His arms were crossed over his chest as he stared at me with the intensity of a hawk over a field mouse.

I gaped back at him.

"She's okay," he said, in monotone. "She had a baby boy. Healthy. Just over seven pounds. We were lucky that she didn't go into convulsions. It was a severe situation and developed quickly."

"Why are you telling me this?" I said bluntly. "You didn't want me anywhere near her or even her room."

"She asked me to. She wanted to make sure you'd stop by to see the baby."

"I understand."

He looked at me somberly. "Do you?"

"Do I understand about Hillary? Yes. About you? No. You're as clear to me as a black hole in outer space." What did I have to lose by speaking my mind? There was never going to be a doula center at Bradshaw. It was crystal clear just how strongly opposed Reynolds was to the idea. At least now I wouldn't hold on to a futile hope that would never be realized.

"You aren't the first person to tell me that. Only, I think the words they used were 'black cat in a coal bin on a moonless night.'" He picked up the coffee cup that was in front of him. "I like to think of myself as inscrutable. It sounds better, don't you think?"

"'A rose by any other name…'" I quoted Tony quoting Shakespeare.

The man is a chameleon that changes colors in and out of a birthing room.

"I feel the need to apologize for what happened upstairs." His brow furrowed and for a moment he looked the slightest bit contrite.

"No need. It was all honest emotion. You hate what I do and probably me, as well. You don't believe in my profession. You think it could be dangerous if a patient's situation deteriorates and I get in the way and you want nothing to do with a doula. I now have no misconceptions that at some time in the future you might ever consider supporting a doula program inside these walls. What's more, I'm now completely convinced that I should not waste any more of your time or mine. I should think you'd be delighted."

"Succinct, to the point and wrong."

I sighed wearily. "Wrong how?"

"I don't hate you. Far from it. I like you."

"You have a funny way of showing it." If it weren't so late and I so tired, I might have minded my mouth a little better.

"Just because you are misguided doesn't mean you aren't pleasant."

"Little ol' pleasant, misguided me." I stood,

picked up my bag and turned my back to Dr. Reynolds. "Good night, sir. This evening wore me plumb out."

He didn't say a word as I walked through the cafeteria door and into the bright lights of the hallway.

Chapter Nine

The next afternoon I waited in the employee parking lot for Lissy to get off work, but it was Tony who dashed out the side door, still in his uniform, and jumped into the car.

"Pedal to the metal, Molly. We've got to get out of here."

I automatically pulled away from the door like the driver of a getaway car in a bad B movie. In my rearview mirror, I saw Lissy and another nurse exit the building. Lissy was talking animatedly, but the other woman was frowning as her gaze scanned the parking lot. Her blond hair was poufed a little too high, her cherry-red lips were just a hint too glossy and her pink cheeks a shade too bright. She examined the parking lot like a policeman with a suspect on the lam.

"I have to go back and pick up Lissy."

"No, you don't. She's going to meet us at the coffee shop a block from the hospital. Now turn the corner before she sees me!"

I turned the corner.

"Who are we running away from, by the way? The Black Widow? Lizzie Borden?"

"No, much worse."

"Worse than an ax murderer?"

Tony, slumped down in the seat so his head didn't show, muttered, "Maybe not worse, but bad, very bad. Wanda Wagner is after me."

"Wanda as in 'I could just gobble up that cute Tony DeMatteo' Wanda?"

"One and the same. She broke up with her boyfriend, a phlebotomist, and now she's after me."

I burst out laughing. Wanda is one of the most forceful, opinionated, my-way-or-the-highway people in the world. When she decides she wants something, she gets it. The phlebotomist had never had a chance when Wanda set her romantic eye on him. And now she is single again and looking for Tony. I, too, might have preferred to run across Lizzie Borden and a newly sharpened ax.

"You should be flattered." I watched Tony sink lower on the floor of my car as if Wanda could see through the door of my vehicle. "She's pretty fussy about her men."

"I'm going to be tracked like a wounded buck, hunted down in the field, dressed out, hung and eaten for lunch."

"I don't like your hunting metaphors, Tony. Too gory."

"It's going to be bloody. I have to work with the woman, and you know how Wanda is when she doesn't get her own way."

I've heard stories. If Wanda wants him to be her boyfriend she'll make it happen or die trying. Tony may have finally met his match.

Tony made me drive around for fifteen minutes before heading for the coffee shop. Lissy was already there, drinking a latte and working the daily newspaper crossword puzzle. Lissy looked up and grinned when we entered.

"Scaredy-pants," she greeted Tony and began to cluck like a chicken.

"Hah. That was pure self-preservation kicking in, like if I'd been attacked by a lion or an alligator."

She clucked louder. When she stopped her chicken imitation she added, "Wanda's crazy about you."

"I suspect that she's just plain crazy," Tony said gloomily. "How am I going to get her off my trail?"

"I hear Alaska is nice this time of year."

"Very funny. Wanda is nice enough. If she weren't quite so loud…or bold…or bossy…or controlling…or colorful…" Tony's voice trailed away and he groaned. "I'm dead meat."

"Tony, every girl you leave still loves you. Work your charm, and it will be fine," I told him, not too convincingly. Wanda has many of the same attributes as a steamroller. It's difficult to argue with a large piece of highway-paving equipment.

"Just stay out of her way until she sets her sights on someone else," Lissy counseled.

"I'm supposed to take advice from a woman whose love life looks like a tornado's swath of destruction? Lissy, you haven't had anything but bad dates for the past two years." Tony looked even more depressed. "Besides, there isn't a hospital big enough to hide from Wanda if she's looking for me."

"Then stay busy," I suggested. "Work every minute you're there. No flirting at the nurses' station, no cozy chats in the cafeteria."

"You're taking all the fun out of my life."

"We're trying to help you," Lissy chastised. "Molly, Tony is busy every night this month, right?"

"With what?"

"We'll figure that out so that when Wanda asks him out he can say he already has other plans."

Wearily I turned to Tony. "Tony, would you come to my house for dinner every night this month? You can cook."

A glimmer of comprehension flickered over his features. "I accept your invitation, and I'll cook for you every night…"

"…that Wanda wants you to go out with her," Lissy finished. "And I want you to cook at my place, too. Molly can't have you every night."

"I'm not sure I like your duplicity," I warned.

"You asked him over, fair and square," Lissy pointed out before swigging the last of her latte.

"Maybe I can get my schedule changed," Tony muttered. "So Wanda and I aren't on the same shifts."

"I'll let you two work that out." I stood up. "I've got my own issues with Clay Reynolds. You're on your own with Wanda."

"A diversion!" Tony snapped his fingers. "Wanda thinks Dr. Reynolds is all right. She'd dump me for him in a heartbeat. All the single nurses would. They think he's hot."

"Dream on. That's a lost cause. Reynolds doesn't have a heart." Then my conscience kicked in. "Forget I said that. It was harsh. I'm sure he loves someone—just not me or what I stand for."

"There's that Christian 'turn the other cheek' behavior in action," Lissy commented

"The other cheek is bruised, too." I sighed. "But you're right. If this is a door that God doesn't want opened at Bradshaw, I need to be okay with that."

"When He closes a door, He opens a window," Tony quoted. "My mother's favorite saying."

I put my hand over his. "Help me watch out for open windows, okay?"

Oil and water, fire and ice, daylight and darkness, that's me and Dr. Reynolds, I thought as I knifed red and yellow oil paints onto the umber background I'd created with my palette knife. I like to work out my frustrations on canvas. Some of my best art has been done that way. My strongest emotions flow through me when I paint—joy, sorrow, frustration, anger, delight—and, thanks to Clay, this painting was going to be a humdinger.

My brother Hugh stretches canvases for me. He's an art teacher at a local high school and owns all the necessary equipment. Because I like to paint on such big canvases—I have a lot of emotion, I guess—he saves me bucket loads of money. This is my largest painting to date, five feet by seven. At least Clay has done *something* useful for me. My frustration with him has pushed me on to bigger and better things—on canvas, at least.

I stood back and eyed my work so far. Something wasn't quite right but I couldn't put my finger on it. Why should I be surprised? My relationship with my inspiration isn't right, either.

The doorbell rang, and my brother Hugh walked in. Geranium squealed and Hildy's tail thumped on the floor. Geri loves Hugh, but it is primarily because he keeps peanut-butter-flavored treats in his pocket. Both Geri and Hildy love them. Frankly, I think he's trying to steal her affection, but it isn't going to work. I'm the one who provides her with clothes—rhinestone-studded jackets, a pink-and-powder-blue boa for her neck—and I also do her hooves. Hugh would never do that. Even if he did steal her, he'd bring her back to me within the week. Geranium, like Miss Piggy of the Muppets, is high maintenance. For one thing, he couldn't afford her wardrobe, which is considerably better than mine or his.

He stood back and studied the painting with me. "What's going on in your life? It must be significant. I haven't ever seen you do anything this big."

"What's wrong with it?" I squinted at the canvas, attempting to see it through his eyes. The blackish background was a good foil for the orange, red and yellow that licked across the canvas like flame. I rarely use so much black or orange, my angry colors, in my paintings.

"Too irate. Needs some balance. Greens maybe, or blue. It's going to be good when it's finished, though. If you get your issue settled that is."

"Some people can read things from one's handwriting. You read my paintings."

He kissed me on the cheek. "You're an open book, Molly. What's troubling you?"

I summed up my encounter with Clay at the hospital.

"Sorry about that. I know how much you wanted your vision to happen at Bradshaw Medical."

"It's not the end of the world. I got my feelings hurt, that's all."

He eyed my painting. "I can see that. What are you going to do about it?"

"Rethink the plan. Rewrite the proposal I had planned to submit to Bradshaw. Paint all my feelings about Clay Reynolds out on canvas."

And burn the canvas.

"I stopped by to warn you that Mom and Dad have decided it's time for a Cassidy bash with all the aunts, uncles and cousins. Maybe you should leave town while you still have time."

Cassidy and *bash* are two words which should strike fear into the hearts of all Cassidy progeny. My father is from a rowdy and prolific family that has family reunions that resemble political conventions—flag waving, debates, strong opinions and baby kissing. Fortunately, my mother's is smaller. Otherwise these bashes would have to be held in a football stadium.

"Mother wants to have a 'family meeting' to plan the party." Hugh opened my refrigerator and took out a bottle of root beer.

"I'm sure I'm busy that day."

"You don't know what day I'm talking about."

"That's okay. I'm still sure I'll be busy."

"She'll plan it for the one moment in the day that you aren't." His voice grew muffled as he stuck his head into my deep freeze. "You're the only one who takes notes when she plans one of these things."

He pulled out the ice cream and two large mugs I keep there. "Where's your ice cream scoop?"

"Do you just come here to have root-beer floats or do you really care about my well-being?"

"A little of both." Hugh filled the mugs with ice cream and poured the root beer over it until it foamed up and ran down the outsides of the icy glasses. "How's Lissy these days?"

"Same as always. She's a great nurse with a terrible love life. The woman needs to find someone special but she's got to quit choosing the wrong men."

"What's wrong with them?" Hugh is the brother who looks most like my father—sturdy and broad shouldered and with a naughty twinkle in his eye. With his untamed red hair, he looks like an oversize leprechaun ready to do mischief. He's always interested in Lissy stories because he seems to have the same kind of luck with women as she has with men—mostly bad.

"Let's see…. There was the race car driver who stood her up five weeks straight, the guy who borrowed five hundred dollars and disappeared into the ether, the coin collector who insisted she empty her billfold at dinner so he could check her coins, the guy who told her he was going for the Guinness World Record for most potato sausages eaten in a one-minute period…"

"Potato sausages?" Hugh shuddered. "I'm Irish and even I don't like potato sausage." He tipped his mug and drank the last dregs of his float. "At least I'm not alone in making bad choices."

"Now what?"

"I thought I'd be nice and let my date pick the restaurant last night."

"Uh-oh."

"One hundred and seventy-five dollars later, after lobster and fillets, a salad made of goat cheese, cranberries and weeds picked from the parking lot, three desserts and a very large tip to a very patient waiter, I decided she isn't for me."

Hugh's budget as a teacher doesn't allow for goat-cheese salad, let alone lobster.

"Sorry, buddy."

He shrugged cheerfully and stood up. "I have to go. Expect Mom to call you soon. Have your answer ready, and don't say I didn't warn you."

He scratched Geri behind the ear until she grunted, tossed Hildy a doggie treat and was gone.

Feeling better after my brother's visit, I decided to go for a run. I pulled on some baggy shorts and a T-shirt. By the time I sat down to tie my shoes, Hildy had her leash in her mouth, waiting expectantly to be taken along for the run.

"Not now, Hildy."

She looked at me and whimpered.

"Later, okay?"

She lay down, leash still in her mouth, put her head on her front paws and whined.

"Oh, all right, you big baby."

Hildy jumped to her feet, wagging her tail, and trotted to the front door.

I'd been had again—as usual.

Chapter Ten

Our favorite path leads us to Lake Calhoun, part of the Chain Lakes on the shores of which Native Americans lived a hundred years ago. It is now a destination for fishermen, wind surfers and swimmers as well as people on in-line skates and joggers such as myself. I enjoy watching the people on skates the most. Some sail along as if they are skating on smooth ice, but it's the less experienced ones I watch. Every crack in the sidewalk, clump of grass, walker or dog on a long leash presents a potentially life-threatening hazard for the novice. No matter how many knee and elbow pads one wears, it still hurts to wipe out.

My brothers taught me to in-line skate. I didn't ask to be taught but I didn't have any choice in the matter. They sat on me, put on the blades, stood me up and shoved me back and forth between them like a hockey puck. Each time they pushed me, they backed up a bit until finally I was actually skating between them, arms flailing, mouth wide but so terrorized that no scream came out.

The memory cheered me, and I began to run faster. If I could withstand my brothers, I could withstand anything. Clay Reynolds was a mere blip on my radar screen, like a crack in the sidewalk. He could take me down, but not for long.

Then to my amazement I saw Dr. Reynolds loping toward me as if he'd materialized out of my thoughts. He was wearing a sweaty T-shirt, perspiration ran down his forehead in rivulets and his tanned face was ruddy with exertion.

I turned to escape, but Hildy inexplicably lost her mind with excitement at the sight of the good doctor and tugged on the leash so hard I thought she might pull me over. Usually she's such a good judge of character, too.

"Hello, Ms. Cassidy." He greeted me properly despite his less-than-formal attire.

"Sir." I'm not very good at being aloof, but I gave it my best shot.

"I didn't know you were a runner."

That's because you know absolutely nothing about me except what you've made up in your mind.

"I try to do five miles a day when I can. I enter a 10K occasionally."

"Impressive." He looked at me as if he were seeing me for the very first time. Then he disappeared behind a big, furry, brown and black head.

Hildy, tired of waiting her turn for attention, jumped up, put her paws on Clay's shoulders and began to lick the salty sweat off his face.

By the time I got her off him, he was sputtering and using the hem of his T-shirt to wipe dog slobber off his face.

"Sorry about that. I thought I'd broken her of the habit. She's a perfectly trained dog when she's working, but off duty she lets her excitement get the best of her."

He spluttered and spit into the grass a few times. Hildy must have landed a wet one on his lips. "The dog has a job? What's it in, real estate?"

"She's a therapy dog."

"Oh, that. I remember seeing her at the nursing home." He eyed her from stem to stern. "What do you feed her? I've never seen a dog that big."

"I call her a German shepherd, but I suspect there's Alaskan malamute hiding somewhere in her lineage. They can grow to be eighty-five pounds or more."

Hildy, satisfied now that she'd had her taste of him, sat down beside me, the picture of ladylike decorum.

We shuffled out of the way of the other runners and a wave of awkwardness flooded through me. Though Clay was someone I never wanted to speak to again, I'd certainly done a bad job of avoiding him.

"Would you like to sit down?" He gestured to a place on the grass.

"I'd rather keep walking, if you don't mind. I need to cool down." I looked at the T-shirt clinging to his body in wet patches. "So do you."

He nodded and we set out. I have long legs but his are longer and I found myself loping to keep up with him. "Slow down. I can't cool off if I have to run to catch you."

He turned to look at me and smiled with no hint of frostiness in his expression. "Feisty, aren't you?"

I tried, but couldn't manage to take offense. His blue eyes twinkled and I realized that he could be quite charming when he tried. Clay shortened his stride to match my own.

"I try. Sometimes it works better than others."

"I do owe you an apology, and you didn't hear me out the other night."

I stopped in my tracks, jerking at Hildy's leash so that she turned to look at me inquiringly.

"Just because I'm opposed to having doulas—or anyone but medical midwives for that matter—in a birthing room, that doesn't give me the right to be rude. I apologize. I was upset." He appeared genuinely contrite, the expression in his blue eyes mesmerizing.

There's a different man buried in there somewhere, I realized, someone compassionate and vulnerable. Maybe it's okay that I don't see that hidden part of him very often. It's a little too appealing.

We crossed the street and walked on the sidewalk in front of the large old homes across from the lake.

When I was a child, my father drove us down this particular street on Sunday afternoons, and we would make up stories about the people who lived in these extraordinary homes. Back then I was convinced that princesses lived inside and every one of my brothers always spun stories about Dr. Frankenstein and crazy hunchbacks warehoused in the attics. They'd watched too many old horror movies when Mom and Dad weren't home to catch them at it.

We came upon a gigantic, Italianate house with elaborate, well-manicured gardens and a heavy wrought-iron fence, which rimmed the yard. Even now, as an adult, I try to imagine what kind of people might live in such an imposing home. The only family I could think of was that of Queen Elizabeth, Prince Phillip and brood.

A small boy on a diminutive bike with training wheels pedaled around the corner of the house and started down the sidewalk toward the gate. He was dressed in what looked like Little Lord Fauntleroy's play clothes—crisp navy shorts, a pristine white shirt, knee socks and a tie—yes, a tie. The boy also wore thick round glasses and a serious expression more suited to archaeology professors than children at play. His dark hair threatened to curl if the humidity rose one iota, and he had incredibly large and serious blue eyes and a sweet, rosy mouth. There was a smattering of freckles across the bridge of his nose.

Before I could comment on this darling child,

he leaped from the bike, let it topple to the ground and came running toward us, legs churning and yelling loudly.

"Daddy, Daddy!" He grabbed the bars of the fence and peered at us through them like a man too long on death row. "You came back!"

"Daddy?" I turned to stare at Clay but he'd squatted down to eye level of the child.

"Of course I came back. Don't I always?" His tone was as smooth and reassuring as the one he used with his patients.

"But what if you didn't?"

"You shouldn't worry about that, buddy."

The child suddenly changed tracks. "Who's that?" He stared at me and pointed a finger through the fence.

Clay gently pushed the finger down. "Don't point."

The boy retracted the offending finger but held the eye lock with me. "Who's that?"

"This is Ms. Cassidy."

"Where is she from?" The boy should be a detective.

"I met her at the hospital."

The child's eyes narrowed and he stared at me. "Are you having a baby?"

I felt blood rush toward my cheeks. "No, I'm not."

"Then why did my daddy meet you?"

"Her job brings her to the hospital sometimes, Mr. Twenty Questions," Clay said.

That seemed enough to satisfy the child and he

swiftly changed gears. "Can I pet her dog?" Hildy put her nose through the curlicues and sniffed curiously in the boy's direction.

"It's a big dog, Noah. I don't think…"

Noah. A nice name. It means "peaceful."

"Hildy is a therapy dog," I assured Clay. "She's perfectly safe."

He wouldn't trust me with a grown woman doing something as natural as having a baby, so I suppose it was only logical that he'd be suspicious of his child and my dog.

"We'll walk around to the backyard," he finally said with a sigh, beaten by Noah's pleading expression. "This gate is locked."

"I'll be right there!" Bike forgotten, the little boy headed toward the mansion.

Clay turned to look at me. "My son," he said unnecessarily. "He's six."

"Do you and your wife have other children?"

"No…she's… I'm not…married, I mean. At least not anymore. My wife passed away."

"I'm so sorry." If Noah is six, Clay's wife has been gone less than six years. Perhaps part of his prickly demeanor is unhappiness rather than bad temper.

He didn't say anything as we entered the park-like backyard. I wonder if weeds even *dare* to grow here.

Clay pulled the gate shut. "You can let your dog off its leash, if you like. It can't get out of the yard."

I bent to unsnap the leash from Hildy's collar.

Her tail began to wag like a furry flag as Noah barreled toward her.

He flung himself at Hildy and threw his arms around her neck.

"Noah." Clay's voice was sharp. "Don't run at animals like that. You could have been bitten."

The little boy backed away, tearing up beneath his glasses.

I bent down until Noah and I were at eye level, and the child gave me a tentative, watery smile. "She's a therapy dog and trained not to snap at people, even if they pull her fur," I told him gently. "Everybody loves her and wants to hug her, just like you do, but I wouldn't try it with a dog other than Hildy, if I were you."

"Does she ever bite you?" Noah asked, his gaze scanning my face in much the same way his father studies his patients.

"No, but she'd lick my skin off if I let her."

He giggled now, trying to imagine it. Then he approached her again, more cautiously this time, and reached out to pet her fur. Hildy dropped to the ground with a thud, rolled onto her back, let her tongue loll out of her mouth and begged for Noah to scratch her stomach. What a clown she is. The little boy chortled with delight.

Noah beamed up at me. "She likes me!"

"She *loves* you."

For the first time I felt Clay's approval rather than disapproval directed my way.

Both Hildy and the child were in their element.

Engrossed as they were in each other, Clay and I no longer existed for either of them.

"He's an adorable child," I commented as we moved out of earshot of the enamored pair.

"Yes." Fatherly pride practically oozed from him.

"You're good with children."

"Others have said that, as well. I have an affinity for kids. I suppose that's why I'm in the field I'm in. I like the idea of ushering them safely into the world. I haven't got a clue what their reasons are for liking me."

Maybe it was because even just thinking about little ones softened his features. He must draw them toward himself as they sensed the magnetism of strength, safety and acceptance he radiated. Of course, we were talking about children and not adults. And especially not doulas.

Clay's expression took a far-away cast. "He looks just like his mother."

Then his jaw tightened and I noticed that tic in his cheek I'd seen in the birthing room and knew enough not to respond. His wife was forbidden territory.

"Would you like something to drink? Lemonade, iced tea or a soda?"

"I don't want you to go to any bother."

"It won't be. There is a small refrigerator in the garage with beverages. Otherwise the butler can bring it down from the house."

"A bottle of water is fine. No use disturbing the help."

He ignored that. "The staff is always looking for something to do. This is my grandparents' home. Since they are rarely here, the only ones working right now are a husband-and-wife team who have been with my grandparents since I was small. They get bored so I stop here and pretend to check on things even though they keep the house immaculate. Cook fixes us a great dinner while Henry, the butler, plays with Noah. Then we all watch television until Noah falls asleep."

So that was his fun night out—partying with his grandparents' cook and butler. Whew. I'm not sure I could keep up with all of that flash and dazzle.

We stepped through the door to the garage. In the dimness I could see the outline of a car—a Rolls Royce, maybe, or a Daimler. Tony would know. He's the car enthusiast. To the right of the door was the re-frigerator. Clay reached in and pulled out two bottles of water.

"Nice digs," I said bluntly. I've never been known for hiding my thoughts too deeply. "And nice wheels."

"Not my taste or style," he rejoined. "I lean more toward a basic three-bedroom, two-story and a staid Mercedes."

I reminded myself never to show Clay my home, which is exceedingly simple and, due to Geranium, is a literal pig sty. It would not be a good idea for this man to darken my doorstep. He probably couldn't survive the culture shock.

We returned to the yard where Hildy still lay on the grass. Noah had snuggled close beside her, and Hildy's paw lay protectively across his shoulder.

"What did they do, fall asleep?" Clay marveled.

"Hildy's sleep trick. Whenever she's around small children and wants them to calm down, she lies down and lets the kids stroke her. It's soothing." I thought of the dozens of times I've used the dog as my own personal sedative—no cost, no side effects and non–habit forming. Well, maybe Hildy is a *little* habit forming....

Clay gestured to wicker lawn chairs with red-and-white-striped cushions on a redbrick patio. It was obvious that the chairs had cost a whole lot more than all the furniture in my living room.

As we were getting comfortable, one of Noah's eyes sprang open.

"I thought you were asleep, buddy," Clay commented.

"I was thinking." His eyes were sharp and clear behind the thick little lenses.

"Yes?"

Noah scrambled to his feet and flung himself into his father's lap. "Can I have a dog? One like Hildy?" He put his hands on Clay's cheeks. "Puleezee?"

"I've told you before, son, that we don't have time for a dog. I'm at work and you're in school. Who'd play with a dog?"

"I could stay home from school and do it," Noah offered generously. "I don't mind."

"Bighearted of you, Noah, but no way."

"Daddy!" He sank into his father's chest and made a moaning sound, the kind that's a cry for attention, not first aid.

Clay scowled at me over the top of his son's head and I shrugged helplessly. As I did, I added one more infraction to the list, causing trouble between him and his son by putting the idea of getting a dog into Noah's head.

So sue me. A playful puppy might loosen the man up.

Unfortunately, words spilled out of my mouth and I spoke before I took the time to realize what I was saying. "Maybe you can play with Hildy again sometime."

"Tomorrow?" Noah squirmed off Clay's lap and came to stand in front of me. "You could bring her to my house after work. Daddy will give you the address."

Clay glared at me with a stern now-see-what-you've-done expression that made me wince.

"No, sweetie, I didn't mean that. I just meant that if you were visiting your grandparents' house and we ran into each other at the lake…"

"Daddy, tell her what time you're going to run tomorrow." The child could organize rings around me, I decided. Maybe I could hire him to straighten out my life.

"That's not what she meant, either, Noah. Molly meant that if we *accidentally* see each other, you could play with Hildy." The curl of Noah's lip, very much like that of his father, told us both what he thought of that lame idea. But the child wasn't done yet.

"Then can I have a playdate with her?"

Noah looked me over with a sophisticated six-year-old eye. "You could play with Molly while I play with Hildy."

I covered my mouth with my hand to hide my smile.

"You already have playdates with your friends on Tuesdays and Thursdays, remember?" Clay choked out. "Your sitter takes you there. Have you forgotten?"

"I know, but I want a playdate with Hildy on Friday."

"People don't arrange playdates with dogs, Noah."

"Can I be the first?"

"A trailblazer, too," I commented, beginning to enjoy seeing Clay squirm under the little negotiator's persistence.

"Ms. Cassidy and I will talk about it and I'll let you know what we decide. Now, no more discussion, okay?"

It wasn't okay, but Noah knew it was as good as he was going to get for the moment.

I stood up. "We'd better move on. Thanks for the water."

Clay stood, too. "Is my apology accepted?" he asked quietly.

Turn the other cheek…even if you know you'll be slapped on it sooner or later.

"Of course."

"Thank you." He looked at me quizzically, as if there was a little CAT scan in his head and he was studying my innards.

I fastened Hildy's leash and we sped off, in dire need of a mind-clearing, emotion-purging run.

Chapter Eleven

❦

"The baby is coming, Molly!" Mandie's voice was terrified even through a bad cell-phone connection.

"I'll be right over." I kicked the blankets off my feet and rolled out of bed. Before I hit the floor I was already tugging off my pajama bottoms.

"You don't understand! It's coming *fast*. My roommate called an ambulance to take me to Bradshaw Medical Center. I feel another contraction coming—" The line went dead.

I tripped over Hildy on my way to the bathroom where I ran a cold washcloth across my face, brushed my teeth and pulled on the clothing I'd set out before going to bed. I glanced in the mirror and saw a wild-eyed, wild-haired woman staring back at me. I'd been sleeping hard, and my face was creased with pillow marks. There was one that bordered on permanent across my cheek.

I grabbed a ponytail band, tugged my curls away

from my face, put a comb and makeup compact into my pocket and hoped that I'd at least have time to tame my hair before Mandie's baby arrived. I wouldn't want one of the first faces it sees to be mine while I'm looking like this.

I was in my car and on my way to the hospital in less than five minutes. As I drove, I ticked off the things in my bag of tricks, trying to remember if I'd included my new music CDs and birthing ball as well as massage tools, essential oils, cold and hot packs, hard candy, a mirror and a hand fan. I also include candy bars for me in case I don't get to eat. I also carry a package of red licorice twists—just because.

Of course, I probably wouldn't need any of it tonight. It would be amazing if the baby hadn't already arrived by the time I got there.

Two a.m. The entrance was empty and the halls silent as I made my way to the obstetrics ward. The mirror in the elevator told me that I hadn't had any success containing the havoc that was my hair. Worse, the pillow creases were going nowhere. As I erupted from the elevator, a nurse pointed me in the direction of Mandie's room.

"Molly!" She was already hooked up to a fetal monitor. Mandie reached out to me like a passenger on the *Titanic* to an empty lifeboat and began to cry.

That was the scene that met Dr. Reynolds when he strode into the room—a frantic, nearly hysterical young mother being tended by a woman who put herself together in two minutes and looked like it. I glanced down at my shoes. There were two shoes all right—one black dressy flat and one brown loafer.

"You?" I squeaked. "But Mandie's doctor is…"

"I'm on call tonight. Her doctor has been notified, and he's on his way, but we can't wait for him. This baby wants to be born." He moved into the room with complete authority and ease. This was his territory, his body language said, and no one was going to second-guess his decision here.

Mandie made a guttural sound and gripped my hand so tightly that the tips of my fingers began to throb.

When Dr. Reynolds moved toward her she began to scream. Not just a small, oh-I've-seen-a-mouse kind of scream, but an I-can-see-your-tonsils-and-you're-breaking-my-eardrum kind of scream. And she wouldn't stop.

Dr. Reynolds halted as though he'd hit an invisible shield.

"I want my own doctor!" Mandie clutched my hand. "And I want Molly." She turned to me, panic in her eyes. "I don't know him, Molly. I don't want him to touch me."

Now, I thought, was not the time to become modest.

"He's a wonderful doctor, Mandie. This is Dr. Clay Reynolds. He was the chief of staff at a large hospital in California until he came to Bradshaw. In fact, he's *great!*"

"I don't know him," she reiterated and gripped my hand even more tightly. "I'm scared, Molly. I don't want a stranger—" Her words were cut short by another contraction.

Reynolds took a step closer. Mandie's eyes grew round and through gritted teeth she said, "No!"

Clay looked at me. "We don't have time to—"

"She's frightened, can't you see that?"

"*I* can, but the baby doesn't know a thing about it. It just wants to make an entrance into this world and it's not going to wait for the two of us to have tea and crumpets and get to know each other."

"Let us have just one second, will you? Please?"

I think that for the first time in his life, Clay actually did what someone else asked in a delivery room. He backed out.

As he did so, I pulled out all the charm, blarney, hardheadedness and dogged persistence that I could muster. The last thing I ever thought I'd be expected to do was to make Clay Reynolds sound like Prince Charming, Sir Galahad and Dr. Schweitzer rolled into one glorious medical package, but I did.

Just in time, too. Mandie's daughter, Justine Molly, was born at 2:55 a.m., announcing her presence to the world with vocal cords that rivaled her mother's.

"Don't you just love Molly, Dr. Reynolds?" Mandie glowed like a Christmas candle as she held the tiny bundle in her arms. "She's helped me so much. I couldn't have done this without her."

I patted her arm, hoping to stop her gushing chatter. Dr. Reynolds looked rather peevish as it was.

"I think a doula is every bit as important as a doctor," Mandie concluded firmly. "Maybe more so because she's been with me through everything and my own doctor didn't even get here on time."

Not wanting to hang around and hear Dr. Reynolds's reaction to that, I backed quietly toward the door and escaped into the hall. Thinking it might be a fine time to disappear, I headed toward the hall leading into another wing.

"Is the coast clear?" Tony peered around the corner, his eyes darting in both directions.

I jumped, holding my hand over my thrashing heart. "You nearly frightened me to death! What are you doing sneaking like that? I almost had a coronary!"

"Sorry. Wanda's off duty and patrolling the halls for me. Rumor has it she plans to ask me out on a date. I've got to hide."

"It's three in the morning and no time for games. Why don't you just go out with the woman, have a nice time and tell her that you aren't interested in getting serious about anyone right now? Honesty is the best policy and all that."

"Wanda is selectively hard of hearing. She only pays attention to what she wants to. *No* isn't a word she accepts, at least not from me." Coast clear, Tony leaned against the wall and tipped his head back until it rested on the painted surface. "How'd I ever get myself into this, anyway?"

"By being cute and charming," I told him. "Serves you right."

"Thanks, I think. I'm on break. Want to go for a coffee?"

"Might as well. I'll be up for the rest of the night, anyway." I told him about Mandie, her reaction to Dr. Reynolds and what she'd said to him about doulas being just as important as doctors.

Tony whistled. "I'll bet he took that well."

"I don't know. I got out of there as fast as I could. I'm only hanging around until he leaves so I can go back to the room, get my bag and tell Mandie good-night."

We reached the cafeteria and Tony put coins in the coffee vending machine. "Decaf or real? Cream or black? Sugar?"

"Real and black. I need all the fortification I can get."

"I'd hoped that you and the good doctor could learn to get along."

I thought of the day Clay and I had met at the lake. "We can 'get along,' Tony. The problem is that we will never agree on the things that are most important to us. He doesn't respect what I do. My passion means nothing to him."

"But…"

"He's the one standing in the way of the doula program. Several people had seemed open to it until Clay arrived. Now everyone has cooled off. No one here is going to go against the ideas of a Bradshaw grandson, especially with a reputation like Clay's. I'm just being realistic, that's all."

"So here we are. I'm tiptoeing around Wanda and her designs on me, you're butting heads with the most powerful doc in the hospital and Lissy is no doubt stewing about another one of her seriously bad dates. What's happened to us, Molly? We had so much potential." Tony sank into a chair and stared at the ceiling.

"We *have* so much potential. We're at a bumpy spot right now. You should have a serious talk with Wanda, and Lissy should stop going out on dates until she figures out what it is she wants."

"I'll do that as soon as you and Dr. Reynolds lay down your swords."

I didn't respond but I already knew that the only way to do that was to quit taking clients who planned to deliver at Bradshaw Medical.

Why not? Just do it, I told myself as I returned to Mandie's room to get my things. I'm welcome everywhere else. I'd even be welcomed *here* if it weren't for Dr. Reynolds's old-fashioned ideas. I don't need him, I reminded myself. I don't even want to be around him! What, I began to wonder, am I doing here, anyway?

I walked slowly and thinking so hard that I forgot

to look up until I ran face-first into the tall, white-coated figure of Clay Reynolds.

"Trying to run me over?" He looked down at me with amusement mingled with frustration.

"That's like a tricycle tangling with a bulldozer," I commented grumpily. "Excuse me. I wasn't looking where I was going. I need to get my things from Mandie's room."

"They are at the nurses' station."

"You don't even want me to say good-night to her?" I was suddenly furious.

"Actually, she was so exhausted that she couldn't stay awake. She told me to tell you 'thank you' and that you should come by in the morning."

"Oh. Sorry." Shame on me for jumping to conclusions.

"She also couldn't quit raving about how wonderful and kind you've been to her."

"It's been a privilege to work with her."

He looked surprised at my curious choice of words.

"I know you think what I do is superfluous and a nuisance but to me it's an honor. I don't know how you feel about God, but He's the guiding force in my life and I believe He wants me to be doing what I'm doing. I'm to be a servant to these mothers, to show them His love and to help them keep the faith—or to discover it for the first time."

"So you proselytize?"

"Preach? No. Sometimes I never say a word about

my faith, but I do witness. I want people to see Jesus in me, not just hear about Him through my lips."

He looked at me as if I'd just said that I have a space alien that accompanies me while I work.

"Don't you believe?" I said softly. "If not, I'm sorry."

His eyes darkened until they were flat, blackened stones. "Let's just say I *used to* believe." His voice faltered. "Sometimes I still miss it. Good night, Molly. And congratulations on your deep connection with Mandie. It got her through tonight." He turned abruptly and strode away, his back straight and his head held high.

The invincible Dr. Reynolds. I stared after his receding back.

Let's just say I used to believe.

So he doesn't believe anymore?

If I understood what he'd meant by that I'd know a good deal more about the baffling enigma that is Dr. Reynolds.

When I got home, I hugged Hildegard so tightly that she whined. Then I scratched Geri behind the ears until she went into piggy ecstasy. Finally I filled my palette with paint and, even if it was nearly morning, I vented my frustration on canvas. I like painting with a palette knife because it's a lot like buttering bread. I pressed the blade flat into the paint, relishing the ridges it created.

Perhaps I should dedicate this piece to Dr. Reynolds. He's the cause of the turbulent feelings going into this work. He's also the reason it's turning into something very different from my usual painting. This time it is in control of me rather than me of it.

Chapter Twelve

"How's the doula business, sis?" Liam spooned another helping of chicken and rice onto his plate. "I heard that you ran into some choppy waters this week."

"Does Hugh tell you everything?" I asked peevishly. I should know better than to stop at my parents' house and have dinner with the family. My brothers can hear Mom's dinner bell from miles away, and there are usually a couple of them putting their size-twelve boots under her table for a meal. Tonight it was my brother Liam and the caboose of the clan, Kevin, two of my family's rusty-headed clowns.

Hugh would probably find his way here for dessert. There was a peach pie cooling on the kitchen counter, and as soon as he was downwind from it, he'd follow the scent.

"Give him a break," Kevin chided. "He hasn't got

much of a life right now. If your life is more interesting than his, let him talk about it."

"My life is not lived for the benefit of your conversations, Caboose," I snapped. "I know that might surprise you, but…" It hadn't been a great week for me, thanks to Clay, and my temper was frayed.

"Now, children," Mother said with a sigh, her round, cheerful face creasing with the familiar frustration my brothers always generated in her. "I thought I'd be able to quit treating you all like babes by now, but no such luck." She pointed the serving spoon she had in her hand in Kevin's direction. "And don't sass me, young man."

"What is Hugh's problem these days?" My father inquired.

"He broke up with his girlfriend."

"Didn't you just break up with a boyfriend, Molly? The one who didn't like pigs?" It always surprises me how Dad keeps up with all of our lives. "You kids should be like your mother and me. Married at twenty and it has lasted forty years."

"They don't make women like our mother anymore," Liam pointed out.

"After her, they threw out the mold." An agreeable voice came from the doorway. Hugh stood there, his red hair tufted and messy, his eyes bright and his smile easy.

"Hardly," Liam interrupted. "Look at Molly. She's one of a kind, too."

"Yeah, but we don't know what 'kind' that is.

Besides, we don't want to date Molly." Kevin shivered at the thought.

It isn't flattering to make your own brother's blood run cold.

"Is that peach pie I smell?" Hugh sniffed the air. He sauntered to the table, hugged each of us and gave our mother a fond peck on the cheek.

My brother, though short in stature, has the world's biggest heart. He'd give someone the shirt off his back—and he has. I should know; I was there. We were serving at a mission food kitchen when a fellow came through the line wearing the most ragged, filthy shirt I'd ever seen. He'd washed his hands and face, though, before coming through the line and there was a dignity about the fellow that his clothing denied. Hugh had seen it, too.

When it was time to leave, my brother disappeared for a few minutes and came back wearing only his white Fruit of the Loom on his back. When I tried to question him, he just shrugged, but outside the mission I saw the ragged fellow smiling widely and standing a little straighter—and wearing Hugh's Joseph Abboud shirt, cuff links and all.

After dinner we all adjourned to the living room where the card table was spread with a work-in-progress thousand-piece puzzle. This one was of a mass of Labrador puppies, feet, tails and tongues everywhere. There is always a puzzle going at Mom and Dad's place. And an eternal Monopoly game that no one has won in three years. Growing up, Solitaire was not a solitary card game. There were always two or three people hanging over the player's shoulder giving advice—most of it bad.

Then Caboose turned up the boom box on the counter, and Irish folk songs rattled the rafters. The music is always loud and the food plentiful here, and this worn but cozy home holds the heartbeat of our family. It is no wonder that we still migrate here whenever we can. Even the next generation of Cassidys has started. My sister Debbie and her family came from Massachusetts for a visit recently and her redheaded—naturally—baby, Cullen, started to squeal the moment he came through the door.

"How is your nemesis?" Hugh asked as he pounced on the puzzle piece I was going for and tucked it neatly into place.

"I didn't know Molly had one of those," Liam commented. "Doesn't everyone love Molly?"

"You had to bring it up, didn't you?" I glared at Hugh, who ignored me for another puzzle piece.

"Do you want me to punch him out?" Liam offered cheerfully.

"Behave," my mother said absently, so accustomed to keeping her kids on the straight and narrow she wasn't going to stop now, even if Liam was on the far side of twenty-five.

"My nemesis is fine, thank you very much."

"What has he done lately?"

"Give it up, Hugh. I don't want to talk about

him. I'm sick and tired of having to prove myself to that man."

Unfortunately, I'm having to do it more and more. Dr. Reynolds's reputation is spreading quickly through the pregnant-mother community, and more of my clients are planning to give birth at Bradshaw because of him.

"The man is a meticulous, exacting control freak. He has a Dr. Jekyll and Mr. Hyde personality. Sweet as pie toward his patients and little kids who don't know any better than to like him, yet a vulture ready to pounce on me."

"I find that odd," my mother said quietly. "People usually don't act that way unless they have a reason."

"I told you. His reason is that he's a meticulous, exacting control freak."

"Don't be so quick to judge," my mother, ever the conciliator, advised. "Now tell me, Molly, do you want ice cream with your pie?"

I hadn't been quick to judge, I thought, as I drove home later. I'd given Clay the benefit of the doubt a number of times, and he'd failed me every time. Clay Reynolds was stomping so hard on my dream of having a doula center in Bradshaw that it was no longer anything but dust.

Help me not to be resentful, Lord. Help me remember that You've called me to do this and You will provide what's good and right. And I pray for Dr. Reynolds. There's a burr under his saddle somewhere. Amen.

Sometimes my prayers are pretty cryptic, but I know God understands. I'm grateful someone does.

Lissy, who'd let herself in, met me at my front door. She was eating a Popsicle. Her hair was in pigtails, her feet barefoot and she was wearing a pair of cutoff bib overalls. She looked like a blond Pippi Longstocking.

"Now if guys could see you like that instead of all dolled up in high heels and makeup, you'd find the right one." I threw my things onto the table by the door. "This is the real you."

"Who'd be interested in a woman who looked like this? Little Jack Horner who sat in a corner? Or candlestick Jack of Jack be nimble, Jack be quick? Or Jack of Jack-and-Jill-went-up-the-hill fame?" She paused. "Do you realize how many guys are named Jack in children's stories? Is that weird, or what?"

"Until you are just yourself and quit attracting the wrong kind of guy, you'll never find the right man."

"Who says I always find the wrong kind of guy?" she said indignantly. "Some of them are pretty nice."

"Think about it, Lissy. One guy you dated had so many facial piercings he looked like he'd fallen headfirst into a tackle box."

"Okay, so he was a little strange."

"A little? The man couldn't get through a metal detector in an airport."

"You've got company." Lissy pointed toward the

living room, deftly changing the subject. "She's been waiting thirty minutes for you to get home."

"Really? Who…"

My jaw dropped in surprise at the sight of Emily Hancock perched properly, like a small bird, at the edge of my couch. Her feet were flat on the floor, her ankles pressed primly together, her Donna Karan suit skirt demurely covering her knees. She held her purse on her lap in a nervous vise grip and her blouse, buttoned to the top button around her neck, seemed to be choking her. A pretty woman, Emily wore artful makeup, her hair coiffed perfectly and her expression… Well, that was completely out of sync with the rest of her.

She looked like Bambi staring into the headlights of an oncoming car.

"Sorry to keep you waiting, Emily. If I'd known you were stopping by…"

"It was an impulse. I hope you don't mind?" There was a hint of a plea in her voice. "I just needed to talk to someone sane."

"Of course I don't mind. Did Lissy offer you anything to drink?"

"She did but I'm not thirsty. My stomach has been a little upset."

"Nothing a glass of milk won't cure. Come into the kitchen."

She stood up and followed me obediently, as if I actually knew what I was talking about. Milk settles *my* stomach so at least it's worth a try.

When we were seated across from each other sharing a package of Oreos and a quart of milk, Emily's color began to return.

"I knew you were just what I needed, Molly. I've been in a state all day. My husband is out of town. He's got several board meetings that demand much of his time so he's not available by phone. My own mother is a nervous wreck and all my friends think I should have my head examined." Emily played nervously with the wrapping of the now-depleted Oreos. Her impressive diamond ring winked in the light. "I didn't know where else to turn."

"Emily, everything is going to be fine. Don't pay any attention to them. I thought we had a deal that you'd ignore the negativity from now on."

"Are you sure you don't think I'm crazy?" She put her hand on my arm and I could feel her tremble. "That I'm risking my life or at least ruining it entirely?"

"By having a baby? Hardly."

"But I'm forty-five years old, something of which my mother reminds me every time we speak. 'I was twenty when I had you, Emily, and it was terrible even then. I was in labor for three days. The doctor said it was the hardest birth he'd ever seen and now you, at forty-five, *choose* to get pregnant? Have you lost your mind?'" she quoted. Her elegant features crumpled in dismay.

"You do a great imitation of her and every other Doubting Tomasina in the world."

"I can tune her out some of the time," Emily continued, "but my friends...if I can even call them that!"

Emily had rudely inconvenienced her circle of friends' social lives when she decided to get pregnant. Now their fourth for bridge would be up nursing a baby when she was the dummy. No long, leisurely lunches at the club. No day-long shopping trips or late-night dessert forays after the theater. A baby at her age? Not only did her friends think it was ridiculous but also downright stifling. She was disrupting their fun. Some friends. "What are they saying now?"

"Same old, same old. That forty-five is no age to have a baby. That I'll regret it. That I won't be able to go sailing or play tennis and that my figure will be ruined."

"As if! You're more buff than most twenty-five-year-olds I know. You have *abs* and you'll be able to see them again as soon as this baby is born."

"They also 'helpfully' tell me that the baby might have something wrong with it and that I was nuts not to have had amniocentesis or genetic testing done. But we knew it wouldn't matter, that we'd love this baby no matter what. What was the point?"

"It sounds to me that by you having a baby, they think you are ruining *their* lives."

"Something like that." Emily smiled wanly. "Just when I need support most, everyone is freaking out on me. No one understands that my husband and I are ecstatic. We've tried forever to get pregnant and had given up entirely. No one else seems to think it's even possible that we could have had a baby now. Our baby is a late-in-life miracle for us—" tears sprang to her eyes "—and everyone else is horrified."

"When the baby actually arrives their tunes will change." I patted her arm. "Maybe they'll even be a little jealous."

"It could be, but they aren't helping right now." Emily stared at me. "I just needed to see you and hear some common sense. It's not easy being one of the oldest mothers on the planet."

I burst out laughing. "You aren't even close!"

"It feels that way."

"Just be thankful that you aren't another Sarah."

Emily looked at me blankly, as if I were talking in riddles.

"You don't know the Biblical story?"

"Not really."

"Sarah and Abraham were husband and wife. Sadly, Sarah was barren. It caused her a lot of hurt and shame because to have children was so important in those times. It was even worse for Sarah because God had promised her husband that his children would become a great nation."

"Yet she was unable to give him a child." Emily smiled weakly. "I see her problem."

"But God promised Abraham that he would have a son even though Sarah was ninety years old and Abraham nearly a hundred."

"Double my age," Emily muttered.

"God kept His promise, and when Abraham was a hundred years old, Isaac was born."

Emily finally smiled. "Then maybe my friends should be grateful I didn't wait any *longer* to get pregnant!" She studied me for a long moment. "You talk about God a lot."

"I love Him," I responded simply.

"And you trust Him?"

"Look at His promise to Abraham. God's timing isn't our timing, but He always comes through eventually."

"If He can get Sarah through a safe birth in her nineties, He should have no trouble helping me at half her age."

"That's what I believe."

"I'll have to think about that."

When Emily stood to leave, she gave me a hug so tight that I almost gasped for breath. "You have no idea how you comfort me, Molly."

"Anytime."

"I'm so glad you'll be with me during labor."

She must have seen a wisp of hesitation in my eyes.

"You are going to be there, aren't you?"

"Of course I am. It's just that things have gotten a little…complicated…lately."

"Tell me how." Emily rested her hand on the doorknob.

"It's nothing for you to worry about."

"Let me be the judge of that."

"As I know I've mentioned before, my dream is to educate more and more women about doulas and how they can help ease a woman's labor. I want to start a center where doulas and clients can meet. I can even imagine doula volunteers working at the hospital on weekends to be available to birthing women who can't afford a doula of their own. Unfortunately, I've run into some opposition at Bradshaw Medical."

Emily remained silent.

"I'm considering not taking any more clients who plan to give birth there. That won't affect you, of course, but in the future…"

"That's ridiculous." She looked indignant. "Is this all Dr. Reynolds's doing?"

"Dr. Reynolds is one of the finest obstetricians I've ever met," I assured her, "but he's not a fan of what I do. His philosophy is that there should be no one but medical personnel present for a birth. He thinks that a doula just gets in the way."

"He hasn't kept up with the times," Emily said indignantly.

"Maybe not, but he's a good doctor. I don't know or understand his reasoning, but I don't think it is wise to cross him. He's got all of his patients at Bradshaw. I'll just have to focus my energies elsewhere."

"There are other doctors at Bradshaw. I'm sure he's the only doctor who has restrictions about people in the birthing room. He can't chase you away."

"Dr. Reynolds has a lot of influence there.... His grandfather and all..."

"I've met Everett Bradshaw and his wife. They're lovely people."

"You *know* them?" I recalled the massive, uninhabited house near the lake.

"I can't imagine that Dr. Bradshaw would agree with his grandson's stand on this."

"But he's not here, and Clay is," I pointed out.

The tables turned and she patted me on the arm, comforting me. "Don't worry about it, Molly. Things will work out."

"You are beginning to sound like me."

Emily laughed. "Maybe someday I'll be the one to help *you*."

I couldn't imagine how, but right now I'm willing to take help from anyone who will give it to me.

Chapter Thirteen

"You've got to talk to him, Molly." Tony stared at me over his milkshake as we sat in one of our favorite haunts, a hole-in-the wall burger-and-malts place not far from the hospital. Grease, salt, red meat and butterfat—Tony's four favorite food groups. He keeps promising me he's going to improve his diet soon. "You can't let him drive you out of business."

"He's not driving me out of business," I explained patiently for the umpteenth time. "I'm not even in business yet. He's just driving me out of Bradshaw Medical. I don't want to spend my life butting heads with Clay Reynolds over whether or not I'm a valuable commodity in the birthing room. I'm not taking it personally anymore. Even the medical midwives have begun to have issues with him, but I can't really fault him. He's exceedingly attentive to his patients. Besides, how can every child on the planet be wrong? They all adore him."

"You should be able to be with your clients there," Tony insisted stubbornly. He reminded me of Elvis today, in jeans and a white T-shirt rolled slightly at the arms. A forelock of dark hair fell over one eye as he sneered at the idea of Dr. Reynolds chasing me away from Bradshaw. Not only that, "Blue Suede Shoes" was playing on the jukebox at the back of the café.

"I have lots of clients who go to different hospitals, Tony. And I am just a doula, not a medical professional."

"*Just* a doula? I can't believe I heard those words come out of your mouth. Are you going to let Reynolds get to you like that?"

I have an approach/avoidance thing going on with Clay Reynolds, I've decided. I've been sitting on his nerves ever since we met, and yet, when I forget how stubborn, obstinate and inflexible he is, I am just like the rest of the single women in the hospital—thinking he's so good-looking that it shouldn't even be legal. I like him as much as I dislike his opinions. It would be much easier if I didn't.

Eager not to go there, I tried to change the subject. I picked one of Tony's hot buttons. "How's Wanda?"

Tony's face took on a pained expression. "She sent me *flowers*. What am I going to do?"

"Take yourself off the market. Find yourself a good woman and settle down."

"What's the fun in that? Besides, what kind of

woman would I look for? You are the only one who has ever given me that…zing." He grinned appealingly at me but I didn't fall for it.

"I only give you a 'zing' because I won't date you. You, apparently, need someone who is hard to get."

"Okay, Ms. Freud. What else do I need?" Tony put his elbows on the table and leaned forward. "This I've got to hear."

What would a good match for Tony be like? I began to tick off the attributes on my fingers. "Easy to look at, witty, good sense of humor, loves poetry and the Bard, highly intelligent and completely uninterested in you. A blonde, maybe, if you couldn't find a redhead like me." I looked at him. "Anything else you'd like to add?"

"No, you pretty much summed it up. Where do you think this dream woman hangs out?"

"What does it matter? She's not interested in you."

Tony beamed his most beguiling grin. "But that's what I like best about her. That and the part about loving poetry. 'To love is to admire with the heart. To admire is to love with the mind.' Theophile Gautier. Know him?"

"Like a best friend," I retorted. "Really, Tony, only *you* know most of these people and their quotes. If you want to find a girl to love, look in the stacks at a library, in an English department at an ivy-covered university or a moldy used bookstore, not the all-you-can-eat places you frequent."

I sighed and took a deep swig of my chocolate

malt. "We're a pathetic pair, wanting what we can't have. Why don't we just settle for less?"

"Because that's not how we're made."

"So you think I should try to talk to Dr. Reynolds again?"

"He owes you an explanation of why he feels the way he does. He's trying to isolate the women who have hired you so they have no support group. That practice is ancient history. He's trying to return us back to the dark ages!" He slurped on his malt for emphasis.

He was being overly dramatic, but I didn't argue with him. It felt a little like that to me, too.

"Here's the deal," I countered, hoping to point out just how ridiculous this all was. "I'll talk to Dr. Reynolds about the situation if you will make a date with a woman with the attributes I listed. And start haunting libraries and used bookstores."

He thought about it for a moment. "It's a dumb idea, but I'll do almost anything to get you to talk to Reynolds. We'll meet here this time tomorrow. You tell me how your meeting with Reynolds went and I'll report on my date. Deal?"

How do I get myself into these things?

I twisted and fidgeted in the reception area outside Dr. Reynolds's office. I hadn't expected to actually see him today when I'd agreed to the deal with Tony. I'd thought I'd come back to Tony tomorrow, hands helplessly in the air, saying Reynolds wouldn't even let me cross his threshold.

The woman at the desk watched me squirm. "Maybe you'd prefer to go into the doctor's office to wait." Then she added, "I'm just filling in while the other receptionist is on break."

No wonder she was being so helpful. She wasn't the real gargoyle at the gate, just a fill-in.

She waved me toward Dr. Reynolds's inner sanctum.

"No, really…"

"It's okay. Go on in."

Rather than cause a fuss, I did as I was told.

Reynolds's private office was a surprise. I'd expected walls of medical books, and a dearth of photographs and personal memorabilia. I didn't see him as a collector type but I was wrong. There was an entire bulletin board of photographs of babies— laughing, crying, red-faced, cute, not-so-cute, chubby, scrawny—the whole gamut. The display reminded me of the one I have at home. There were also childish crayon drawings, lumpy clay figures and macaroni art displayed, right next to a small but real Picasso sketch.

The man is a contradiction if there ever was one.

I sat down in a finely upholstered leather armchair, leaned my head against the back and closed my eyes. The calm before the storm. It wasn't until I heard a small cough that I realized I was not alone in the office. Someone was sitting behind the desk.

I could be forgiven for not noticing right away. After all, the individual's head barely cleared the top of the writing surface.

"Noah!"

"Hi. Are you waiting for my daddy, too?" He wielded a green crayon and peered at me curiously through those thick lenses of his. The little professor at work.

"I am. Does the receptionist know you're in here?"

"I don't think so. Nobody was outside when Daddy and I came."

"I see." I strained to see what he was working on. "Is that a green cow?"

He gave me a disgusted look usually only bestowed on town idiots. "It's a horse."

"I see."

He sighed, knowing I really didn't see at all. "The horse from *The Wizard of Oz.*"

My thick-headedness must have shone through.

"You know, the horse of a different color?" His little-professor look was more charming when I wasn't the one under scrutiny.

A dim bulb lit in my brain. "Now I get it. Cute."

"A visual play on words, or something like that," he said. Then, seeing my confusion, added, "That's what my dad calls it, the horse of a different color, I mean."

"So you and your daddy talk like that, using big words?"

He looked at me disparagingly. "How else would we talk?"

Of course. How silly of me to ask. Clay had managed to make his six-year-old son into a sixty-five-year-old man. He knew how to take the fun out of everything.

Noah pushed his glasses up the stub of his nose and peered at me again. He had the same disquieting dark blue eyes as his father. I squirmed under his childish scrutiny.

"How's Hildy?"

Ah, Hildy, an ice breaker if there ever was one. "She's good. I'll bet she'd like to see you again."

Noah stared at me with a wistful expression on his small features. "I want to see her, too." He paused. "But what I really want is a puppy of my own. Daddy says no."

"Do you have any pets?" I found myself both fascinated and charmed by this little boy who talks like an old man.

"Fish." He said it contemptuously as he might say "cockroaches" or "bedbugs."

"Fish are nice," I ventured. "Are they goldfish?"

"Koi," he informed me. "In a pond."

"I see." A nice, cozy pet. Clay might as well have gotten the child a plaster cast of a dog.

"There are some saltwater fish, too," he continued. He'd gone back to coloring his green horse as he spoke. "But someone comes in to take care of them. Dad says they're 'fussy.'"

They aren't the only ones!

"So I've heard," I said aloud. "You like animals a lot, don't you?"

"I'd have a *million* of them if Daddy would let

me." He spread his arms wide and the green crayon flew out of his hand and landed on the floor. "*Two* million! A *zillion!*"

"I know of another Noah who liked animals, too. At least he must have—he shared his boat with them for more than two hundred days."

That got Noah's attention. "He lived with them?"

"On a ship called an ark."

"Ark? Ark…ark.." Noah giggled. "Ark, ark, ark" he chanted, sounding a little like Hildy. "That's a funny word."

"Hilarious," I agreed. "Do you want to hear about him?" We might as well pass the time pleasantly, I thought. It was bound to go downhill as soon as Noah's father arrived.

"Okay." Noah slid down from the chair and circled the desk to stand in front of me. "Can I sit in your lap?"

My heart melted. I opened my arms. "I'd like that."

"Me, too." He scrambled onto my lap, his slight body warm and smelling like soap and wax crayons. His childish body fit into the curves of mine and every maternal feeling I've ever had reared its head. Though I tried not to, I fell madly, wildly, crazily in love.

"There was a time, long ago, when the people on the earth were very bad. Everybody was doing awful things, things that God didn't like."

"My mommy knew about God," Noah said.

"Oh?" He had to have been very small when she died, I thought.

"She left me a present, and God was in it."

Now how did she manage that? "What was the present?"

"Books," he said, looking delighted. "Lots and lots of books. My grandma says my mommy read them when she was a little girl and that she wanted her child to read them, too. Some of them have God in them. In one, He's making the whole world and then somebody gets swallowed by a whale and this lake dries up and a whole bunch of people cross it and then Whoosh! the water all comes back and drowns the bad guys who are chasing them." He turned to look me square in the eye. "Don't you know about this?"

The Bible according to a six-year-old.

"I do. Your mommy must have had a book of Bible stories."

"Yeah, that's it." Now that he'd gotten that settled, he returned to the subject at hand. "Tell me about the guy with my name. And tell me about his animals."

By the time we'd gotten to the part about the dove bringing back an olive leaf in its beak to show the residents of the ark that the earth was drying, we were both so engrossed that neither of us heard the office door open.

"What are you two doing?"

Noah and I both jumped, startled, as if we'd been caught coloring in Clay's medical books or unwrapping all his tongue depressors.

"Just telling your son the story of 'Noah and the Ark.' He wanted to hear it."

"It's good, Daddy! There were all these animals and Noah wanted to save them so he took them on his boat…." That triggered something else in the young but agile mind. "If he could take all those animals, why can't I have a puppy?"

"You seem to be a bit of a troublemaker even during your off hours," Clay commented, his voice pleasant but his eyes steely. "And what makes you think I want my son to know the story of 'Noah and the Ark'?"

I hadn't even considered that possibility. "I didn't realize 'Noah and the Ark' was off-limits. Your son said his mother left him a book of Bible stories…."

Clay's eyes, which had been cold and hard, suddenly changed, as if something very painful had just pricked his heart. He looked at his son again. "Yes, she did."

"Hildy is a mal-a-mutt and a worming shepherd, Dad. Can we have one of those?"

"Malamute and German shepherd, not mal-a-mutt…." Clay looked at his son and smiled. "We'll talk about it later. Right now Ms. Cassidy wants to talk to me. Why don't you go ask my receptionist to take you to the cafeteria to get a soda?"

"And ice cream?"

"I suppose."

"And candy?"

"Don't push your luck."

Noah raced to the door before his father could change his mind and we heard his childish voice

Oh, Baby!

pipe, "Dad says I can have soda and ice cream and maybe candy if I'm really good. Will you take me?"

Clay closed the door. "What is it you wanted to see me about, Molly?" He walked across the room and took the chair behind the desk.

I thought again of my conversation with Tony and chastised myself for being so stupid as to agree to this. "I wanted to clear the air between us," I began, wishing my voice didn't sound so reedy and thin in my own ears. "We got off to a bad start. I realize that you don't like doulas—or anyone but necessary staff—around during deliveries, but I feel the need to understand why you have such negative feelings about doulas."

"You get in the way."

That was succinct. Still, I couldn't leave it at that.

"This is the twenty-first century, not the nineteen-thirties. Back then they used to order bed rest for a new mother for days after. Things change." I swallowed and added, "Sir."

"You're questioning my skill and knowledge as a physician?"

"No, I'm not, but if I understood *why* you felt the way you do, it would be easier for me to accept."

He looked at me coldly, his handsome features imposing and a little daunting. "I have no need to explain myself to you."

My mouth opened and closed like one of Noah's saltwater fish. "No, you don't, but all I'm asking for is the courtesy of—"

"I'm sorry, Ms. Cassidy, but I don't feel like being courteous today." He stood, rising to his imposing six-foot-something height, making me feel very small at five feet six inches. "Now I'd like you to leave my office."

"I'm being kicked out?" Incredulity laced my voice.

"Only if you call it that." He took a step toward the door and I scrambled out of my chair and dodged out of his way.

Outside, I leaned against the hallway wall to catch my breath. "That…that…*man!*" The only happy part about that little encounter was the fact that when Clay had stepped toward me, he'd ground Noah's green crayon into his fancy Persian carpet.

Chapter Fourteen

"I can't believe he actually said that to you!" Lissy dished heaping mounds of spaghetti onto each of our plates. Tony and I had decided to meet at my place rather than the burger joint. I'd called Lissy and Hugh and told them they could come for dinner if they would cook.

"Believe it. There's a core of…of…"

"Ice?" Hugh offered.

"No, worse than that…there's a core of *titanium* in him. He's absolutely rigid and unbending."

"Well, he's the doctor," Tony said philosophically. "At least you tried."

"And how about you? Did you ask someone…unexpected…out on a date.?"

"What's this 'unexpected' part?" Hugh asked before forking a meatball the size of a tennis ball into his mouth.

"Tony was supposed to ask out a woman—a beautiful poetry lover who's smart, witty and has no interest in him whatsoever."

"Where did you find her?" Hugh asked. "Maybe if she doesn't want him, she'd be interested in me. I'm Tony's polar opposite—short, red-haired, lacking in charm…"

We all groaned at that.

"And I hate poetry."

Tony looked sheepish. "I went to the library at the junior college near my apartment. I figured that if a woman liked poetry, I might find her in with Keats or Shelly."

"If she's already with one of them, why would you want her?" Hugh asked.

We glared him down.

"And?"

"And I found a great book of sonnets. Unfortunately the only women at the library who were over twenty-five years of age were also over sixty-five."

"You should have checked out the English department," Lissy suggested.

"Full of bearded men with leather patches on their elbows. They all smelled like pipe tobacco."

"Then you didn't look hard enough. I know there's more out there than the stereotypical professor."

"I'm going to remain single for the rest of my life," Tony said. "If I can't have Molly I don't want anyone."

"And you can't have her," I assured him.

"We're a fine bunch, all losers and misfits in love," Hugh observed without rancor. "Will you pass the meatballs?"

My phone rang as I was getting ready for bed. Emily Hancock was on the other end of the line.

"How are you feeling?" I inquired.

"Like Methuselah. My friend had a baby shower for me and for her oldest daughter who is also having a child. I feel like I'm about to give birth to my own grandchild. All these enthusiastic young mothers were talking about jogging strollers, sports bras for nursing mothers and 'getting their abs back.'

"*My* friends were talking to me about getting enough fiber after the baby is born, prune juice and those panty shapers that hold your tummy in. My friends kept staring at me like I was barmy and the younger mothers thought I was old as dirt."

"Other than that, how are you feeling?"

Emily burst out laughing. "Good, actually. Dr. Reynolds says I'm doing 'beautifully' and that he expects no problems with delivery. He says I have the body of a twenty-five-year-old, which makes me feel a little better. He's such a good doctor. I can't brag about him enough…."

She noticed my silence. "Still having a disagreement with him?"

"More like out-and-out war, but I don't want to talk about it. He is a good doctor. Just stubborn and old-fashioned." *And annoyingly cute when he's not being difficult.*

Emily seemed about to say more, but before she did, Hildy took a running leap and landed on the bed, knocking my phone to the floor.

Just what I need today, a real-life version of *Family Feud,* I thought as I watched the Hatfields and the McCoys—actually the Hendersons and the Morgans—go to their corners and prepare to come out fighting.

I knew it was going to be bad when the parents of the mother-to-be had asked me to keep "those people," the family of the baby's father, away from their daughter Marsha. Then, only minutes later, the parents of Ted, the father-to-be, had asked me the same thing. The only two who seemed unaware that World War III was brewing in the waiting room were the excited parents, a young woman of twenty and her equally youthful husband. They had, according to Marsha, eloped because their parents could not agree on a) a site for the wedding, b) a restaurant for the reception, c) a band, d) a baker for the cake, e) a florist, f) which of a myriad of nieces and nephews would be ring bearers and flower girls or g) a wedding planner. I didn't think the argument over the wedding planner was necessary—who needs a wedding planner when there's already so much input floating about? What they really needed was a referee.

Now, all the energy these two families had not been able to expend on a wedding had refocused onto the birth of one small baby, a boy, whom Marsha and Ted insisted they would name Chicago because that was the city in which he was conceived. They both ignored the fact that their families had lineages filled with the names Harvard Milfoil Henderson II, III, IV and V and James Paul Vincent Ogilvee Morgan Jr., Sr., etc. etc. etc. The infant wasn't likely to arrive for a few more hours yet and already the grandparents were duking it out in the waiting room.

This is where a doula comes in handy. If you can't get the National Guard to come to the hospital to supervise a birth, I'm the next best thing.

"Dr. Reynolds is right," I told Tony when he stopped outside my client's room. "I'm going to quit my job as a doula and do something easy for a change. Do you know much about negotiating peace treaties between warring nations? With my experience I should be able to pick up a job like that easily, or maybe something at the United Nations. Too bad the Cold War isn't still on. I'll bet I could warm it up faster than I'll be able to thaw these two families."

He eyed a balloon bouquet coming down the hall which nearly had the delivery boy airborne. It was being followed closely by a basket of teddy bears that would rival the FAO Schwarz bear collection on Fifth Avenue. They were, no doubt, heading for

Marsha's room as both families attempted to buy off the baby with extravagant gifts.

"A little competitive, I take it?"

"And the families can't stand one another. Something about a business takeover twenty years ago. Apparently Marsha and Ted didn't tell their parents they were dating until it was too late to break them up."

"Ouch." Tony winced. "I'm glad I'm going off duty in a few minutes. By the way, I've got a date tonight."

"Wanda?"

"A woman from the college. I found her in the library stacks."

"Just like a reference book? How lucky for you."

"I'm holding fast to our deal. Now all you have to do is make peace with Dr. Reynolds."

"Since when was that part of our deal?"

Tony took me by the shoulders and forced me to look at him. "You know that in your heart you are going to feel you failed with this doula thing unless you give it your best shot. And your best shot is Dr. Reynolds."

"It's over and done, Tony. I'm not beating my head against that wall anymore. He'll never appreciate what I do. Forget it."

"Then I'm canceling my date."

"Don't be ridiculous."

He leaned forward and kissed me on the cheek. "Remember what I said."

Tony was gone before I realized that Clay Reynolds had come into the hall and was staring at me. Why is it that every time Tony shows me any affection whatsoever the man turns up?

Fortunately we didn't have to speak because Marsha Henderson's father stormed up to him, his face dangerously red. If this delivery didn't happen soon, they'd be treating a middle-aged male stroke patient in a birthing room. "I demand that those people not be allowed to see my daughter. They're going to upset her. Shifty, devious, underhanded, business-stealing…"

"I heard that, Henderson," Mr. Morgan said. "The only thing that will upset her is that you are out here making a fool of yourself. It's not your fault you don't know how to run a business. Why my son—"

"About that son of yours sneaking around dating my daughter behind my back? I should have gotten a restraining order…."

"You're going to have to run interference, Ms. Cassidy." Dr. Reynolds appeared thoroughly disgusted by the nonsense going on outside his patient's room. "My patient doesn't need to hear or see any of this."

Oh, sure, *now* he needs me. Granted, I was supposed to be inside the room with Marsha but in the long run, I knew I'd do more for her out here, keeping her baby's grandparents from pummeling each other.

"I'd like to tell her," I said. I looked at the two bickering grandfathers-to-be standing nose-to-nose gesticulating furiously. "Then I'll come out here and see what I can do."

"Very good." He hesitated briefly before adding, "Thank you."

Suddenly, amazingly, Clay and I were on the same side of an issue.

Marsha and Ted gave me the go-ahead to marshal the impending war, relieved to let their parents be someone else's problem for a while.

I returned to the hall and caught Mr. Henderson's arm just as he was pulling back to pop Mr. Morgan in the nose. Sometimes having to deal with brothers is a definite advantage. I have skills honed in battle. I drew an imaginary line down the middle of the room. "Hendersons on that side, Morgans on this. There will be no crossing the line, no getting within two feet of the line. Talking is to be allowed only in civilized voices."

"Young woman," Mr. Henderson blustered, "do you know who I am?"

I studied the bellicose man across from me. Then I turned to the belligerent Mr. Morgan. "Actually, I see who both of you are. You are parents who love their children yet can't get over themselves long enough to realize a miracle is happening in there." I pointed to the birthing room. "I also see people who want a happy, healthy grandchild to love. You guys are both on the same side, don't you see that?"

It was deadly silent in the room. Finally Mr. Morgan began to scuff the imaginary line with the toe of his shoe. "If we're on the same side, what did you draw this line here for?"

The question hung in the air until Mr. Henderson laughed. It was an unoiled-hinge sort of laugh, harsh and raspy, as if it hadn't been in use much lately. Gradually the nervous, tittering laughs of others joined him.

When I tiptoed back to Marsha's room, the opposing forces were shuffling their feet and looking foolish but the bomb had been defused, for the moment, at least. Time enough for a baby to be born before the skirmishes began again.

Clay caught me in the hall later, just as I was about to leave the hospital. He touched my arm and I felt a tingling shiver bolt up my arm. Static electricity, I hoped.

"Have I said thank you for handling that situation so well?"

"About a dozen times." For once I'd proven my worth. Ted and Marsha and little Chicago had had nearly an hour of uninterrupted, nonhostile family time together before they all fell into an exhausted, happy sleep.

"Are you headed for the parking lot?" He fell into step with me. His walk was smooth and athletic, a glide, really—like a panther.

"Yes. I'm exhausted. That was more excitement than usual."

"I'll walk you to your car." He looked as collected, pressed and starched as he had when I'd seen him hours earlier. While I, on the other hand, was limp and sweaty and looked as though I'd been sent through the wringer of an old-fashioned washing machine and hung out to dry.

We walked in silence and for once I actually almost felt comfortable with him. "Here's my car." My very un-Mercedes-like car.

"I'll wait until you get in and get the car started," he said gallantly, something one doesn't see much of nowadays.

"That's not necessary. I'll be fine."

He looked at the darkened sky and then at me. "No way," his expression said.

"Oh, all right." I opened my door and got into the car. I stuck the key into the ignition and turned it. Nothing. I wiggled the key and tried again. Nada. I pulled the key out to examine it, determined that it was indeed the right key and stuck it back into the ignition. Still nothing.

"Trouble?" he said. It sounded more like "I told you so."

"I must have left my lights on. I've got a road service card somewhere. I'll call for a jump." I pawed through my billfold and came up empty. Then I recalled that I'd been cleaning my purse when Ted and Marsha called. "I left all my credit cards on the table at home. It must be with them." I dug in my purse some more before I decided that I'd left my cell phone in the same place. "I'll just go into the hospital and call a cab. No problem."

"No need. I'll drive you home." He was like a brooding storm cloud on my horizon, standing there, waiting for me to do something else that smacked of incompetence.

"I don't want to inconvenience you."

"You won't be."

"I really don't think…"

"You'll inconvenience me more if you don't just quit arguing and get into my car."

I might have protested more but I'd expended all my energy on the Hatfields and the McCoys. It would be easier to have my car jumped in daylight, anyway. I gathered my things and trailed him across the parking lot to…what else? A Mercedes sedan, the dream car he'd talked about.

He opened the passenger door and gestured me inside. It smelled of leather and musk, soap and masculine cologne. I leaned against the headrest and sighed.

Clay rounded the car and got inside. In a smooth motion he started the car, put it in gear and wheeled out of the parking space. There he sat, tapping a fingernail on the steering wheel.

"Well," I said, cranky that he was wasting time. "Aren't we leaving?"

"I don't know where you live. You'll have to give me your address first."

Flushing, and glad the light in the car was bad, I mumbled my address.

Chapter Fifteen

"Turn left here." I was relieved to see my home ahead. Riding with Clay cranked my nerves even tighter than they'd been while I was inserting myself into the face-off between Ted's and Marsha's mothers.

The women had bickered in the hallway nonstop over who the baby would call Grandma and who would be referred to as Nana. Both ladies had had enough face-lifts to put their eyebrows in their hairlines, and neither wanted the moniker *Grandma* quite yet—bad for one's image on the tennis court or at the club, apparently.

How two sweet, unworldly kids like Ted and Marsha had sprung from the loins of these people is beyond me. Fortunately they had managed to ignore the claptrap around them and focus on giving birth.

"Here we are." Clay pulled into my driveway. The streetlight revealed that, thanks to Hildy, there were large yellow patches of dead grass marking my lawn and that Geranium had rooted three holes in the flower bed. The place looked like it had been overrun with moles the size of small children. It was too dark to appreciate the riot of flowers in terra-cotta pots along the front porch or the swing with its newly upholstered seat.

Not that I was out to impress Reynolds, anyway, I reminded myself. He has certainly never tried to improve my concept of him.

"Don't you leave a light on?" He frowned at the darkened house.

"The porch light is burned out. I meant to ask Tony or my brother Hugh to change it, but I forgot. I'll do it myself tomorrow."

He turned off the ignition. "Then I'll walk you to your door."

"That's not necessary. I'm accustomed to—"

"I'm *un*accustomed to leaving women on the street to find their own way home in the dark." He left me no option but to be accompanied to my front door.

He took my elbow and with a firm touch marched me to the porch.

It's nice to be treated like a lady. The irony is, of course, that while he'll gallantly escort me to my door, he'll also happily chew me up and spit me out at work. The man is a study in contradictions. What had made him such a conundrum?

I couldn't dwell on it, because my house key had gone missing in the bottom of my purse. I pawed through it much like Hildy digs a hole to bury a bone, tissues and pens flying into the air. No key. I handed Clay my billfold, sunglasses, a notebook and pencil, lip gloss, powder, doggie treats and hair clips as I rummaged. Still nothing. Finally I dumped the rest of the contents onto the floor. Candy, paper-clips, breath mints and pennies scattered across the floorboards before I saw the key glimmer from beneath a coupon for dog food.

Even that wouldn't have been so bad if there hadn't been an escalating hullabaloo inside the house. Hildy never makes a fuss when I come home alone, but she knew that there was someone else on the front porch with me. Until she made sure I wasn't in danger, she punctuated the gut-tural noises in her throat with fierce yips and barks. Then she began to run at the door and jump against it in a desperate attempt to get outside to protect me.

"Who's working the battering ram?" Clay mut-tered.

And Hildy wasn't the worst of it.

Geranium had been in the sunroom when I'd left for the hospital. She usually stays there when I'm not at home, but she does occasionally venture into the rest of the house. From the sound of it, she'd joined Hildy's noisy chorus and was making some of the most eardrum-piercing squeals in her vocabu-lary. If I hadn't known better, I would have thought there were ten or twelve animals on the other side of the door, most of them man-eating.

Clay's deep blue eyes grew wide. "What's going on in there?"

He is cute when he is discomfited.

"Oh, nothing. If I can just get my key in the lock…"

"Is it some kind of weird alarm system?"

"You might say that," I said vaguely, hoping to slip through the door without having him see exactly what was inside. The Morgans and the Hendersons had worn me out and I didn't have it in me to explain one more thing.

No such luck.

My door swung open and Hildy shot past me in a blur and hit Clay square in the chest with her front paws. He staggered backward and caught himself on the porch railing, barely escaping a backward tumble into one of Geri's hollowed-out pits.

Hildy, her lips pulled back, stared at Clay for a beat before recognizing him. Then her tail began to fan slowly and she backed off to let him recover from his precarious perch against the railing.

"Good girl," I assured her. "He's okay. He's one of the good guys, remember?"

Regaining his footing, Clay ran his fingers through his hair as he followed me. "I guess I didn't have to worry about you not being safe…." His words trailed off and his eyes widened to round circles as he stared past me into my house. "What's that?"

My sister Krissy, who lives only a few miles from me, had stopped by while I was out. An adept seamstress, she thinks it is funny to sew outfits for Geranium. She'd been to my house with her latest creation, a bright pink garment with snaps which fit much like Geri's little denim jacket and ended at the middle of Geri's back. The bonus was a frill of pink nylon netting sewn around the hem. Plainly, Geranium looked as though she were wearing a tutu.

"A pig in a tutu?" I answered, hoping to sound as if everyone in the neighborhood had one. "That's what it looks like to me."

For a moment, I thought Clay might leave and go check himself into detox.

"What's on its face?"

So busy was I enjoying Clay's discomfiture, that I hadn't noticed that Geri's snout was streaked with a suspicious brown glop. She'd had her nose into something she shouldn't have and I had a pretty good idea what it was.

She snuffled happily around my legs as I leaned over and touched my fingertip to the goo. I held it to my nose, trying to detect a scent. Then, to Clay's horror, I put the muck on the tip of my tongue to sample it.

"What do you think you're doing? That's a pig. You can't do a taste test on a pig's snout!" He looked as though he might throw up.

I smacked my lips and smiled at him. "Chocolate pudding," I announced.

"Wha…"

"I had a huge bowl of the stuff in the kitchen. I

evidently forgot to put it in the refrigerator before I left. Hildy must have knocked it off the counter."

He grabbed for the back of a chair to steady himself and stared at me in bafflement.

I sighed at the expression on his face. "You'd better come inside. You don't look well."

"What else is in there? Alligators? Opossums hanging from the light fixtures? Skunks?"

"No, no and no. Too snappy, too lazy and too stinky. Come on in."

I switched on an interior light and Clay trailed me inside and shut the door behind him. Geri trotted after me, her little hooves clicking on the hardwood floor. Her tutu, which was made of a shimmering net, glimmered and twinkled in the light.

Nothing was amiss in the living room. The kitchen, however, was a different story. A bowl lay on the floor. It and the floor had been licked clean, but the wall where the bowl had first hit had a splatter pattern on it that would have delighted a CSI detective. The pair had also managed to push my chairs into a hodgepodge and knock a centerpiece off the table. A sampled and discarded piece of plastic fruit—a banana—lay on the floor.

"You two got into a lot of mischief, didn't you? I left you guys alone too long today. Sorry. Hildy, do you want to go out? How about you, Geri, do you want to get out of your party clothes?"

While Clay stood in the middle of the room, his

head turning from side to side as if he'd found himself in a carnival fun house and couldn't find the way out, I let Hildy into the fenced-in backyard for a run and began to unsnap Geranium's tutu. She snorted and snuffled at my hand and squirmed happily as I scratched her neck. I wiped the rest of the pudding from her face and urged her through her pet door to the outside. Only then did I turn to Clay.

He sat on a kitchen chair with a thump. His arms and hands hung limply between his knees, and his mouth was open, jaw slack. Poor fellow looked like he'd been hit in the face with a two-by-four.

"I've got iced tea, coffee, sodas, pomegranate and apple juice."

He didn't respond.

"Coffee, then. Strong and black."

He was still staring at the pet door as if Geri would return dressed as something else—Batwoman, Marie Antoinette, perhaps, or Cruella deVil.

He roused as I made the coffee. "What on earth is this place?"

I glanced around. On its easel, my big, wild, thickly painted canvas dominated the living room. The Medusa hat I was making for my sister curled itself across the back of a chair. Clients' baby pictures that I hadn't yet organized were taped to the cupboards, and childish artwork covered the refrigerator. Pictures of my big, rowdy family were framed and positioned all over the room—Hugh in a leprechaun costume. Liam garbed in a multicolored robe for a community theater production of *Joseph and the Amazing Technicolor Dreamcoat,* Caboose in an Elvis costume for a charity gig he'd attended. There was a picture of my parents dressed as the couple from Grant Wood's *American Gothic* and a bumper sticker Lissy had recently given me, "We Can Spray for Mosquitoes—Why Can't We Spray for Men?"

"I like to call it home."

"No, really. Did I fall off the porch and hit my head? Am I unconscious? Dead?"

"No such luck. Have a cookie. They're my favorite, monster cookies." I handed him a plate-size cookie full of oatmeal and M&M's.

"Monster? Why am I not surprised?" He looked gloomily at the cookie. "I've been spun into an alternate universe and I'm afraid I'll never get home again."

"It's true you aren't in Kansas anymore, Dorothy, but if you click your heels together, you'll discover that you knew how to get home all along."

Naughty as it was of me, I was enjoying this. For once I had the upper hand, and the assured, self-confident Dr. Reynolds was on unstable footing.

My family has that effect on people sometimes.

What unnerved me was the feeling I had as Clay sat in my kitchen without that superior expression I've grown to dislike. I felt drawn to this Clay like a moth to a flame. Fortunately I'm smart enough not to get burned,

"I'm beginning to understand you a little better," he commented.

"That's unsettling." I sat down on the chair across from him and curled my legs beneath me. "I still don't understand you at all."

"There's nothing to understand. I'm a doctor, a good one. I like things by the book, orderly. I'm a stickler for tradition and propriety. I'm a father and have a bright, articulate son. That's all there is to me." He looked around, still dazed by the bright lights and strong colors I live with. "But this…"

"I'm a doula, a good one. I like things to be spontaneous and fun. I thrive on chaos in my personal life and order in my professional one. I'm bored by convention and am in favor of creativity and imagination. I'm not a parent but I have dozens of children in my life. I'm a Christian. And that's all there is to me."

"No wonder we've been butting heads," he said ruefully, rubbing his own as if it still ached from the conflict.

"Night and day, oil and water," I said, voicing my thoughts. "Flim and flam, up and down, in and out, black and white—"

He held up his hand. "I get the idea."

"But I was on a roll."

"You're always on a roll, Molly. You are a perpetual-motion machine, one of those punching dolls that you can hit but it never falls down. You bounce back and keep going."

Did I hear a hint of respect in his voice? Not many days ago I would have taken that as encouragement to keep trying to institute my program at Bradshaw, but not tonight. This punching doll has been knocked down one too many times. I need a rest.

"Are you admitting to me that you are a stick-in-the-mud?" I broke my cookie into several pieces and nibbled at it daintily.

"I didn't say that." His hair was tousled, and somehow just walking into my home had set his collar askew. He looked much more approachable that way.

"But it's what you meant. I hate to be blunt, Dr. Reynolds, but…"

"Uh-oh, here it comes."

"…since henceforth I will be turning down clients who have you as their physician, I don't need to tiptoe around your sensibilities anymore."

He looked up hopefully, a light in his eyes. "You're quitting?"

"No. I'm quitting *you*. I can't cope with your negativity toward me anymore."

"So you're *firing* me?" He appeared dumbstruck.

It's a look I enjoy seeing on a man once in a while.

"You could say that. I'd advise you not to ask me for a recommendation anytime in the near future. I do have a couple of clients who see you, but they'll give birth soon and then you'll be out of my life."

"And you'll be out of mine." He looked far too happy about that.

Chapter Sixteen

He was suddenly genial, more so than I'd ever seen him. I hadn't planned to make him quite *this* happy.

I poured his coffee before going to the refrigerator to take out a carton of chocolate milk and a squeeze container of chocolate syrup. I set them, a straw and a glass on the kitchen table.

"What are you doing?" Clay watched me like a specimen beneath a microscope.

"Making my favorite drink." I poured milk into the glass and then squirted a goodly portion of chocolate syrup in, as well. I stirred it with the straw and took a deep sip. "Yum. I like my chocolate thick and dark."

"What else do you like?" He frowned at me as he asked the question.

"Chocolate chips mixed with coconut and eaten by the handful, Mexican food made with a dash of chocolate in the sauce and most anything made by Hershey's. Why?"

"Those were my wife's favorites, too."

"Ah, a discerning palate." I was surprised he mentioned his wife but had the distinct sense that I was not to go there unless he took the lead.

He swilled back a cup of coffee. "You remind me of my wife in several ways. She too, had a nice singing voice, and knew the words to 'The Brady Bunch.'" He looked inexpressibly sad as he said it. "She loved animals, as well."

But you don't have anything but cold-blooded fish at your house now.

He shook himself like Hildy does when she comes out of a scummy pond, shaking away memories like Hildy shakes off water. "Never mind. Just an observation, that's all."

Clay stood up and walked toward my painting. I'd added the greens and blues Hugh had suggested and it didn't look nearly so psychotic as it had earlier. "Do you paint a lot?"

"Most of the ones in this room are mine. I tend to paint out my emotions." I let it drop but noticed him blink and stare once again at my work in progress. His diagnosis? Probably insanity, lunacy or severe psychosis.

He looked around the room and headed for a bright piece that looked like a Monet painted on a Tilt-A-Whirl. "I like this. Did you do this one?"

I swallowed thickly. "Not exactly."

"What does that mean? 'Not exactly'?"

"I helped a little but I'm not the artist."

"Who is, then?"

At that moment Geri popped her snout through her pet door and grunted.

A strange expression crossed Clay's face as I tossed her a bedtime snack and shooed her back to her quarters.

"The pig did it?"

"I didn't know it would turn out so well. I just kept putting washable paints, the kind that small children use in school, on her hooves and let her walk around on a piece of canvas. When my brother Hugh stretched it and put it on a frame, I was blown away by how attractive it was." I walked close to him and pointed to the small but distinct shape in the corner. "There's her signature, a hoofprint."

"Of all the artwork in this house, I picked out one painted by a pig?"

Our shoulders brushed as I looked up at him and grinned. "Do you want to guess which one is Hildy's?"

He rolled his eyes. "Say it isn't so."

I pointed to a canvas that was done in all greens and looked like ferns in a forest. "She did it with her tail. Cool, huh?"

He stared at me as if I'd just touched down from a long-distant trip across the galaxy, collecting stars and exploring black holes.

"I'm beginning to worry about Tony." Lissy sat in my kitchen holding a bottle of nail polish. Every time I waved the empty brush at her, she thrust it out so I could get another gob of Pink Nightie, Geranium's favorite nail color.

I finished painting Geri's last hoof. "Hand me the decals, will you? And that little box of rhinestones."

"You spoil that pig."

Lissy opened the container in which I kept Geri's bling. I shop at the beauty-supply store, haunting the place for discounts on sparkly things for Geri's hooves. It's bad enough to have to paint ten human fingers or toes, but Geri's four feet demand an even larger supply of nail enamel. I get her hoof moisturizer online, however, as it's not a commonly called-for item.

I looked down at Geri as she sat between my legs, one hoof in my hand, patiently waiting for me to finish her pedicure. There's nothing she likes better than lots of attention, and she is well behaved for any sort of beauty treatment.

"She's not spoiled," I retorted. "She just smells that way. Now what were you saying about Tony?"

"He's turned into a wild man at work. He's busy every minute. When he isn't doing his own work, he's doing someone else's."

"Hiding in plain sight," I deduced, "from Wanda and her designs on him."

"Exactly."

"I still think he should take her out and explain that he's just not interested."

"Wanda isn't the kind of person who takes no for an answer."

I thought of the persistence with which Tony pursues me. "He isn't, either."

"Still, I'm worried about him. He looks stressed."

I carefully pasted the last of the butterfly decals on Geri's hoof and dried it a bit with my hair dryer. She trotted off looking very pleased with herself.

"Why don't you ask him what's really wrong," I suggested. "I see him coming up the sidewalk right now."

Almost before I was done speaking, the bell rang and the door flew open.

Lissy was right. Tony did look strained and frazzled, not his normally suave, confident self. He bolted into the house and closed the door behind him. Then he went from window to window in the front of the house and pulled the shades. Only then did he fling himself onto my couch and breathe a sigh of relief. "I don't think she followed me."

"Wanda is not *that* bad," I reminded him.

"No? She wants to constantly feed me."

"You should love that."

"Sweet rolls on the front seat of my car, bundt cake in my locker at work and brownies in my mail box? I'm being stalked by a foodie!"

"Wanda is a good cook." Lissy rubbed her flat belly. "I'd eat it if you'd give it to me."

Tony's expression of consternation didn't fade.

I sat down next to him on the couch, right on the

bad spring that I keep meaning to get fixed. "Now tell us what the real problem is."

"Wanda…" He spread his hands helplessly as if she were a force of nature, not a person.

"She wouldn't get to you if something else weren't going on," I pointed out.

He deflated like a punctured balloon. His shoulders drooped and his head sank toward his chest. "I just came from my sister Gina's place. She's a mess and it's breaking my heart. All she thinks about is why she can't get pregnant. Now she's got this idea in her head that God has 'abandoned' her because she's prayed for a baby that hasn't come."

"How long have they been trying?" Lissy handed me a cup of tea, sat down on the chair across from Tony and curled her feet beneath her like a cat tucking itself in for a nap.

"Over three years."

"They're still young. That's certainly no reason to give up."

"You tell her that. I've tried but she won't believe me." Tony scraped his fingers through his dark hair. "She's really down. She's convinced that she's made to be a mother and this is killing her."

"Hope deferred," I murmured, more to myself than to Tony. "Proverbs. 'Hope deferred makes the heart sick, But desire fulfilled is a tree of life.'"

"What does that have to do with Gina?"

"I believe that we should never give up hope and that things happen for a reason, that's all. No matter how much we may not like it, it's all about God's timing, not ours. And it's all about trust. He can do things that we can't even begin to imagine."

"It seems to me that God's clock is off where my sister is concerned. She's thirty-three and that biological ticking of hers sounds like a freight train in the house." Tony scraped his fingers through his dark hair. "It hurts my entire family to see her blaming herself and God."

I took a handful of animal crackers from the bowl on the coffee table and put down my tea. "Have you ever wanted something so badly that you could taste it and yet, no matter what you did or prayed for, it didn't come?"

"A train set, for one," Tony said, "but a train set and a baby are hardly the same thing."

"I've always wanted a BMW," Lissy chimed in. "But I've got a long way to go before my savings account will allow that."

I ignored Lissy to press Tony. "Did you ever get a train set?"

"Yeah, but I was twelve and was more interested in sports by then."

"So you *did* get what you'd hoped for."

"But it was too late."

"You mean you never played with the trains?"

"Of course I did. Not for myself so much, although it was enjoyable, but because it was something my little brother and I could do together. He's six years younger and it was the one thing we had in common. We'd play for hours." Tony grinned. "Sometimes I even let him be the engineer."

"So you *did* have fun with the train?"

"I had fun because he was having fun. It's part of the reason my brother and I have a close relationship today. Otherwise, without the trains, we'd likely have gone our separate ways."

"So hope deferred isn't necessarily a bad thing, is it? In your case, although you didn't get it when you'd planned, it still worked out."

"Probably for the better," Tony admitted, "now that I think about it."

"So even though you didn't think God knew what He was doing when you prayed for that train and it didn't come, the timing was actually perfect. It came at a time when something even more important could happen—you could build a real friendship with your brother."

Tony scowled. It didn't do a thing to mar his handsome features. "But a train set isn't a baby. My sister won't buy it."

"Even if, in the end, the delay is for the best?"

"I'm not sure what better time there could be. Besides, no one likes taking no for an answer."

"I do understand the impatience, Tony. I'm convinced that I'm supposed to begin a doula program at Bradshaw, but it's not happening. Maybe God has a better place in mind, one I don't know about yet."

Tony leaned forward and brushed his index finger along the line of my cheek. "Molly Cassidy, the eternal optimist."

"God's in charge. How can we be anything else?"

Chapter Seventeen

I pulled into the parking lot behind the free clinic and was surprised to find an empty parking lot. Usually on Saturday mornings the place is packed like a sardine can.

Feeling rather festive in the colorful skirt I'd purchased against Lissy's better judgment, I swirled into the waiting room. I'd had a great night's sleep, a long, hot shower and three cups of coffee so rich and black that it would, if my father's old saying were correct, put hair on my chest. I felt ready for anything.

Well, almost anything.

"Where are all our patients?" I greeted Gretchen Sykes, a nurse I've worked with many times here at the clinic. I'm normally a receptionist, girl Friday and all around gofer. We try to pack in as many patients as we can with our usually short staff so when I'm not at the desk I might be counting Ace bandages or mopping the restrooms.

"We drove most of them away."

"Did you stand at the front door and make faces as they came up the sidewalk?" I dropped my bag onto the desk chair. I always carry knitting with me wherever I go. Usually the desk is too busy to get too much done, but today looked promising. Maybe I could finish my sister's hat.

"We've been giving away free tickets for the circus. Unless someone is desperately ill, they're not coming in today." Gretchen looked pleased. "These people need a diversion from hard times. The tickets were a great idea."

"Who thought of it?" I began to straighten the desk to make room for today's paperwork.

"Rumor has it that Everett Bradshaw made the decree."

"*The* Everett Bradshaw? Chief Bigwig? I didn't think he was here enough to pay attention to those sorts of things."

"He may not be here, but he's paying attention," Gretchen said. "I work for Dr. Ogilvee. He says that Dr. Bradshaw has his finger of the pulse of everything concerning Bradshaw Medical, including the free clinic. 'Eyes in the back of his head and wiretaps in every hall' is the way he put it."

"Sounds subversive and devious to me."

"Not really. Dr. Ogilvee admires the man enormously. He runs a first-class operation and that's the reason why. He calls Bradshaw a 'benevolent dictator.'"

Subversive, devious dictator. Clay had inherited his grandfather's genes except for the benevolent one.

"I'm positive there won't be much happening this morning." Gretchen glanced at her watch. "I've been here since 8:00 a.m. and haven't seen a soul. Even the doctor hasn't arrived yet. Would you mind terribly if—"

"I covered for you? I don't mind if the doctor on duty doesn't."

"I checked it out with the office at the hospital. They said that it was okay with them if it was all right with you. It's a free, volunteer clinic, after all. They know that most of the emergencies today will probably involve eating too much cotton candy and peanuts, which, by the way, the ticket holders also get free. If you need me, I'm only five minutes away. My husband and I are going on a cruise next week and I'd love to start packing."

"Who's the doctor du jour?"

"I don't know. The new schedule isn't up yet."

"Go ahead, pack your bags. Even I should be able to handle an empty clinic."

Gretchen gave me a hug. "You're the most loyal volunteer we have, Molly. Everyone who works in the reception area says that without you to keep things together the clinic wouldn't run nearly so smoothly."

I hugged her back. "Then I'd better take advantage of this quiet day and get all the filing done."

"You're a doll. Holler if you need me."

I watched her leave and, in a fit of orderliness,

decided that today was the perfect day to redo the filing system.

Taking advantage of the quiet and the open space, I spread everything out on the floor in the waiting room and sat down in the middle of it to work. Horizontal thinker that I am, I always see things more clearly when I've got all of my work spread out around me. It drives my family crazy but it also explains why I'm both neat and messy at the same time. I think messy but am good at creating order out of chaos. One more complicated aspect of my personality, I guess.

I was at the peak of messiness—which comes just before I pull things into order—when the bell over the front door rang. I jumped to my feet but not before spilling a box of pens and a glass of water.

"I'll be with you in a moment." I grabbed for the paper towels and began to mop up. "Minor accident here. Nothing important got wet." I turned toward the desk. "May I help…*you!*"

"We seem to be doomed to run into each other at every turn," Clay Reynolds said pleasantly. He was dressed in casual clothes: body-fitting denim jeans and a polo shirt. A jacket was hooked in the crook of his finger and held casually over his shoulder. His hair still held a hint of dampness from the shower and curled haphazardly at the nape of his neck. "May I ask what you're doing?"

I felt heat rush up my neck and into my cheeks. "Organizing the office."

He studied the chaos around my feet. "So that's what you call it."

"It's how I do it, that's all. I'll have it all picked up and filed before I leave. I'd never leave a mess like this...." My voice trailed away as I realized he was smiling faintly, as if catching me in a jumble vaguely pleased him.

A sigh escaped me. "And you don't care a bit because you expect me to foul things up one way or another."

"Now, did I say that?"

"Basically, yes."

"That was about having you underfoot during labor and delivery. I don't mind a bit if you make a mess in a receptionist's office."

It took everything in me to ignore the statement.

Clay glanced around. "Where are the patients? The doctor who was supposed to be here today came down with flu. He just called and asked me to cover for him."

"'Physician, heal thyself,'" I murmured.

Clay looked at me strangely but didn't comment.

"They're all at the circus." I explained about the free tickets the clinic had been giving out.

"My grandfather is a generous man," Clay commented. "And always thinking of others." His expression changed. "I always aspire to be like him."

Then you'd better start with a personality class. Learn not to be rude to doulas.

He glanced at me as if he were reading my mind. "I'm not doing so well in your book, am I?"

"I'm not sure there's a good answer to that question," I parried.

"Pleading the fifth. Good idea." He shrugged into the jacket. "What have you got for me to do until a patient wanders in?"

I glanced at the floor. "This project I'd better finish myself."

"I'm glad for that." Distaste was plain on his face as he studied the jumble.

"It's okay. No one expects the doctor to do anything but see patients."

"There aren't any patients to see." He glanced around the office, still looking for a task to keep him busy.

"You could make labels for these files." I handed him a pile I'd already sorted. "How's your handwriting?"

"Silly question. I'm a doctor, remember? My handwriting is terrible."

"Do they teach you that in medical school or did you miss penmanship in third grade?"

"Both. I can type, however."

That was how Dr. Reynolds and I came to be working cozily side by side, waiting for patients that didn't come.

There were two or three, of course. One boy needed stitches after falling from his bunk bed during a fight with his brother. Another family came in looking like albino rabbits, each sporting a severe case of pink eye. But Clay handled all of that with aplomb and promptly returned to his job making labels. By one o'clock we'd accomplished what would have taken me hours to complete if I'd had to do it alone.

It was surprisingly satisfying to close the last file drawer on a job well done.

"Thank you for helping me." I smiled at Clay. "I really do appreciate it. Those files have been bothering me for weeks but when I'm here I'm usually too busy to make any headway with them."

"You're more than welcome." He studied me appraisingly. "You really care about this clinic, don't you?"

"I care about the patients and love the fact that they have a place to come for help." I hesitated. "I care deeply about everything I do."

He didn't take the bait, so I continued. "I don't think I've ever seen a doctor in here who has actually paid any attention to what happens at the front desk. I've always wished they would, just so they could understand the amazing job the clinic is doing."

"I see what you mean. I had no idea."

Why couldn't we get along like this all the time—civilly, courteously, amicably? I wondered. Of course, we probably could if I changed careers.

I bundled together my untouched knitting bag and prepared to leave.

Clay, who had been watching me, said, "How about lunch?"

"Me?" I couldn't keep the shock out of my voice. "With you?"

"I've heard of more ridiculous things." He had that smile on his face again, half smirk, half grin.

But not many.

My head, completely apart from rational thought, bobbed an assent.

"What about Noah?" I stammered, hoping to extricate myself from what my body had decided without me.

"He's with a sitter. They are visiting a great-aunt of mine. She and Noah enjoy each other. He won't be home until later."

"Where do you want to go?" I sounded as resigned as I felt.

"Do you usually do dessert first?"

I blinked owlishly. "How did you know?"

"Lucky guess, that's all." There was that grin again.

"But I'd better eat solid food today. I had cookies for breakfast."

"Monster cookies?"

I nodded. He is getting to know me a little too well.

"Sushi okay?"

I shuddered and gagged. "Too raw."

"Cajun?"

"Too spicy." Did the man have a cast-iron stomach?

"Soup and sandwich?"

"Perfect. You lead with your car, I'll follow."

"No need. You can ride with me, and I'll bring you back here to pick your car up."

That was not exactly what I had in mind. I need to keep my distance from the good doctor. I don't want to get to know my dream dasher too well.

Then he added, "I insist."

When a Bradshaw progeny says "jump," I say "how high?"

He chose the restaurant well, a small mom-and-pop affair called Al and Bess's Good Eats, which was tucked away in a strip mall and served the best chicken-wild-rice soup I've ever tasted. That's saying a lot in Minnesota where wild rice is plentiful. It was after the normal lunch hour, and we were the only diners there other than an elderly couple who held hands and gazed into each other's eyes like newlyweds.

"I didn't know this place existed," I admitted. "You've only been in town a short while. How did you discover it?"

"I visited the Twin Cities a lot as a child, remember? My grandfather always made a point of eating in small, independent restaurants. No eating in places that he can find in any shopping center across the country, that's his policy."

"Smart man," I took a bite of a Reuben piled high with corned beef and dripping with dressing, just the way I like it.

For a moment I forgot who we were talking about, *the* Everett Bradshaw. I'd also overlooked for the briefest second who I was dining with—the illustrious grandson, heir to the Bradshaw throne.

"What are you staring at?" I demanded as I realized that he hadn't taken his eyes off me since I'd tackled the giant sandwich.

"I like women who eat."

"They don't last long if they don't." I took another bite.

"My— Someone else I knew enjoyed food as much as you seem to."

Someone as in who? As in *wife?* He didn't elaborate.

Bess of "Al and Bess" fame approached our table. "Dessert, folks?" She did a double take and gaped at Clay. "Clay Reynolds, is that you? I haven't seen you here in ages!"

"Hi, Bess, it is me. This is Molly Cassidy. We worked at the free clinic today."

She turned to me. "Nicest family in the world, the Bradshaws. Absolutely the best. Dessert is on the house! What would you like? Truffle pie? Peach melba? My special bread pudding with cream?"

"I will never turn down your bread pudding, Bess. It was a highlight of my childhood."

The older woman blushed. "Still as charming as ever, then." She turned to me. "And you?"

"I'm pretty full. I usually eat dessert first to prevent this from happening but…"

"She'll have the truffle pie. We'll share."

Bess nodded and scurried off.

"We'll share, will we?"

"You know you want to. How else would you have been able to decide between the two?"

I hate it when he's right.

Chapter Eighteen

I closed my eyes and allowed a spoonful of the creamy custard from Clay's bread pudding to melt on my tongue. On a scale of one to ten, this was an eleven....

Clay's voice broke into my food-induced reverie. "If you'd rather have the bread pudding than the truffle pie, I'll trade."

Clay, when he isn't ruining my life, can be very charming.

Dreamily, I opened my eyes, savoring my taste bud bliss. "But it's your favorite." He didn't speak. Instead he stood up and sauntered to the counter where Bess and Al were rolling silverware into paper napkins and securing them with paper bands. "Another bread pudding, please."

"I'll make this one bigger," Bess assured him. She glanced at me and then back at him. She leaned forward and murmured, "I like a girl who eats."

Of all my sterling qualities, my appetite is not the one for which I really want to be remembered. Then Clay brought to the table another serving of the warm bread pudding, flooded with caramel sauce and cream, and all my reservations fled.

At the moment I really didn't care if my tombstone said:

She Loved Bread Pudding,
R.I.P.

With far too much amusement he watched me finish the pudding. That was nothing next to the look he wore when I downed the truffle pie, as well.

"Impressive," he said, admiration in his voice.

He really *does* like women who eat.

He picked up the bill despite my protests. "Cheap date," he said offhandedly as he handed Bess a fifty-dollar bill and waited for change.

My stomach did a traitorous, treacherous flip at the word *date*. Clay, on the other hand, seemed oblivious. Date and Dr. Reynolds? Inconceivable; surreal, at best. Yet here we were, walking back to his Mercedes, behaving as if we actually liked each other.

"Big plans for this afternoon?" Clay asked as we slid into his car and buckled our seat belts.

"Nothing special. My brother Hugh's birthday is coming up. My mother and my sister Kelly, too. I also have some baby showers on the horizon. I thought I might go shopping." I patted my purse. "I just got paid so now's the time."

"Seems to me you're planning to spend your entire paycheck on others." He turned his head to look at me. "Nothing for the hungry mouths at home to feed?"

"I bought dog food, yarn and art supplies last week. And bling for Geri's hooves."

"I'm sorry I asked. For some reason, I thought you'd say you'd paid the mortgage, put groceries in the cupboard and funded a 401(k). How foolish of me."

"My brother Hugh says I manage my money like I live my life—by the seat of my pants."

"And do you?"

I rolled down the window a crack. Just being in the same car with this man causes me to overheat.

"No, but don't tell Hugh. He's got this idea that I'm flighty as a hummingbird and as sensible as a pile of bricks. He's wrong, of course, but he's decided that I'm his burden to bear and I don't want to disappoint him."

"How would you do that?"

"Hugh's a planner. He's already resigned himself to never marrying, and he thinks I'm too hopeless to actually settle down. Someday he believes he'll have to take me in as a charity case because I will end up a bag lady with a grocery cart full of knitted hats, paints and baby pictures." I lowered my voice. "Don't tell him I've got more money in the bank than he does. It would devastate his image of me."

"Does your family *try* to be wacky or is it genetic?"

I dug in my purse for a piece of gum and handed him one. "Genetic, I think. If you were to come to the Cassidy bash my family is having, you'd understand."

"What happens at these things?"

To my surprise, he sounded genuinely interested.

"My aunt Siobhan gives all of us the third-degree because she feels the need to know everything that's happening in the family. My uncles tell stories, the rest play music too loudly and, unfortunately, sing. Everyone eats too much, the little kids play until they drop in their tracks and my siblings and cousins tease each other unmercifully. It's just the usual family get-together."

When we paused at the stoplight, Clay turned to look at me. "I'm beginning to believe that there is nothing 'usual' about you." He paused and when he spoke again it was as if he were winching the words up one by one from the depths of a long-unused well. "Do you want some company while you're shopping?"

"What?" I couldn't believe my ears.

"Shopping. Do you want company?" He sounded annoyed, as if he hadn't wanted to say it twice.

"Why?" It wasn't very polite but he'd blindsided me with the request.

"Noah's birthday isn't long off, either. I'd forgotten about it until you mentioned your own family birthdays, that's all."

How does anyone forget his child's birthday?

"Of course. I'm particularly good at choosing gifts for six- and seven-year-old boys. My brother Caboose taught me that. Besides, Liam says my brain is permanently stuck somewhere between the ages of six and seven, anyway."

"Noah will be delighted. He's not always enamored with the gifts I give him."

Why am I not surprised?

"What did you give him last year?"

"Clothing, a contribution to a 529 college savings plan, colored pencils and—"

"I'm dying of boredom just listening to you! Poor kid. I'll bet he's tried to forget his birthday, too."

"You don't have to insult me." He didn't appear terribly offended, however. Amused was more like it.

"What did you do for his party?"

"I took him out for dinner."

"Where? Something kid-friendly, I hope."

"A sushi bar. Noah likes sushi."

"Barf, gag! What kind of father teaches a child to like sushi? A shark? He should have been at…" I rattled off a half dozen kid-friendly places.

"He also likes escargot and calamari," Clay said defensively. "He was pleased."

"Worse yet." I turned in my seat so I could look directly at him. "I tell you what, I'll let you go with me today, and I will give you expert advice on gifts for small boys. Deal?"

A plethora of emotions crossed his features at my

suggestion: surprise, shock, horror and, oddly, relief.

"Maybe…"

"You can't abuse the child with another birthday of sushi and contributions to a college fund. You need fun—bumper cars, games, pony rides, funny hats, balloons, face paint, you get the idea."

"Face paint?" he echoed doubtfully.

"You'd better hurry. This may take all day."

Clay's medical knowledge must have crowded the entire concept of play and fun out of his brain. This was apparent from the moment we stepped into the Mall of America, the largest shopping mall in the entire world.

"Wouldn't it be easier to just look in the phone book for a couple specialty shops and…"

"The 'specialty shops' you frequent are called 'banks.' Feel free to contribute to the child's college fund, but don't call that and a sushi bar his birthday party." I shook my head gloomily. "We have a lot of making up to do. Just tell me you've never given the child furniture or appliances for his birthday."

Clay hesitated. "Does a new bed in the shape of a car count? Or an alarm clock?"

I groaned. It was worse than I thought, much, much worse.

Leading Clay Reynolds through the mall was a little like taking my mother on safari. He was a tourist in a land of strange and wonderful curiosities.

"Don't you ever shop?" I asked as he stood in the middle of the bead store looking befuddled while I shopped for beads with which to make my sister a birthday present.

"A whole shop devoted to—" he picked up a lumpy brown bead "—whatever this is. What happened to the dime stores and grocery stores they had when I was a kid?"

"You've had your head in medical books much too long," I informed him. "Do you actually go to the grocery store?"

He reddened a little. "I order online."

"Clothing?"

"Same thing. I don't have time to waste walking around stores."

"It's no wonder you're the way you are," I muttered under my breath.

Unfortunately, he heard me.

"What is that supposed to mean?" He put his hand on my arm and an unfamiliar sensation surged up my arm.

Shaken, I took a step backward, away from the source of my confusion. "I, uh, nothing."

"The way I am in the hospital, you mean?" The playful expression disappeared from his eyes.

"Listen, Clay." I hoped we were still on a first-name basis after my inopportune comment. "My suggestion is that what happens at the hospital stays at the hospital. This is about our families, not us. Okay?"

He was quiet for a long moment, allowing me

plenty of time to mentally kick myself back and forth, up and down the long hallway. *Lord, I'm sorry for being so self-centered. This isn't all about me. He has feelings, too. Help me to respect his opinions whether they are mine or not.*

A slow, lazy smile spread across his features. What a spectacular-looking man he is when he isn't frowning, scowling or glaring at me. I hadn't personally received the full measure of his charm until just now, and it was like a floodlight springing to life before my eyes.

"Okay."

A sense of relief seeped through me. *Thank you, Lord! Help me hold my tongue and banish a bitter spirit in me from now on.*

I picked out enough beads to make necklaces for both my mother and my sister and towed Clay back into the mall.

"What shall we look for first for Noah's birthday?"

"He's outgrown most of his play clothes and somehow he keeps losing his socks—"

"You are not buying that child socks for his birthday."

"Okay, Miss Mall Maven, what do *you* think I should buy?"

"How much can we spend?"

Clay looked startled, as if money were not even a consideration in the equation. Of course, with him it probably wasn't. In a family like mine, however, we'd always had to consider the state of our piggy banks. We'd been happy, though. The box the refrigerator came in or a small table covered with bedsheets to make a tent could give us hours of pleasure.

"Why? What are you thinking of getting him?"

"How do you feel about a dirt bike?"

"Too dangerous."

"A train set?"

"He has one."

"A lawnmower?"

"Very funny."

"I need to think," I told him. "I've got to get into the mind of a six-year-old boy."

"How do you propose to do that?"

I glanced around the hallway in which we were standing and felt the floor shudder as a roller coaster careened by in the amusement park. Of course. Is there any better way to get into the mind of a child than at an amusement park? Especially one with a carousel, a Ferris wheel and roller coasters.

"Come, I'll show you."

We were at the ticket booth before Clay realized what I was up to. "You aren't going to get me on any of those things. I do not need to be inside Noah's head to buy him a present."

"How does he enjoy the presents you get him?"

"Just fine."

"Does he jump up and down?"

"Not necessarily."

"Squeal with delight?"

"That's your pig, not my son, who squeals."

"Then you haven't given him the right present." I slapped my credit card onto the counter to buy tickets. "Which ride do you want to go on first? The roller coaster or the Ax?"

Chapter Nineteen

Bad idea. Very bad idea. Very, very bad idea.

Serves me right, too. In my zealous enthusiasm to show Clay what fun was like, it slipped my mind that I am terrified of heights, dislike being dizzy and, because I am not a bat or an opossum, resist hanging upside down. I especially loathe dangling upside down and spinning head over heels while suspended ten stories off the ground. Unfortunately, I didn't recall any of this until it was too late.

"Come on, Clay, it will be fun, I'm sure of it." I tugged on his hand much like I imagined Noah might. This man needed some serious shaking up.

He tipped his head back to see the ten-story-high ride that looked like an enormous ax standing on end. At the bottom of the ax was a passenger platform onto which people were eagerly piling. Surely anything that creates that much enthusiasm can't be all bad.

"Have you ridden on this thing?"

"No, but it's time. I have a teeny-weeny fear of heights, but now is the time to face it." I eyed him with disdain. "Unlike some people I know."

"You are nuttier than peanut butter, Molly, you do know that, don't you?"

"Cluck, cluck, bwack!" I took a page out of Lissy's book when she was teasing Tony.

"And I'm not a chicken." He looked at me with exasperation. "You do a lousy chicken imitation, by the way."

"It takes one to know one." I was having so much fun I forgot that I, too, have a coward's gene in my DNA.

"Come on, then. At least I'll be able to impress my son when I tell him I rode the Ax." He glowered at me. "Since I'm such a lousy gift giver."

I grinned triumphantly.

It wasn't until I saw the size and nature of the restraints in the seats on the passenger platform that I began to second-guess the wisdom of this idea. There were forty people cheering and yelling "Let's go!" while Clay and I stared at each other, the enormity of what we were doing only now crashing down upon us. But it was too late.

We were lifted into the air, and the passenger platform rose as the ax at the top fell in a sweeping motion to the floor of the park. The passenger platform paused at the top, allowing us a view of the amusement park from ten stories up. Then the platform spun upside down, and I was thrown against the restraints and we were catapulted toward the concrete floor below. The ride became a pendulum, swinging back and forth, back and forth and spinning in 360-degree arcs. The riders' platform acted independently of the swinging ax, sometimes whirling us head over heels, creating rapid directional changes and unexpected forces.

And to make matters worse, some crazy person yelled, "Swing faster! Faster!" It took me a second to realize the demented person was sitting next to me. Clay was actually enjoying this!

I opened my mouth to protest, but the platform turned and I was hanging head down, looking at the concrete floor below. The protest turned into a cry for mercy as we twisted, flipped and turned, plunging toward the ground and then catapulting upward again.

My scream was lost on the air, trailing somewhere behind me like the jet stream of an airplane making white streaks across the sky.

When I finally opened one eye to see if I was dead or alive, Clay was staring down at me.

"Ride's over." He took me by the armpits and walked me like a puppeteer manipulating a marionette to a nearby bench. "Can you stay there without falling over?"

"I think so," I whispered, a sailor who hasn't lost her sea legs yet.

"Good. Don't go anywhere."

As if.

Clay returned in a few moments with a carbonated soda in hand. He put the straw in my mouth. "Suck. You probably shredded your throat screaming, and it will settle your stomach if it's still churning."

The cold wetness felt wonderful on my lips and the sugar hit didn't hurt, either. I felt myself gradually coming back to earth.

"So you do more doctoring than just delivering babies," I mumbled faintly.

"A regular Renaissance man," he agreed cheerfully. "That was fun. Want to do it again?"

I groaned. "Not in this lifetime."

"I have to admit it, Molly, you were right. I'm staid and stuffy. I should be enjoying life more. How do you feel about roller coasters?"

I pointed in the direction of the kiddies' rides where a mini roller coaster whipped around the track. "That's the biggest I'll go on."

"If you aren't going to be any fun, maybe we'd just better shop for Noah."

He was way too cheery for my taste.

"Did you get any gift ideas while you were hanging upside down?" I tried to stand up but my legs seemed to have other ideas.

"Actually, I did." He lifted me off the bench and stood me upright on watery legs. "How do in-line skates and a helmet sound?"

"Like a recipe for a broken arm." My legs buckled and I sat down again.

"Downhill skis?"

"Same recipe, different broken body part." Had I created a monster?

"A chemistry set."

"Better. Of course, he could blow up your house."

"I'll work with him. It might be fun for both of us."

"How about throwing in a parakeet and an ant farm?"

"No birds."

"Ants, then. Clay, the boy needs some sort of pet that he can call his own. Even an ant is better than nothing. Besides, they can lift twenty times their own weight and have three eyes. Little boys love that stuff."

He looked at me curiously. His eyes were lovely when lit by a smile. "Is this coming from a woman who at one time or another has *owned* an ant farm?"

"Years ago. The older I am, the bigger my pets get."

"What's going to be next, a milk cow and an elephant?"

I nodded thoughtfully. "Good idea. I like it. The cow, I mean. My yard isn't big enough for an elephant."

"You are incorrigible, do you know that?" He leaned against a post, arms crossed over his chest. His expression was a mix of amusement and dismay.

"Don't try to sweet-talk me out of this. As soon as I can stand, we're going to buy an ant farm." I attempted to stand again. My legs had turned into cooked spaghetti. "Or you can buy it and come back for me."

"I wouldn't dream of it. You're the expert. Maybe you'll feel better after we shop a while longer." He took my arm and helped me up, then put his arm supportively around my waist. I grabbed the circle of his leather belt, needing to hang on to something.

"Maybe we should shop for you now that we've got Noah figured out."

"Me?" Where did that squeak in my voice come from? "But Noah…"

He pulled a mall directory and map out of his shirt pocket. "There are a couple places in here that should have what we're looking for. We'll stop there on the way out. Now, what do you need? Clothes? Shoes? Women always want shoes."

The merely surreal was quickly spiraling into the exceedingly bizarre, I realized as I sat in a small specialty shoe store trying on shoes and being grateful that I had not only given Geranium a pedicure, but myself one, as well. Clay had morphed into a man of virtue and patience that I hadn't believed possible. He good-naturedly sat in the chair next to me, giving me a play-by-play of his opinion of the shoes the clerk was showing me.

"Too flat… Too ugly… I wouldn't even put those things on Geranium…."

I love shoes but rarely buy anything other than sturdy things with good arch support and little style. I'm on my feet a lot, often on tile floors, so anything with high heels or any sort of style is highly impractical.

"Man, I could do surgery with the points on those toes. I didn't know foot binding was coming back into fashion,"

The clerk glared at Clay and pursed her lips. I'm sure she wanted to smack him but held her tongue. I know the feeling.

He stood up and sauntered to the far side of the store and picked up a glorious shoe, one I'd noticed as we'd walked in. "How about this?" He dangled the shoe from his forefinger by its slim black back strap. "Stylish, sophisticated, good arch support, can be dressed up or down, able to serve the same function as that other old standby, the little black dress."

The clerk stared at him with new respect in her eyes.

"And more expensive than my car payment."

He glanced at the price tag on the sole. "Hardly. Not much more than those." He pointed to my Birkenstocks.

"They are if I only wear them to church on Sundays."

"What about your family get-together, the Cassidy bash, or whatever it is?"

"I usually don't dress up that much…. My family wouldn't know who I was…. Hildy might eat them…."

He turned to the clerk. "She'll take them."

Suddenly Clay was her best friend. "I have a lovely evening bag that would match perfectly. Would you like to see it?"

Clay glanced at me and grinned. "Molly would love to."

I was stunned to walk out of the store with shoes and a purse that I would never have purchased on my own. I also felt a little giddy. I'm good at denying myself things, and I loved the shoes. The part that astounds me is that it was Clay Reynolds who talked me into buying them.

In the hallway I turned to the right, but Clay grabbed my arm. "This way."

"I thought we were going to buy Noah's gifts."

"We will. But first, I like the look of this little store over here." He steered me toward a women's apparel store, one of those places that has only two or three things in the window on gaunt models, which guaranteed that the prices would be king-size.

"You have good taste." I had to give him that. "But I don't shop there."

"Why not?"

"The question is, why do you care?"

"You've been manipulating me to your way of thinking about Noah. I'm just returning the favor. This is how *I* think *you* should shop."

Ouch. Touché.

"I don't have any money left after purchasing those shoes."

"When was the last time you bought a new dress?"

"Not long ago. I found the skirt while I was shopping with Lissy."

"An evening dress, one that might match those shoes."

"A while, I guess." I counted backward in my head. "Five or six years, maybe. I live a very casual life, you know." I was loath to add, but it bubbled out anyway, "I suppose my friends might be getting sick of the same dress, but I reaccessorize...."

He gazed at me, one dark eyebrow lifted speculatively.

"Okay, I'll look, but this is all weird, just plain weird." I flapped my arms. "You hate me. You don't want me anywhere near you and yet you think I need new party clothes?"

"I never said I 'hate' you. And the only place I don't want you near me is in the hospital. Besides, you've been aggravating me for weeks. It's fun to return the favor."

I felt my lower lip jut out. "I liked you better cold and obnoxious."

"Don't worry, today is an aberration. It won't continue. I'm just having a little fun. The last time I went shopping like this was just before..." His words trailed off and I saw pain pierce through him as plainly as if he'd been stabbed by a sword.

Before he lost his wife.

I put my hand on his arm. "Okay, come on. Have your fun, but I'm not speaking to you again after today."

He rallied and some of his smile returned. "Good. You're very noisy. You disturb my peace and quiet."

You, Clay Reynolds, disturb a lot more than that in me.

I tried to pout but the dresses were too pretty. What's more, Clay, shockingly, has a very good eye for style. Every dress he recommended I try on fit like a glove. The ones I chose on my own were a parade of deteriorating fashion disasters.

"Why are you so good at this?" I asked, as the clerk wrapped up a trim black sheath that was going to look stunning with my new shoes.

He chuckled. "Actually, I had a good teacher. My grandfather's sister was a bit of a clotheshorse in her day and she often dragged me with her when she went shopping. I adored her, so she could have asked me to go to Siberia with her and I would have said 'How much do I pack?' I learned by osmosis. That, and the fact that she'd always tell me why she liked a dress or why she didn't. She explained the styling and the workmanship."

"You had an odd upbringing."

"Not necessarily odd, but certainly different from yours."

"And now you're duplicating your upbringing for Noah."

He stiffened. "What do you mean by that?"

"You were treated like a little old man and that's how you treat him. You overprotect him, you know."

"And you're an expert on that?"

I laughed. "I was the exact opposite of over-protected. Mom always said if there wasn't blood, it probably wasn't serious. I wrestled with my brothers, dangled from trees and ate mud pies. And look at how I turned out!"

He eyed me and I realized that might not have been the wisest example to use to secure my argument.

Chapter Twenty

"I don't know about you, but I'm hungry." Clay, loaded down like a pack horse with bags and boxes, looked up and down the parking lot for his vehicle.

"You've been working hard." I took one of the larger bags from his hand. "It's not easy to boss me around."

"You're telling me. It's like pushing a boulder uphill in a thunderstorm." As if he hadn't insulted me at all, he added, "After we put this stuff in the car, I know a great place on the St. Croix for dinner."

My mind whirring, I trailed him to the Mercedes. I couldn't explain, even to myself, how I can feel comfortable with him while knowing what he thinks of my ilk, but I can. If he is willing to leave work at the hospital, I am, too.

He put the bags in the trunk before courteously

opening the car door for me and rounding the car to the driver's side. When he dropped into his seat behind the wheel, I blurted, "I don't get it."

"Get what?" He buckled his seat belt and turned the key in the ignition.

"If I'm so difficult, why did you spend the day with me?"

"Because, in spite of being a pain in the neck, you're funny, cheerful and the only living human being to ever get me on a carnival ride that was ten stories off the ground."

"So, I'm determined and relentless, too. A worthy foe."

He glanced at me sharply. "If you're talking about Bradshaw Medical and my opinion of birthing rooms that look like Grand Central Station, no. You can't win that one."

"Too bad. I thought I was getting to like you."

"Now why would you do that?" He seemed to enjoy the repartee.

"You're actually fun when you haven't got a chip the size of Nevada on your shoulder. You've been a relatively good sport, you had patience enough to go shopping with me and you have probably been as cheerful as you know how to be."

"That's a ringing endorsement. I'm overwhelmed." He pulled into traffic going east on the freeway and relaxed in his seat. A faint smile tipped the corners of his lips and lit his eyes, improving the already impressive scenery.

"Why are you nice to me outside the hospital and when we are there such a…a…"

"Swine?" He filled in the blank.

"No. I like swine. You're a *fiend* at Bradshaw Medical." I immediately felt a twinge of guilt. "No offense or anything."

"None taken. I will always be a 'fiend' where my patients are concerned, particularly if I believe there is anything happening that is not in their best interest. Nothing you can do or say will ever change that."

I could see his steely determination in the set of his jaw and, although I didn't agree that a doula was not in a woman's best interest, I have to admire the ferocity with which he protects his patients.

"Frankly, I'm not even sure why today happened," he continued. Then his blue eyes began to twinkle like my brothers' do when trying to aggravate me. "You didn't annoy me nearly as much as you do when you're doing your doula thing at Bradshaw." He softened the statement with a smile as charming as the ones Noah could shower on me.

"The makings of a perfect relationship." I sighed. "I'm sure great friendships are forged on foundations like this."

"Tolerance and compromise. The building blocks of rapport."

"That's for warring countries, not human beings."

"Oh, yes. I forgot." He looked completely at ease as we drove across the river toward Hudson, Wisconsin.

Today Clay's charm definitely outweighed his stubborn pigheadedness. There I go again, insulting pigs.

It was fruitless to speculate any further, so when we arrived at the restaurant overlooking the St. Croix, I made up my mind to enjoy the food and not think of the inevitability of next time Clay and I were bound to cross swords.

There was just enough wind to keep the mosquitoes from biting, and the air was comfortably warm as we sat on the outside deck overlooking the river. The St. Croix, a tributary of the Mississippi, was dotted with large boats. Everyone seemed to know Clay at the place, and he was led, without question, to be best table overlooking the river.

"You've been here before."

"A time or two. I recommend the bruschetta and the artichoke dip as appetizers, the prime rib for your entrée and the chocolate cake for dessert."

"If you think I should eat all that, we should have bought my dress a size larger."

"Want to share?"

Share? Now that's a concept. I come from a family in which there are always skirmishes over food. My brothers decided long ago that I, as a girl, didn't need as much food as they did and certainly no dessert. To have a man suggest sharing an entire meal with me is an anomaly of the highest order.

"Is that deer-in-the-headlights look a yes or a no?"

"Yes, I think."

He ordered before turning back to me. "What are you staring at?"

"You're beginning to scare me. Who are you? Is the man at the hospital your evil twin, or what?"

He laughed and laid his hand on the table so that it brushed mine. "You're growing on me, Molly. And I appreciate anyone who cares about my son's feelings. It's the least I can do to show my appreciation. You turned my attitude on its head toward Noah's birthday."

"That was the carnival ride, not me."

"Let's just enjoy the evening. I've put the hospital out of my mind for the night. I'm not a chameleon. I know that tomorrow my attitude about having you or any doula with my clients is not going to change. I'd like to think that today is about Noah and you. What do you think?"

There was nothing I could do but agree. Today was an island in the storm.

Dusk descended into a clear, cloud-free night, and the candle on the table flickered on the planes and angles of Clay's features. Relaxed, he looked so much like Noah that I knew exactly how Clay himself had looked as a child. Noah's childish features would eventually take on the ruggedness of his father's, including the finely chiseled chin and sensitive mouth.

"How is it to raise your son alone?" Had such a personal question come from my own mouth? "Sorry," I added quickly. "You don't have to answer that if you don't want to."

"You've already seen what a lousy job I've done of his birthday in the past. It's no wonder you're curious." His eyes focused somewhere behind me as he spoke.

"I didn't think that at all!" I paused. "Well, maybe a little."

"You're a compulsive truth teller, aren't you?"

"'Truthful lips endure forever, but a lying tongue lasts only a moment.' That's in Proverbs. Besides, I'm not savvy enough to lie. I couldn't keep straight what I said and to whom. Truth is definitely easier."

He leaned back in his chair and studied me through lowered lids. "Noah's IQ is off the charts, but socially and emotionally he's very much a six-year-old. I've always been glad he isn't one of those precocious brats that no one can tolerate. The reason I decided to leave California and come to the Twin Cities is that I think Noah will thrive here. The schools are good, my grandparents have a home here so he'll see family and—" he smiled a little "—I like to ski, particularly cross-country. I do biathlons."

I must have looked blank.

"It's a combination of marksmanship and skiing."

My eyes narrowed. "Do you hunt?"

"No. And I'm not lying just so that you won't jump up and storm out of here. I'm not interested in killing anything. I'm a healer, remember? I am brutal to a field target, however."

I imagined Clay on skis with a rifle strapped to his back, a rather enticing masculine image.

"You are an athlete, then?"

"Armchair type, mostly, these days, but I hope to change that this winter. I might add a little downhill to Noah's repertoire. How about you?"

"I grew up with brothers. I played hockey, as the puck…football, as the ball…softball, as the one who had to climb the fence and go into the neighbor's yard to retrieve the ball." And the evening was half-over before I realized that Clay had deftly turned the topic of conversation from himself to me and kept it there.

The next afternoon Tony and Lissy stopped by with a supreme pizza, a liter of soda and an ice-cream cake. Hildy's ears came to attention and Geranium poked her snout through the pet door at the first whiff of the food.

"What's the occasion?"

"We're celebrating." Lissy put the ice-cream cake in my freezer and headed for the silverware drawer. "Tony got a promotion."

I eyeballed him. "He doesn't look all that happy."

"He's the new nursing supervisor."

"No kidding? That's a big deal. Now you are in charge of making the nursing schedule."

"And interviewing applicants for Nurses' Services. He'll be the one checking up on the nurses' work, too."

"Administration and paperwork," Tony grumbled. "It will cut down my opportunities for direct nursing care."

"There must be a pay raise in it for you," I pointed out.

"And he has Wanda to thank for it." Lissy looked particularly amused by this.

"She put in a good word for you?" I dealt out paper plates and dug in a drawer for napkins.

"Let's just say she motivated him to success." Lissy opened the pizza box and took the first slice.

"I know I haven't been around Bradshaw Medical for a few days but things must be changing rapidly."

Tony slumped lower in his chair and stared gloomily at a sliced olive lying on the table.

"He was so busy avoiding her that several patients commented to the administrator how attentive he was. He quit taking breaks so as not to be caught in the lunchroom with Wanda. With all the extra time on his hands, he turned into über-nurse. By trying to hide from her, he made himself stand out from everyone else. Hence—" Lissy gave a little curtsy "—he's the new nursing supervisor."

"What's so bad about that?" I gave Hildy a bit of crust from my plate as she sat on the floor next to me. Her style of begging is to sit at my feet and look emaciated. That's a difficult stunt for an eighty-five-pound dog, but somehow she manages it.

Tony sank deeper in his chair. "Now I'm going to have regular office hours and she will know where I am at all times. And I'll have to oversee her work as her supervisor. I'll never be able to get away. I'm trapped."

"She's a professional. She won't monopolize your time."

"No? She will be waiting outside my office door to pounce every time I leave the office."

"I'm sorry you are so cute and charming, Tony," I said. "Because you are my friend I wish you were short, stooped and balding."

"And had a lisp and a twitch," Lissy added helpfully.

"But no such luck. You'll just have to deal with it."

"You've heard me say it before. 'Love sought is good, but giv'n unsought is better,'" Tony quoted. "Why can't Wanda figure that out?"

"You mean that if Wanda *waited* for you to give her your love, it would be more meaningful?"

"That would be a long wait," Lissy rejoined. "Probably until the end of time."

"Let's say grace," I said as I put a slice of Canadian bacon, pineapple and pepperoni on my plate.

After two slices of pizza, I licked my fingers and studied Tony. "Scripture says we're supposed to give thanks in all circumstances. There must be *something* good about your promotion."

"He'll be privy to Dr. Reynolds's thoughts about you," Lissy pointed out.

No wonder Tony is depressed.

I'm ambivalent about the good doctor and he's even more unsure about me.

"How's your sister?" I asked as I cut into the cake.

"I tried to tell her what you said about the train

set but she wouldn't have any of it. She doesn't listen to anyone these days. It takes time away from her obsession with getting pregnant."

"Hope deferred isn't necessarily a denial of what we want. It can be a postponement."

"Try telling her that," he groused.

"I know another benefit of Tony's new position," Lissy said, attempting to change the subject. She had a bit of chocolate ice cream on her chin, which Tony leaned forward to wipe away.

"And that is?"

"He heard at a meeting that someone wants to make a documentary at Bradshaw!"

I leaned forward, feeling sick in the pit of my stomach. "What documentary?"

"I don't know much about it." Tony shrugged. "Just that some team of moviemakers wants to film a documentary in the hospital."

"Do you know what the documentary is about?"

"Yeah, what is so interesting at Bradshaw over any other hospital?" Lissy asked. "Bradshaw is small. How'd they even find out about the place?"

Say it isn't so. Say it isn't so!

"I didn't get the whole story," Tony said absently, absorbed, as usual, with his food, "but it sounds like someone invited them to Bradshaw."

It can't be.

"Weird," Lissy concluded and dismissed the topic. "I have to go home, guys. Tony, you drove. Are you ready?"

I saw them to the door and waved cheerfully as they backed out of the driveway. Then I shut the door, leaned against it and sank to the floor. Hildy came over to lick my face.

I was in trouble now, more trouble than for anything I might have done in a birthing room. I'd opened a Pandora's box that was going to cause an unimaginable amount of turmoil.

Chapter Twenty-One

Don't invite trouble.

If it's not broken, don't fix it.

Pretend it isn't there and maybe it will just go away.

I recall playing hide-and-seek with Caboose when he was only two years old. Instead of actually hiding, he would stand right where he was and cover his eyes. His logic was that if he couldn't see me, I couldn't see him, either. Right now, it's the only game I can think of to play.

A documentary being done at Bradshaw Medical. What foolhardy soul would invite someone to do that?

Someone with more enthusiasm than common sense, more passion than practicality and more zeal than prudence. In a word, me.

I'd started the snowball rolling months ago, long before Clay was a blip on Bradshaw's screen. It hadn't been much of a snowball, either, just a note to a small production company that had done some of the videos used in birthing classes. Feeling clever, I'd whipped up a brief letter and sent it to the name and address of the production company from the backside of the video's box.

> To whom it may concern,
> I am a birthing coach (doula) who recommends your videos to my clients. Doulas, professional birth assistants, support not only the laboring mother but also the father and hospital staff. The origins of this tradition are thousands of years old yet it is relevant and contemporary for today's world. I thought you might be interested to know that statistically, women who are attended through labor have shorter labors, use less pain-relief medication and have fewer Cesareans. I attend women from early labor to delivery and am a support partner, freeing the parents-to-be to focus on the birth of their child. I thought you might be interested…

I'd never heard a word from the company and had assumed it ended up in the round file at the base of their desk—just more garbage. Until now.

Just the *idea* of a video informing the public about doulas would make Clay apoplectic. If the hospital board wanted to use Bradshaw for the taping, Clay would have to be put in restraints to keep from bodily chasing the production crew off the premises.

How was I to know back then that someone as rigid as Clay would become the voice of Bradshaw? It had seemed like such a good idea at the time.

I grabbed Hildy and buried my nose in her fur. "Oh, Hildy, girl, I'm going to be in big trouble if Clay ever gets wind of this and discovers I'm behind it. What was I thinking?"

Hildy put her big paw on my knee and whined sympathetically.

"I'll just act dumb. I'll never bring it up. No one at Bradshaw would agree to it anyway." I'd seen how carefully everyone listened to Clay's opinions. He'd probably never even hear about it. Nothing to worry about, I told myself as I headed for bed. No use wasting sleep over this. A request like this would get lost in administrative paperwork. It was purely an accident that Tony even heard the gossip.

By the time I went to bed, I'd convinced myself this was an insignificant blip on my radar screen.

In reality, I should have been worrying. Or looking for a new state in which to live.

"Candy?" Mattie B. Olson offered me a large box of Godiva chocolates as we sat together in her room at River's View with Hildy at her side.

I took a chocolate hazelnut truffle. "Where did you get a box of candy like this? It's enormous."

"I'm one of the lucky ones in here," Mattie said.

"My family is very attentive. Unlike some of the residents who are alone, I have people who stop by often—and bring me fattening gifts." She patted her stomach. "Even though they know I want to keep my girlish figure."

"Are you hinting that we should go visit someone more in need than you?" I teased gently. We'd already made the rounds, Hildy and I, and we'd saved Mattie for the last.

"I certainly am not!" She smiled at me and her blue eyes danced with light and youth that belied her age. "Fortunately, one of my nephews is a gerontologist and he has educated the family on how important it is to 'keep me in the loop,' so to speak."

"Even if your nephew were a mechanic, everyone would keep you in the loop. I'm sure you are a delight at a party."

"Sadly, I *am* known as the party girl in my family. When surrounded with a bunch of somber surgeons trying to save the world, anything is better than a discussion of the benefits of laparoscopy versus standard surgery. Even in my father's days of practicing medicine, he and my brothers would have conversations as interesting as watching paint dry."

Mattie looked at me with amusement, her face, though lined, still beautiful.

"Your family isn't like that, is it, Molly?"

"Mine? No. Compared to yours we look like a

three-ring circus complete with a dozen clowns. Which reminds me…"

"Yes?" Mattie leaned forward, curiosity in her expression.

"We're having a party next weekend. A Cassidy bash. That means every relative within traveling distance will be there. The in-laws, the out-laws and everybody in between. After a bash one year, it took us two weeks to sort out that a stranger had wandered in, eaten dinner, partied with us and wandered out again. Each of us assumed he'd come with someone else."

"Oh, my." Mattie looked delighted. "Tell me all about it."

"The bashes pretty much happen on their own now. Someone puts out the word that there's going to be one and the rest of the family burns up the phone lines telling everyone else. Since it's at my parents' house this time, Mom's in charge of the food. Dad cleans the garage and the basement because we need the extra room. Liam and Caboose are always in charge of setting up the backyard for the kids—horseshoes, badminton, a full sandbox— and cleaning our old playhouse.

"My uncle Kenny is a musician so he gets together a little family band. Anyone can play. If someone doesn't have an instrument, Mom hands them a pair of spoons. Staying in tune has no special merit in Cassidy music. It's all about the noise and the fun. We eat, tell wild stories, sing and generally carry on like fools into the wee hours of the morning. My uncle Matt retreats to the corner to sing 'My Wild Irish Rose' to Hildy, who is the only one who will listen. Then we hug, kiss, promise to do this again soon and say goodbye. My family spends the next week recovering and cleaning up the mess. Then someone gets the bright idea to do it all over again."

"Mercy, me!" Mattie clapped her hands. "It sounds wonderful! I wish I could give an infusion of your family's energy into mine."

"You're welcome to come to our party, Mattie. I'd come and get you if you like."

She put her hand over mine, and I saw tears flooding her eyes. "Just being asked is enough, my dear girl. I'm not up to so much fun, I'm afraid. It would be a shock to my system, but thank you for being so generous."

I leaned forward and kissed her white head. "Whenever you're ready, Mattie, let me know. We'll have a bash just for you."

I thought about my elderly friend all the way to my place. When I arrived, my door was open and Lissy had made herself at home inside.

"What's your ideal man like, Molly?" Lissy was curled into the corner of my couch eating coffee ice cream directly from a pint-size cardboard carton. She waved her teaspoon in the direction of the magazine lying open next to her. "This article says that if you don't share the same values as the man you love, you will have a difficult time making it as a couple."

"I agree with that." I picked up the magazine and looked at the long list of values to choose from: honesty, integrity, success, fortune, ambition, loyalty, perfection, faith, family, career, love, safety, fame, power, nature, beauty, service, compassion... The list seemed endless, all the things someone might hold dear.

Long as it was, I knew immediately what my choices would be. "Faith, family, service and stewardship." I glanced at Geri, who was plopped in front of the television seeming to watch a rerun of *Green Acres*. "Stewardship of the earth and the animals God gave us."

"Then those are the things you should look for in a partner—someone who believes as you do, thinks family is a priority and is nuts about weird animals."

As Lissy said it, I imagined a series of zookeepers knocking on my door, all hoping to make a match with me.

"Tony is all about food and family, faith and education and the poetry. Until he finds a woman who has his values, he's not going to be happy," I commented. "What are your values, Lissy?"

She stared at the ceiling, thinking hard. "Family is a big one. I've missed mine terribly since I moved here from Denver. Faith goes without saying. Something I value but don't get enough of is beauty—design, art, music, those kinds of things."

"I didn't realize…"

"You wouldn't. I used to play the guitar and do ink and charcoal sketches, but there's no time anymore." She sounded wistful. "I've made a lot of poor choices in men. Maybe if I'd looked at their values first, I wouldn't have had so many disappointments. Unfortunately I have an internal clock of my own ticking away, reminding that I'd better get busy or I might not find someone to love."

A question skittered into my mind. What were Clay Reynolds's values? I could guess—fatherhood, healing, new life, success, achievement, safety. The things he held dear all coalesced in the birthing room.

"You have an odd look on your face," Lissy observed. "What's that about?"

"Nothing important." I bounced to my feet. "Want to watch a movie? There wasn't much left to choose from at the video store so I got a comedy. Slapstick always cheers me up."

"I didn't know you needed cheering."

"I don't, but there's nothing like preventive medicine."

I was glad Lissy turned toward the television set and away from me. A realization had hit me like a sledgehammer during my conversation with Lissy. It's no wonder that Clay and I can't get along at the hospital. I bring to the table everything his values are not. I'm messy, impulsive, touchy-feely and impetuous—perilous things to a man of science.

Then again, it doesn't really matter. There are plenty of hospitals and plenty of men out there. I don't have to care what Clay Reynolds thinks.

Chapter Twenty-Two

Shades of Tony.

I tiptoed down the hall of Bradshaw Medical at one o'clock in the afternoon, hoping to make myself invisible. It wasn't Wanda that I was hiding from, however, but Clay. I have to see him sooner or later, but my preference is definitely for later.

Emily Hancock had called at noon to say her labor had begun and asked me to meet her at the hospital.

"Dr. Reynolds told me I should come in right away," Emily had said. "You know how overprotective he is. This baby won't arrive for hours, but he wants to monitor an old woman like me more closely."

"You aren't an old woman. Forty is the new thirty, haven't you heard? He's equally cautious with everyone."

"I know. It's probably because my husband, Charles, is out of town that he wants me to come now."

"You're alone? I thought he'd come home from the mission trip."

"He did. Charles had a meeting in Boston today. He'll be home as soon as he can get a flight."

"Why didn't you call me? I would have come immediately."

"Dr. Reynolds took me by surprise. I didn't expect him to tell me to come right in, so I asked the gentleman who lives next door to drive me."

"A neighbor? Emily, you have a much bigger support system than that."

"My friends and mother have been so difficult. They're all better off hearing of the baby after it's born. I don't want naysayers around me right now. The last thing I need to hear is 'I told you so,' or 'You're too old for this.'"

"I'll meet you at the hospital."

"You are a gift from God, Molly. I mean that."

I didn't argue with her. God gave me the skills I have for a reason, and I'm willing to use them in any way He chooses, no matter what Clay Reynolds thinks.

By the time I arrived, Emily had already checked into a deluxe birthing suite with a big-screen television, easy chairs, thick drapes and a refrigerator filled with sodas and juice for thirsty family members.

"Nice digs," I commented as I entered. "You deserve it."

The bright smile she'd greeted me with began to waver.

I studied her features. "Scared?"

The cheery facade weakened even further. "What if Charles doesn't make it in time? I can't do this by myself."

"You don't have to. You have a great doctor and staff. And you have me."

She reached for my hand. "Don't leave my side, Molly. Promise?"

"I, ah…"

"Promise!"

"Okay, but what if Dr. Reynolds doesn't want me?"

"He'll listen to me." She said it with such assurance that I almost believed her.

If he does, she's a better woman than I am.

The door opened and Clay strode in wearing scrubs, a stethoscope draped around his neck, a file in his hand. "Hi, Emily. So today is the day. How long did you say it would be until Charles's plane arrives?" He stopped walking so suddenly I thought he'd leave skid marks on the tile floor. "You…" His glare would have frozen water.

"Soon. Until then, Molly is his stand-in."

"I don't think—"

"It doesn't matter what you think," Emily said. "This is my choice. Molly has been invaluable to me, and I know that she is what I need right now."

My eyebrow rose involuntarily. I've never heard anyone speak to Clay this way. What's more, I certainly hadn't expected it to come from the mouth of fragile, ladylike Emily Hancock. Even more amazing, Clay actually seemed to accept it.

"If it's what you wish, Emily. You already know *my* views on the subject."

"I do. And I disagree with them. Molly stays."

He glowered at me when Emily turned her head.

Well, all-righty, then…

As the hours passed we found a rhythm in backrubs, games of rock, paper, scissors, crossword puzzles and more backrubs. In my bag I had CDs of Emily's favorite music and a photo of her husband to use as a focal point in case the real thing didn't make it in time. I also read aloud to her from women's magazines. The time passed with surprising speed.

Every time Clay walked into the room and saw me his face registered an expression I chose to believe was inspired by the smell of the candles I'd lit and not my presence. He'd told me it would be his way. Until now, I think I'd chosen not to believe it.

"How are you doing, Em?" He leaned over her in the bed like a father might over his child.

"Slow but sure. The contractions are closer, but Molly is great at distracting me, so I don't think about them too much."

"She is that, distracting, I mean."

Emily eyed him and then me. Her patrician face registered something I couldn't read.

"You are a bit stuffy, Dr. Reynolds," Emily observed.

I held my breath, waiting for the hammer to drop, but he merely smiled at her.

"I hardly think *stuffy* is the best word to describe me," he chided gently.

"Rigid, then. It's a new day. Even old ladies like me get pregnant—and it's safe."

"You can never take too many precautions...."

"All the safeguards in the world can't stop some things from happening." Emily looked at him with something that bordered on tenderness.

It was an odd exchange. What was between these two that was not visible to my eye?

"Have it your way," he said cheerfully. "Just get that baby born."

Then he turned around and gave me a look so fiery it would melt steel. "And don't mess anything up," his expression said.

"Did you and Dr. Reynolds know each other before you became his patient?" I asked Emily once he was gone.

"Why do you ask?"

"You seem to know him rather well."

Emily was about to answer when her eyes grew round and she clapped her hand on her belly. "Oh! That was a big one. They're coming faster now."

An understatement. Within the next thirty minutes Emily began progressing rapidly. Clay appeared to check on her with two nurses following in his wake.

After a brief check he said, "It's going to be soon, Emily. I'd recommend that we clear the room and..."

"Molly isn't going anywhere and don't try to convince me otherwise. Your job is to deliver this baby and…." She winced. "Maybe you should do it now."

If Clay had had his way, he might have stalled forever. Fortunately Baby Hancock had a different schedule in mind.

Oliver Thomas James Hancock was born at 7:15 p.m. His father, Charles, arrived at 7:35 p.m., as red-faced from exertion as his wife.

He burst into the room to see his wife holding their son. "Emily!" He moved forward slowly, as if the marvelous sight was a mirage that might shimmer and disappear at any moment.

I turned away to give them privacy, and my gaze fell on Clay.

For a moment I saw wistfulness on his features. Then he began to glower at me as if wishing I'd dematerialize and go pester someone other than him.

It was Clay's bit of bad luck that Charles chose that moment to notice me. Emily's husband strode across the room and gathered me in a bear hug that lifted me off my feet and nearly suffocated me.

"Emily raves about you, Molly. She's convinced that every woman needs someone like you in her life. I don't even know how to say thank you."

"No need," I murmured awkwardly, feeling Clay's gaze boring into my back. "It's my job."

"It's more than that for you, my dear." Charles patted me fondly on the head like I was his favorite Labrador retriever. "Anyone can see that."

* * *

Clay found me later, in the cafeteria, scarfing down cheesy nachos with jalapeños and a foot-long hot dog.

He threw himself down on the chair across from mine without a word. I kept eating.

"You certainly won that round," he commented.

"I didn't know I was fighting." I dragged a chip through the orange cheese glop and put it in my mouth.

"That's a laugh. You've been fighting me tooth and nail since I arrived."

"I have not. You are the doctor. I'm just a lowly doula. You are the rooster, and I am at the bottom of the pecking order. How could I fight you?" That approach-avoidance thing I suffer when Clay is around flared up again.

"Maybe not outwardly, but inwardly. I see your disappointment in me in your eyes."

I held my chip suspended in midair between the basket and my mouth. Was I so transparent?

"Listen, Molly, you know this isn't about you personally. It's just that in my experience..." His voice trailed away.

What made him so adamantly opposed to this? I wondered. It wasn't as if this were a life-and-death thing. Or *had* he lost patients...

My train of thought careened over a cliff.

"Did you... Have you..."

"I'm not going there with you, Molly. Let's just say that I have a lot more experience than you do, not all of it good. It will be good for both of us if you aren't here at Bradshaw so often."

"Absence makes the heart grow fonder?" I joked weakly, even though my knees were rattling and I felt like I might suffocate.

"Maybe." He smiled, almost gently this time. "But I doubt it."

Fortunately the upcoming Cassidy bash gave me something to think about other than Clay's rebuff.

"Molly." My mother's voice sounded harried on the phone. "You've got to do my grocery shopping for me. Your brothers and father are cleaning the garage and the basement, putting the yard together and setting up a tent. Liam is running errands for me on his motorcycle. I'm in the midst of baking soda bread and won't be done for hours. I…"

"Just give me the list, Mom. I'll take care of it."

A huge sigh of relief gusted across the line. "I knew I could count on you, Molly. I can always count on you."

Yup, good old reliable me, perfect daughter but menace in the delivery room.

"Remember that I'm making coddle and will need pork sausage, streaky rashers, potatoes and onions…"

As I strolled up and down the aisles of the warehouse store looking for pork sausages and bacon, the streaky rashers my mother had requested, I couldn't quit thinking of how much Clay's assessment of me had shaken my confidence.

I had never, not once, questioned my calling until

he'd come along. Sadly, last weekend I'd gone online looking for jobs. Yesterday I'd even stopped myself from picking up the phone to call the school at which I'd taught to see if any teachers were planning to leave or retire. Clay's attitude had me questioning myself.

All I had left to pick up were baked goods. My family has a sweet tooth the size of a school bus. I was busy piling sweets into my cart when I looked up and saw Clay Reynolds staring at me.

I dropped an angel food cake into my cart, nearly cracking it in half. "You!"

"I suppose I shouldn't be surprised that you aren't glad to see me." He wore casual jeans, tennis shoes and a soft blue sweatshirt that had seen better days.

"I didn't know you shopped in bulk," I said, a brain-dead remark if there ever was one.

That seemed to amuse him. "I don't, but this was the best place to find one of these." He pointed to a large wooden play yard with a tree house, slide and swing. "I'm getting it for Noah for his birthday. I thought an ant farm and a chemistry set might not make up for years of sushi and savings bonds."

So my thoughts weren't completely worthless. He was attempting to turn Noah back into a little boy.

He peered into my cart. "There's enough food in there to stock the hospital cafeteria."

"My family is having a party."

"Yes, I remember."

I was grateful that a clerk with a tape measure

interrupted us. "I took some measurements and think the crate will fit into the back of your vehicle, sir. You can pay for it at the front and we'll bring it out."

He turned to speak to her and while Clay was otherwise occupied, I grabbed an oversize box of cookies and made my escape. There was nothing left to say to him. Besides, I'm sick and tired of his two personas—affable outside the hospital, surly inside.

Unfortunately he caught up with me at the cash register where the clerk was counting and scanning the many cartons of eggs I'd purchased. "If you don't mind my asking, miss, what are you going to do with all these eggs?" the woman asked curiously as she ran the scanner over the cardboard cartons.

"Savory pies."

The clerk looked blank.

"They're like—" I tried to think of a comparison "—an Irish Egg McMuffin."

"I see."

Of course she didn't see at all.

"Who is coming to this party of yours?" Clay studied the heaps of groceries.

"Just the Cassidys and their families. They're a hungry bunch. My mother and aunts fix the traditional standbys, someone brings Irish stew and Mom puts a ham in the oven. Occasionally, if there are teenagers present, we order out for the younger ones—pizza, mostly."

"Is nothing sacred anymore? Pizza? Do they even make a good mutton and potato pizza these days?"

"Very funny."

"You're still upset, I see." He didn't seem terribly troubled about it.

"You didn't exactly greet me with open arms at the hospital."

"I've told you…"

"I know, I know." I was so frustrated I began to splutter. "But I still don't get it."

"Calm down. Don't let that Irish temper get the best of you."

Translation: Don't make a scene, Molly.

"We don't have tempers. We're the most amiable people on earth!"

"Right. Now pay the lady for the food and let's get out of here."

I would have sent Clay packing, but I needed help loading the food into my mother's van. Fortunately his back is as strong as his stubborn streak and he packed the vehicle with ease. When we were done I turned, hands on hips, to face him.

"Thank you very much. You can go now."

"I'm in no hurry."

No? Well, I am!

"What are you going to do with all that stuff?" He tipped his head toward the van.

"Drop most of it off at my mother's. The rest I'll take home and turn into salads for the party."

"Need help?"

"From you? I don't think so."

"Oh, come on, Molly. Lighten up. I enjoy your

company—when we aren't in the hospital, that is. You're good for a few laughs." He sounded more like one of my brothers than my nemesis.

"I'm your own personal *I Love Lucy,* you mean? What about Noah?" I held up a hand to stop him from saying anything. "No, don't tell me. He's visiting his aunt again. You're off duty and because you lead such a dull and dismal life I'm the only one you can think of who might entertain you. Am I close?"

"Right on the money." At least he's cheerful about his pitiable state.

"Clay, that's pathetic. Here's the deal. I love my work. It's what I'm born to do, and you don't respect it. What's the point of spending time together when we drive each other crazy?"

"Because it's better than being alone?"

The words felt like a punch in my chest. He was right. We are two badly mismatched people who don't have time or energy to look for Mr. or Miss Right. We are only in each other's company because it's preferable to being alone.

He picked up on my hesitation. "I make great salads."

I thought of the heads of broccoli, cauliflower and lettuce in my vehicle. It was going to take me hours to turn it into party food.

"How great?" I felt myself capitulate.

"You'll be astounded." He looked boyishly charming. "Wait and see."

"Don't think I'm letting you do this for any other reason than that I need the help."

Frankly, what I really need is to have my head checked. I don't want him anywhere near me and yet I'd asked him to my home.

"This is strictly business," he assured me.

Monkey business.

Chapter Twenty-Three

By the time he got to my house, I'd washed the cherry tomatoes, cauliflower and broccoli. All Clay had to do was to chop cauliflower, broccoli and onions into small pieces. That should be a breeze for a doctor. Surely he likes knives. He is a trained surgeon, after all.

He sidled into the house as if he belonged there. Before he could say anything, I put a knife in his hand and pointed him in the direction of my island. "Chop," I ordered.

Obediently, he did as he was told. Remarkable. I thought it was genetically impossible for him to do that.

Having Clay by my side in the kitchen is altogether different from working beside him in the hospital. He's pleasant, for one thing. And large.

I stumbled into him on my way to the refrigerator.

Clay grabbed me by the elbow to steady me.

"Careful. I haven't set a broken bone in years. You don't want to be my practice case."

"I must have spilled something on the floor." I looked straight down, avoiding his eyes. I also pulled away from his grasp, which was making me as unsteady as the guilty glob of mayonnaise that had made me slip.

"Did Noah call you? He demanded to have your number," Clay said casually as he went back to work with his knife.

"He did. I told him I would have to talk to you before I set up a playdate for him and Hildy. I was surprised to hear his voice on the phone. What a sweet child he is."

"The child is as persistent as…well, as you… when it comes to getting what he wants."

Clay leaned in front of me to grab a dish towel and his sleeve brushed mine.

"I'm surprised you allowed him to call."

"He woke me up at five in the morning, and I agreed to it before I'd had coffee, that's all. You don't have to do it, you know. He'll only beg me more for a dog if he gets to spend time with that canine of yours."

"I told him I'd have to check Hildy's schedule."

"A dog with a calendar and social life. Amazing."

I turned, not realizing that Clay had moved away from the chopping block, and I ran face-first into the front of his shirt. He smelled fresh and masculine, like soap, cologne and fresh air.

I skittered backward quickly. Although the encounter was very pleasant, it was probably wise not to have too many of them.

"Nice." I picked up a broccoli floret. "Very consistent in size. You could get a job as a sous chef."

"I'll keep that in mind if the medicine thing doesn't work out." He reached for the last head of broccoli.

"You look good in an apron, by the way." I'd made him tie a large white flour sack dish towel around his waist. The one around my waist made me look lumpy, but on him, even a flour sack looked good.

"You are almost done chopping, too." I peered at the counter.

"There's not another head of broccoli in the entire state. Did you count the number of heads of this stuff you had me chop?"

"What about those?" I pointed to the onions.

He shivered a little. "I don't do onions."

"What?" I took the hands-on-hips, feet-firmly-on-the-floor position I use with my brothers when they are being obstinate. "Were you frightened by an onion as a young child? Force-fed French onion soup?"

"Don't put your hands on your hips and lecture me," he said.

I dropped my hands to my sides.

"Onions smell." He made a face to show his distaste.

"Clay, doctors have cast-iron stomachs. What's a little onion odor?"

"I don't do onions. You figure out how to get them to quit smelling, and I'll chop them."

"I'll help you. We'll get them done quickly."

"No smell or no chop." He propped his hip against the counter in a cocky stance. He looks great in my kitchen....

I gave myself a mental slap. *Don't go there, Molly. It would never work and you know it!*

Of course I know it. That doesn't mean I can't admire the scenery.

I didn't want to admit that I hate chopping onions, too. They make me gag. Otherwise I wouldn't have given the job to Clay.

"I've got a book of household hints and tips. I'll bet it will tell us how to do it."

Clay looked at me as though I'd thrown my oar in the water before trying to paddle to shore. Still, I headed for the bookcase.

I have every recipe book ever published, according to my mother. I had to drag out most of them and stack them on the floor in order to find the one I wanted.

"Here it is," I crowed, looking for the page indicated in the index. "Onion odor."

"I've been out of circulation too long," he commented as he picked up a cherry tomato and popped it into his mouth. "I had no idea material had been written on such esoteric subjects."

I read the paragraph on chopping onions and rechecked the cover to determine if the book was for real or if my sister had given it to me as a joke. It was for real, I decided, so we might as well try what it suggested.

I opened a loaf of bread and took out two slices. "Here." I thrust one at Clay.

"I'm not hungry."

"It's not for you to eat, it's for you to put in your mouth."

He looked at me inquisitively. "Isn't that pretty much the same thing?" He studied the slice of twelve grain.

"Like this." I demonstrated by putting the slice in my mouth and holding it there, most of the bread hanging out like a shelf under my nose.

"Then what?"

I took the bread out again to speak. "The bread makes a barrier so that while you're chopping onions, the smell won't get in your nose."

"You have got to be kidding."

"That's what the book says. I've got to get this salad marinating. Come on, Clay, be a sport." Then I used a ploy that always worked on my brothers. "Or is it too hard for you?"

"Is that a challenge?" His eyes narrowed and I knew I had him.

These competitive types fall so easily.

I divided the onions in half. "The one who finishes chopping his or her onions first gets a free dinner from the loser."

"If this doesn't work, I'm quitting." He stuck the bread in his mouth.

"Then chop fast."

That's how my brother Liam found us, chopping wildly, onions flying onto the counter and the floor. Clay and I had our mouths stuffed with bread—it turns out that just one slice isn't enough—and racing to the finish. I'd even stuffed a little in my nostrils to keep the stench at bay.

I reached to take the bread out of my mouth but Liam held up his hand. "Don't say a word, Molly. Whatever explanation there is for this, I don't want to hear it. I want to play with the possibilities, to visualize just which of your brain cells has disintegrated and to consider how long it is until you are carried away in a straitjacket. I'm already imagining how I'll tell Mom and Dad you have a bread fetish. Please don't ruin my fun by trying to explain what you're doing."

Liam walked across the kitchen and picked up my stand mixer. "Mom wants to borrow this. I'll be leaving now. You two just carry on. I'll never breathe a word of it to anyone." He backed out the door and I heard his whoops of laughter as he made his way to the car.

Clay whipped the bread from his mouth. "Now you've made fools of—" He got a full breath of the scent of onion. "These things are strong!"

"Sorry. I meant to get the mild Vidalias. I guess I got into the wrong bin."

Clay's eyes watered and when he thoughtlessly wiped them with his hand, he rubbed the onion juice on his hands into his eyes. With a roar, he headed for my bathroom.

I quickly threw the onions into the salad mix and sealed the bowl. I had most of the mess cleaned up when he returned to the room. He'd stuck his entire head under the shower to wash away the smell. His shoulders were wet and his dark curls spiked in every direction.

"Where do you keep your towels?" He looked as mad as the proverbial wet hen…er…rooster.

"A pipe sprung a leak in the basement and I used them to mop up. They're all in the washing machine." I looked around the room and grabbed the first thing I saw.

In a supreme bit of bad timing, Tony chose that moment to ring my doorbell and stick his head inside to yell, "Anybody home?" He sauntered in to find Clay sopping wet in the middle of my kitchen, drying his hair with a dish towel covered with dancing pots and pans.

He looked from me to Clay and back again. "I think I'd better not ask what's going on."

"Good idea."

"Perhaps this isn't the time to invite you to a poetry reading, either."

"Maybe not."

"Or mention that I have tickets to a local production of *Romeo and Juliet?*"

"No kidding?" I perked up. I'm a sucker for *Romeo and Juliet.* "Who's putting it on?"

Clay spluttered and shook himself like Hildy does after a swim.

Tony looked at him strangely and then, to my amazement, strode across the room and planted a kiss on my lips. He lowered his eyelids and whispered just loud enough for Clay to hear, "I'll call you later." And he left.

I turned back to Clay, who looked more put-out than ever.

Men. They were acting like two roosters both interested in the same hen. Chalking it up to an aberrant testosterone surge, I handed Clay another towel, this one covered with spoons and flowers.

He glared at me but didn't look nearly so fierce with that particular towel on his head. "Poetry? Shakespeare? What gives?"

I stuck my nose in the air. "I'm far more sophisticated and interesting than you give me credit for being."

"And Tony?"

"He has the soul of a poet. He's the hospital poetry guru. Elizabeth Barrett Browning, Percy Bysshe Shelley, Shakespeare, Frost, you name it, he quotes it."

"All this right under my nose, and I didn't know it?" Clay appeared genuinely surprised.

"You aren't right about everything, you know. I'm the perfect example of that."

Before he could respond, the doorbell rang and I went to answer it.

"Ms. Molly Cassidy?" a bouquet of flowers inquired. Then a head popped from behind the colorful spray. "Flowers for you, miss." He thrust them at me, turned and sauntered toward his delivery van, whistling. It must be a happy job, delivering flowers.

"What's the occasion?" Clay was dry now, looking no worse for wear. He smelled only faintly of onions.

"I don't know." I set the vase of on the table and lifted out the card tucked in the flowers.

You are amazing, Molly. I can't thank you enough for supporting me. I hope I can do something for you someday. Hugs,

Emily Hancock

I tried to tuck the card into my pocket but Clay grabbed it and read it aloud.

"Do you get things like this often, Molly?"

"Sometimes. Occasionally. Usually. Yes."

"I see."

What exactly did he see? That mothers find me valuable during labor? That I wasn't a menace to society? Or that my insidious job was infiltrating and contaminating the hospital? I couldn't tell if Clay wanted to congratulate or fumigate me.

To my surprise, he didn't comment about the flowers.

Even more to my surprise he said, "It's not poetry or Shakespeare, but there's a film festival running at the U. And I know a great place for ribs. What do you say?

I say yes. Definitely yes.

Chapter Twenty-Four

Ribs are a messy business. By the time we were done with the all-you-can-eat rib buffet, I had barbecue sauce in my hair, on my blouse, and two handprints where I'd wiped my hands on my jeans. Clay, thankfully, made sure I wiped the sauce off the tip of my nose.

"I enjoyed watching you eat more than watching that obscure movie we just saw," he commented, as we strolled together on a sidewalk that led around one of the city's many lakes. "You do everything with gusto, don't you?"

"Why not? This isn't a dress rehearsal. We only get one life this side of heaven. Might as well make the most of it."

"Do you really believe in heaven?" Clay inquired, hands in his pockets and his gaze on an airplane overhead.

"Do I believe... Of course I believe! Don't you?"

"I want to. I thought I did. I just haven't seen many signs lately that it's more than wishful thinking." His remote, sad tone hurt my heart.

"What happened to you, Clay? What made you doubt?"

"It's a long story. One I choose not to go into." His voice grew flat and emotionless.

I leaned forward intently. "Eternity is too important to ignore, Clay."

He looked down at me and his expression grew soft and vulnerable in a way I'd not seen before. "You aren't the first one who has told me that. There are a lot of faith-filled people in my family."

"Just so you know, I'm here if you want to talk about it."

"Why do you care?"

"I'm no doctor, but I am sure when I say that you'll feel much better once you realize that you really can rely on God."

"I'll think about it. How about that?"

Maybe he was just placating me, but it was a start.

He looked puzzled. "I don't understand why you still speak to me. I've given you a bad time in the hospital and I don't plan to quit."

"'Do unto others as you would have them do unto you.' 'Love your neighbor as yourself.'"

"That's it?"

"That's why I tolerated you in the beginning.

Now, when we aren't at work, I actually like you a little bit. When you aren't being an obnoxious, insufferable know-it-all, you have some latent charm."

"Why does that backhanded, more-criticism-than-praise compliment please me?" he asked, half amused, half frustrated.

"Because it's honest?" I ventured. "When you are accustomed to having people fawn over you and listen to and obey your every word because you are a Bradshaw, my type of candor is refreshing."

"I knew there had to be a reason." He chuckled and took my hand in his.

Why was the most dreamy walk of my life with a guy I'd fight tooth and nail the next time a client of mine delivered in his hospital? A decent romantic moment wasted—how sad. I haven't had that many of them lately.

We walked a few minutes without speaking. The night air was velvety and the stillness was soothing.

"Have you got big plans for the weekend?" I asked eventually, breaking the silence between us.

"Not really. Noah is going to my sister's home in Wisconsin to visit his cousin. It will be pretty quiet without him."

"Do you get lonesome when he's away?"

He took a long time to answer. "Sometimes I think lonesome is my default emotion. I go there no matter what happens."

I surprised even myself when I responded, "If you don't want to be lonesome, you can come to the

Cassidy shindig. You'll be pleading for peace and quiet within the hour."

He stopped walking and I felt him staring at me. "Do you mean it?"

Did I? I must have.

"Sure." I gave him my mother's address. "Be there or be square."

"What decade did you say you were born in?"

"Very funny." I thought for a moment that Clay might even put his arm around me as we walked. Fortunately he has more self-control in such matters than I.

"You invited him home to meet your family? What are you, nuts?" Lissy, hands on skinny hips, glared at me. "Even Tony and I didn't get invited to a bash until three years ago. This man is an interloper!"

"My family can take care of itself," I reminded Lissy, "but thanks for caring. It just slipped out. I didn't mean to do it, but he did help me with the salads. It seemed only fair." That and I was a little moonstruck at the time. My tongue had been temporarily disconnected from my brain. "Besides, I give him two hours at the party before he runs away screaming. Just wait until Uncle Jerry pulls out the bagpipes."

"I thought bagpipes were played by Scots."

I sniggered. "True, but we Cassidys believe they were invented by the Irish as a joke, and the Scots just haven't caught on yet. Jerry's my uncle by marriage," I reminded her, "not blood."

She threw her hands in the air. "You're right. Dr. Reynolds won't last."

I was still counting on that as I helped my mother set out food on the long tables we'd borrowed from the church basement. Tables really can groan, especially under the weight of full Crock-Pots and warming trays, chafing dishes and bowls of ice to hold salads.

"Do you think we overdid it?" Mother asked, eyeing the bounty.

"Have you forgotten the last party?"

"We'd planned for leftovers and ended up with only the butt end of a ham, three buns and a dish of stew your aunt forgot was in the oven."

"I think the relatives starve between parties. Remember the year Liam and Uncle Jerry ate an entire ham?"

"It was a small ham, as I remember, but maybe I'll call your father and tell him to pick up an extra…." Mom wandered off clucking to herself.

I didn't dwell on it because something hard and heavy hit me in the back of my legs, and I nearly fell to the floor.

"Geri, quit it!"

My pig, dressed in a leprechaun costume my sister had sewn, bumped my calves for the umpteenth time demanding attention. Krissy had outdone herself this time. She'd sewn a wee green jacket with tails and buttons and even found a shiny green cardboard leprechaun hat to which she'd attached a bit of stretchy elastic. It fit perfectly to Geri's head. Geranium doesn't have much of a chin—she's pretty much pork fat all the way from her bottom lip to her chest—but Krissy had managed to make it work.

I don't normally take my pets to these things. The children tend to overfeed them. It's a special problem with Geri because she eats anything. Because I don't want a nauseous pig in my car on the way home, I'd made a sign to hang around her neck. Please Don't Feed the Pig! Hopefully most of the children can read by now. Hildy, I'd left at home with a new bone. I might have left Geri there, too, but she did have the leprechaun suit to model. What's more, she's awfully cute nosing around under the table, a tubby Irish pig.

Hugh arrived early, knowing I'd be there with Mother, putting last-minute touches on the party. Of all my brothers, he's the most thoughtful. I credit that to his delicate, artistic nature. The other boys had had their brains marinated in sports from the time they were born, and although they do have sensitive sides, they've been callused over by Monday-night football.

My brother Liam is the most incorrigible of all— a flirt, a tease, a handsome heartbreaker. And he'd never think to come early to help out, though the others might entertain the notion for a moment before tossing it out.

"I'm glad you're here," I greeted Hugh as he planted a kiss on my cheek. "Mom needs your help."

"Why wouldn't I be here? I'm the one without a life, remember?"

I pulled away to stare at him. "Hugh, that doesn't sound like you."

"No? Well, get used to it. It's the new me." He dropped into a chair and stared at my pig/leprechaun rooting under an area rug.

"Your date wasn't successful last night?"

"A disaster. I took her to the new Mexican place in Uptown. She hates Mexican food. Then we went to a pop concert. Afterward she told me that she only likes heavy metal. When I dropped her off at her house, she couldn't get out of the car fast enough. I can't believe I read her so wrong."

I sat down next to him and put my hand on his arm. "Sometimes women will tell a man what they think he wants to hear—that they enjoy Mexican food, for example, or easy listening—just to go out. You can't help it if they aren't being honest."

His beautiful green-gold eyes looked sad. "I really thought I checked it out with her, Molly. And I blew it."

"Maybe she blew it." I patted him on the arm. "Why tell you Mexican food is okay if she doesn't like it? She needs to be honest, too."

He studied my face. "Like you?"

I thought of some of my conversations with Clay. "Maybe I'm just a little *too* honest sometimes. I could hold back a little bit."

"That's not possible for you, sis. You're passionate by nature. Things just spill out of you."

The doorbell chimed and Hugh opened it to find Lissy and Tony on the other side.

Lissy looked marvelous in a pair of jeans and a billowing white poet's shirt with a broad silver and turquoise belt at the waist and dramatic silver and turquoise earrings. Hugh, who was used to seeing her in grubs around my house, did a double take.

Tony wasn't too shabby himself in a crisp white shirt, sleeves rolled partway to his elbows, collar tipped up at a rakish angle and snug, sharply pressed jeans. His black hair was just a shade too long and curled at his collar. All my female relatives will swoon at the sight of him. Fortunately, Tony is accustomed to that.

"We're the first?" Lissy glanced at the tables of food. "Wow, look at this spread."

The doorbell rang again. "You were first, but not for long. Make yourself at home."

Uncle James and Aunt Sarah were the next to arrive, followed by my father's other brothers and sisters and their spouses, their offspring and a few grandchildren. My own siblings drifted in, as well, and in the middle of the mass arrival, Clay appeared. He introduced himself to my relations with graciousness and ease.

When the relatives passed me, they all gave me nods of approval, as if I'd finally caught a fish big enough to mount.

I gritted my teeth when I saw my father's oldest sister forging down the sidewalk.

"Here comes trouble," I whispered to Hugh. Aunt Siobhan believes she is matriarch of the clan and has taken it upon herself to be as vocal as possible about the things she feels the family needs to remedy. Hugh and I, because we are both single, are at the top of her to-do list. An unmarried Cassidy is a defective Cassidy, in Aunt Siobhan's mind. Sometimes I wonder how such a lady with such a lovely name—it's pronounced Shiv-awn—got such an overbearing personality.

She entered the house as if blown in on a strong gust of wind, with Uncle Kent, a mild-mannered accountant, in tow. Her gaze took in the crowd, and I could practically see her checking names off a mental list to see who was present and who would need to be chastised on Monday for their absence. Then her eyes quit moving and became fixed on a spot somewhere over my shoulder. I turned my head to see what she was staring at.

Clay. He'd bent forward to listen attentively to my father spin out some tall tale. Occasionally he nodded thoughtfully, as if he were hearing the secrets of the universe instead of Dad's rambling, long-winded joke.

"Who is that?" she demanded imperiously.

Sometimes I wonder how she and my mild-mannered father had sprung from the same DNA.

Hugh glanced at Clay. "It's a friend of Molly's. A doctor."

Siobhan beamed a high-wattage smile on me. My aunt is a regal-looking woman, more handsome than beautiful with her high cheekbones and angular jaw. "Really? Molly, I must say I'm delighted. I'd nearly given up on you ever settling down. Now I see that you were just waiting for the right one to come along."

"But Clay and I aren't..." Then I closed my mouth. Let my aunt think what she wants. It will keep her off my case, at least for tonight.

The she turned her laser eye on Hugh. "And do you have someone here, too?"

I kicked my brother in the ankle before he had a chance to answer. "Lissy is here," I said.

"But..." He began to protest and then saw where I was going with this. "Yes, Lissy. She's a good friend of Molly's. I'd like to get to know her better."

We were telling the truth, I reminded myself. Just not all of it.

Siobhan patted us both on the heads like we were five years old. "I'm delighted with the two of you." Then she scanned the room again. "Have you seen your cousin Michael? I hear he's thinking of dropping out of school. I need to put a stop to that immediately."

She sailed off, her chest held high, like the figurehead on the prow on an old English ship headed out to sea. And we were free.

Hugh and I high-fived each other and grinned.

"I think I'm going to really enjoy this party for a change. I won't be Siobhan's project for the evening."

I glanced around the room. Uncle Jerry was pulling out his bagpipes, and Liam had cornered Tony to discuss motorcycles, Liam's favorite topic.

"You'd better find Lissy and start hanging out with her so our beloved aunt doesn't get suspicious."

Hugh nodded. "I'd recommend you do the same with Clay."

Once again unforeseen circumstances had thrown us together. Fortunately for my brother and me, there are a lot worse people to hang out with than Lissy and Clay.

Chapter Twenty-Five

"So you're a doctor," Uncle Henry said as he eyed Clay, "and you deliver babies just like our Molly does."

"I don't deliver babies," I interrupted, hoping to divert Clay's ire, but Uncle Henry would have none of it.

Clay, however, didn't seem to mind. He'd already realized that anything said in this crowd was probably worth ignoring. He was wise to pay no mind to any of it.

"Did Molly tell you about our cousin Finn?" My uncle's eyes began to sparkle and I groaned inwardly.

"I don't believe she did." When Clay tries to be charming, he succeeds admirably.

"Finn and his wife, Mary, live in the old country, out on a backward farm with no electricity or running water."

"I had no idea that it is still that way in parts of

Ireland." Clay listened attentively, his high, intelligent brow furrowed with concentration as my jokester uncle reeled him in.

"Oh, indeed. Last year Mary went into labor with their firstborn. It was mighty exciting. I'm surprised Molly didn't tell you about it."

Clay looked at me with one eyebrow raised. I shrugged helplessly and gave Clay a point for being patient with Henry, who takes a bit of getting used to.

"The country doctor came by to help her deliver. Finn was a worried mess, you know. He kept pacing and fidgeting until the doctor, trying to keep Finn busy, told him to hold the lantern so he could deliver the baby."

My uncle's eyes began to sparkle. "And lo and behold! A handsome baby boy was born!" Henry slapped his hand on his thigh enthusiastically. "And then—wouldn't you know?—the doctor says, 'Hold the lantern higher, Finn, I think there's a second baby coming.' Finn did as he was told and there she was, a beautiful daughter."

Clay smiled encouragingly at my uncle.

"Then the good doctor told our Finn to move the lantern a bit to the left and a little closer, as it appeared that a *third* baby was coming." Uncle Henry's eyes grew wide.

"Triplets?" Clay murmured.

"Yes! Another beautiful baby girl. Of course by that time, our Finn was more than a little nervous.

"'Doctor,' he said, 'maybe I should put the lantern down now. I think it's the light that's attracting them.'"

My uncle's wheezy laugh filled the room as Clay realized he'd been had.

"Don't mind Hank," my father said, carrying a fresh plate of ham. "The best six years of his life were spent in fifth grade."

I tucked my arm through Clay's and led him as far away as I could from my barmy relatives. Aunt Siobhan had Tony in her clutches, and I couldn't find Lissy or Hugh. They'd escaped the insanity without my noticing.

"I'm sorry, I should have warned you about Uncle Henry," I said as soon as Clay and I got to the back of my parents' yard. "There's no one in the gazebo. We can hide there."

Now that darkness was descending, we'd be shielded from the madness. Geranium trotted behind us, her hat slightly askew, so I prodded her into the gazebo, as well.

"Poor baby, I didn't mean to subject you to all of this. I know it's humiliating...."

"It's okay, Molly. I can take care of myself," Clay said.

"I was talking to Geranium."

He sighed. "I guess I should have known. You'd never called me 'baby.'" A charged pause filled the air. "But I suppose almost anything is possible here."

My gratitude for the night knew no bounds as embarrassment turned me bright red. The idea of calling Clay "baby" in any context was inconceivable.

"Geri! Geri! Here piggy, piggy, piggy," a childish voice called from the patio.

"One of the kids wants Geri," I murmured. I prodded my porky pig toward the gazebo door and helped her out. She grunted mildly and trotted toward the calling voice.

After I closed the door, I retreated to the shadows of the bench next to Clay. "I know you didn't think much of me before. Now you will probably never speak to me again. I realize that my family is colorful, but they are usually normal, sane and productive people. These family gatherings are where they let their hair down…and down…and down…."

"Of course I'll speak to you. I've said it before, you're a lovely person, Molly."

"Stay out of Bradshaw birthing rooms and we can be buddies?"

"Exactly."

"I'm as passionate about my beliefs as you are about yours. We run on parallel tracks, Clay. I don't see any way for us to meet in the middle."

His silence was deafening.

When he finally spoke his voice sounded ragged and resigned. "I realize you don't know me very well, Molly, but you'll have to trust me when I say I have had a lot more…experience—" his voice caught on the word "—than you."

"And education, too. But I'm good at what I do, and mothers love me...."

"It's a bridge I won't cross."

"Parallel tracks it is, then." I felt strangely sad as I said it. I'd enjoy having this man as a friend, but the obstacles were insurmountable.

Scripture warns against being unequally yoked in faith. Being unequally yoked in how we view each other's work is no small thing, either. That's two strikes against us.

"Is it just because of our work or is there something else?" Clay inquired softly. He shifted, drawing his body closer to mine.

"I'm a believer and..."

"I've mislaid my faith?" He rested his arm on the back of the gazebo bench and circled my shoulders, his hand rested casually—precariously—close to my arm. "I miss it, frankly. I come from a family of deeply Christian people...." His voice trailed away and I knew that he'd gone somewhere in his past that I was not invited.

"If I can help..."

He took my chin in his hand and turned my face toward his. "You already have. You remind me of fun and laughter. I feel alive around you. I promised I'd think about this, remember? I'm known to keep my promises."

A flicker of hope teased at me. It was actually more than I'd expected. God was working, no doubt about that.

"Besides..." He leaned forward and for a moment I thought he might kiss me. Any romantic idea was banished from my head by squeals and laughter outside. It came from the direction of the old playhouse in the backyard, one my father had built for us when we were children. A wooden ladder inside the playhouse led to the roof and to a rope ladder, which provided the playhouse with a second story in the branches of the old elm. Dad once threatened to tear it down, but such an uproar went through the family at the idea that he decided to maintain it for the next generation by shoring it up and replacing the rope ladder.

"What's happening?" Clay stood up and poked his head out of the gazebo door to scan the yard.

"Who knows with my family? Whatever it is, it sounds big."

The sounds were bordering on hysterical.

"Maybe someone needs a doctor. We should check it out."

The only kind of doctor my family needs is a head doctor, but I followed him out of the gazebo, anyway. The ruckus was on the other side of the lawn where my relatives were gathered around the little playhouse, hooting and pointing upward. Someone beamed a flashlight into the branches. My gaze followed the pointing fingers and I realized exactly what—or who—they were pointing at.

My brother Hugh, his face as red as his hair, was sitting on a thick branch, like a leprechaun caught in a tree. But that wasn't as weird as what else was in the old elm. Lissy was out on the branch with him, clinging to Hugh's waist looking terrified that she might fall.

"Looks like Hugh has a new girlfriend," Caboose announced. "No wonder he hasn't been able to keep any of the old ones. Hugh, bring her down from there and take her on a decent date!"

If looks could kill, Caboose would have been toast.

"Hugh Cassidy, I thought I taught you better than that!" my mother yelled into the tree. "She's going to ruin her pretty clothes."

Jokes were flying fast and furious as Hugh and Lissy remained trapped, the beam of the flashlight playing on their humiliated faces.

"Yeah, Hugh, listen to Mom!" Liam yelled. Then he gave a loud, obnoxious whistle. When Lissy and Hugh looked at him, Liam clicked a picture of them with the digital camera in his hand.

Liam's hobby is taking ridiculous photos of family members and blackmailing them later. Nice guy, my brother Liam.

It was time for Molly to the rescue. "Go back in the house, all of you! You should be ashamed of yourselves. I'd climb a tree, too, to get away from you!" I started pulling on Caboose's arm. "Go, go!"

One by one, the group broke apart and reluctantly moved toward the house. Some of them walked backward so they could continue to observe the goings-on.

"They'll never get to earth with you watching," I pointed out to whoever would listen. "It will be much easier for Lissy and Hugh to come down from the tree without an audience."

I waved my hands and they scattered like chickens.

Finally the stragglers, my brothers in particular, disappeared into the house. Liam was already handing his camera around to show others the condemning photo.

"They're gone," Clay announced. He, too, had a ridiculous smile on his face but at least he had the courtesy not to comment. "Let's go to the house, Molly."

"No, wait." Hugh's voice from the branches was bleak. "There was no place to talk so we…well, we were just going to come down when they found us, but Lissy is scared to get on the ladder."

"It was fun coming up, but now it looks so far to the ground," she said plaintively

I looked at Clay. "It's got to be you," I said. "I'm not strong enough. If she fell we'd both come tumbling down."

He nodded and headed into the playhouse, up to its roof and mounted the rope ladder. He secured himself as best he could before opening his arms.

"I'm here, Lissy. You won't fall and if you do, I'll catch you."

"And who will catch *you?*" She and Hugh shimmied toward the ladder together. Lissy tentatively put a foot on the ladder. "Oh, never mind, I'd probably rather die of a fall out of a tree than of embarrassment."

With Clay urging her on, Lissy slowly made her way down. They disappeared through the hole in the roof and emerged from the door of the playhouse. Lissy wore an expression so morose that I burst out laughing. Hugh appeared beside her quickly, having had the benefit of years of experience going up and down that particular tree.

"I want to crawl home," Lissy moaned.

Hugh's cheeks were so red they looked sore.

"Frankly, I think it's wonderful," Clay drawled as he brushed imaginary dust off his trousers.

We all turned to stare at him. *Wonderful?*

"I was wondering how to get a break from the chaos myself. Molly and I found the gazebo. Your way was much more inventive."

"You think so?" Lissy breathed.

"Brilliant. Hugh, you, of course, must be a master at foiling that gang in there." Clay nodded toward the house and gave a mild shudder. "They're out of my league, that's for sure."

Hah. Yet I saw my brother's shoulders lift as Clay deftly provided him with a response to the family waiting inside.

"They drove us to it, didn't they, Hugh?" Lissy said.

"They did. The whole pack is nuts." Hugh turned to me. "Save you, of course."

I didn't feel like arguing.

"I'll bet you'll go into the house," Clay said, "and tell them if they weren't all so curious you might be able to court a woman like she should be courted."

"You're right," Hugh said, his smile returning. "The best defense is a good offense. I'll tell them off before they get a chance to start their teasing." He turned to Lissy. "Are you game?"

"I could get tears in my eyes," Lissy offered helpfully. "Maybe they'll think they made me cry."

"That's good," Hugh said. "Yes, make them ashamed of their behavior. It would serve them right.... Those meddling busybodies need someone to stand up to them...."

"And Liam and his camera need to be separated," Lissy added. They moved off, hatching their plan to save face.

"Thank you." I turned to face Clay.

"For what?"

"For reminding Hugh that he knows how to handle those jokers in there. For a minute I thought he'd lost his sense of humor."

"No wonder you are so spirited, Molly. It's self-defense."

I put my hands on my hips and stared up at him. "Keep that in mind when you try to cross me again, Dr. Reynolds."

And before I realized what was happening, Clay leaned forward, and his lips brushed mine, knocking whatever bit of sense I'd had in my head clear into the neighbor's backyard.

"Clay, I…"

But I couldn't finish because at that moment Aunt Siobhan called out, "Molly, come to say goodbye. We're leaving!"

He smiled, took my hand and walked with me toward the brightly lit house.

Hugh had several of our siblings and cousins backed against a wall and was haranguing them for their bad behavior. The smirky grins on our relatives' faces were beginning to fade. Caboose, a relentless teaser and almost as bad as Liam, apologized to Lissy. I could see by her expression that she'd begun to enjoy the kerfuffle.

Geri, her leprechaun's hat still askew, was asleep under the table with two small children. Her little legs stuck straight out from her body, and one of the girls was holding her hoof in her hand like little best friends who'd dozed off after playing too hard. I thought I also heard a faint piggy snore but I could have been imagining it.

Aunt Siobhan plowed toward Clay and grabbed his face between her palms. "You're a darling man. I'm so happy Molly finally got some sense. A doctor! Imagine! I hope we see you again soon, dear boy."

"Dear boy" smiled charmingly at my irrepressible aunt. "It's been my pleasure. Your family is delightful."

Siobhan looked around and smiled almost tenderly. "It is, isn't it?" And she was off to kiss someone else good-night.

What's more, all the females in the family managed to sidle over to give Clay a good-night kiss on the cheek. I, on the other hand, got several thumbs-up signs and one silently mouthed "You go girl."

If they knew of the battle Clay and I were waging, I doubt that at the moment even one of my relations would have taken my side over his.

Tony sauntered up to me holding three plastic containers. "Your mother is sending me home with food. Isn't it great?"

"Women love to feed you, Tony."

"What's your secret?" Clay inquired curiously.

He could use a few tips, I thought to myself.

"'Love all, trust a few, do wrong to none.' Billy Shakespeare always advises me well." His eyes twinkled, and the reason for his appeal was obvious.

"Where did Lissy go?" I glanced around the room.

"I lost my date," Tony continued. "Your brother took Lissy home. I think they had a few more things they wanted to say to each other."

"I'll bet."

"They made a great recovery," Tony said. "Hugh came storming into the house scolding everyone for being impolite. People started apologizing until I think they almost forgot they'd caught him stuck in a tree with a lady." Tony kissed me on the temple. "Thanks for the party. Best one yet. I'll talk to you tomorrow."

My mother joined us in the entry, wiping her hands on her apron. "Our little bash was a success, don't you think, Molly?"

"Tony says it's the best he's attended, and he knows a good party." Impishly, I added, "Hugh and Lissy brightened it considerably."

Mother shook her head. "They are a nice couple. I hope they realize it for themselves."

"You can see that? Until tonight I'd never really put the two together in my mind."

"Molly, dear, I didn't raise all you children and live with your father's family without getting some people smarts. I know a good match when I see it. Now go home, both of you."

"What about cleaning up? Clay can go. I'll stay to help."

"Nonsense. Your father is going to help me." She twinkled. "It's the least he can do for inviting that crowd to our house." She waved us off. "Scoot. The two of you."

And we did, before Mother could change her mind.

"Can I give you a ride home?" Clay asked.

"I've got my own—" I glanced down the street. "Where's my car?"

Before Clay could answer, the front door of the house swung open again.

"Molly," my mother said, "Caboose borrowed your car. He said you should get a ride home. Geri can stay here until morning. Do you want your father to…"

"I'll take her," Clay said quickly.

Mom nodded and closed the door.

"The insanity never ends." I sighed. "I'm sorry about this."

"I'm not."

I tried not to put too much interpretation into those two words, but I couldn't help myself.

He wants to be with me! He's going to ease up on his stance at the hospital because of this. We can start to see each other.... Something more permanent... Aunt Siobhan wants a doctor in the family....

I rode in a haze of fantasy all the way to my house.

"Here we are."

I reached for the door handle before realizing that Clay was making no move to leave the car. I put my hand back in my lap.

"Maybe you don't want to answer this," he began, frowning. "If you don't, just tell me it's none of my business. What's the deal with you and Tony?"

I stared at him. "What does Tony have to do with anything?"

"You two are obviously...you know." He squirmed as if the leather car seat was shrinking beneath his girth.

"No, I don't think I do. What are you talking about?"

"Love sonnets? Kisses? His being overprotective every time I'm around? He's a better guard dog than Hildy. He's got a Keep Away sign posted on you that's a mile high."

That's how Clay saw it?

"He's one of my best friends in the world, that's all. He's asked me to marry him for so long that it's a constantly running joke. Tony's biggest concern for me is that he doesn't want to see me get hurt."

"Why is he so edgy around me?"

I felt a flush bleeding through my body. "Maybe he thinks you're…dangerous."

"You mean he believes that you might be susceptible to my latent, highly inconspicuous charm?"

My heart did a flip at the expression in those expressive blue eyes. "Apparently so. Your charms aren't *that* inconspicuous." I paused. "Or else he's afraid you'll chase me out of Bradshaw or sour me on being a doula, or both."

He pondered this bit of information but kept his conclusions to himself. "I'll walk you in." Clay rounded the door to my side, and as always—except in the birthing room—he was a perfect gentleman.

Hildy gave a single welcoming woof, having already put the sound of Clay's car under Friendly in her mental data bank.

Suddenly I was fantasizing about what it could be like for Clay and me. *He'd thought Tony and I were romantically linked. He* cared *that we might be!*

I floated into the house without touching the ground.

When I fell asleep, I was sheltered in the billowy bliss of cloud nine, my dreams sweet with the idea of harmony between Clay and myself.

Chapter Twenty-Six

Dreams may come true. Nightmares certainly do.

I floated through Sunday in a rosy haze, unable to believe what had happened between Clay and me on Saturday night. He'd been everything I'd hoped when he let down his dour shell and revealed the man he could be—funny, perceptive, charming, gracious, patient and altogether delightful.

Aunt Siobhan left a voice message for me while I was at church that underscored the success of the previous evening. "Molly, that's a wonderful young man you brought to your parents' last night. I hope to see more of him. *Much* more of him." Having Aunt Siobhan endorse Clay was a stamp of approval equal to that of Clay asking my father for my hand in marriage.

I spent most of the afternoon polishing nails, mine and Geri's, trying new looks for my hair and experimenting with the items in my makeup bag that I rarely use. I'm not typically so self-indulgent, but last night with Clay had made me feel more playful than I had in a long, long time.

It wasn't until Emily Hancock called that I realized my future might not be as rosy as I was imagining.

"Hi, Molly, how are you?"

"The real question is how are you and your baby?"

Emily giggled like a teenager. "I cannot tell you how ecstatic we are or how much fun we are having. We have a new lease on life." She hesitated before adding, "This child has brought my husband and me closer to each other in so many ways. We're like newlyweds, Molly."

"And how are your friends and family?"

She burst out laughing. "Envious! My friends are here every day to hold the baby. They've all noticed a change in us and are amazed by it."

"So they don't think you're crazy anymore?"

"Crazy in love with my baby and my husband. But I should get to the real reason I called. You, of course, know that my husband, Charles, is on the board at Bradshaw Medical and…"

"He is?" I was shocked. "I had no idea."

"I never told you? I thought I had."

"So that's why you said you'd met Everett Bradshaw and his wife." *And were able to be so blunt with Clay.*

"Yes. We've been to their home several times over the years. A lovely couple. That's why I'm calling. I've been raving to Charles about you, and now that he's met you, he's a fan of yours, as well. He thinks you should be getting the word out about the women who work as doulas."

"I'm doing my best."

"I know that, but my husband thinks on a grand scale and he's come up with a wonderful plan."

My stomach wasn't so sure about a wonderful plan for doulas. "What is that?" I ventured.

"Some time ago, a documentary maker approached the board about doing a documentary at Bradshaw. Apparently someone had written to them and suggested it."

Tony's bit of gossip had been correct.

I'd hoped they'd ignored my letter or forgotten all about it, but no such luck.

"My husband has become involved with the documentary video company."

"Great." I tried to sound cheerful but was imploding within.

"They are a great company and very excited that Charles and the board have now expressed interest in the doula idea again."

I felt the guillotine beginning to move toward my scrawny neck.

"Isn't it great? What fabulous exposure you'll get."

"Yes, of course, but how…"

"That's the best part!" Emily sounded exceedingly pleased with herself. "The video company's next project was put off—something about a junta in the country they were going to visit. Instead, they are fast-tracking the doula idea."

"F-fast track?" I stuttered.

"Yes. Charles suggested they use you as one of the doulas in the video. Do you have any clients who will be delivering at Bradshaw in the near future?"

"Just one. Her name is Penny and she's a patient of Dr. Reynolds." My last patient at Bradshaw, thanks to his irascibility.

"Do you think she'd be willing to be involved in the taping? My husband is spearheading this and the board is one hundred percent behind it. You didn't tell me that someone had given a donation to the hospital to support a doula program there! In your name, no less. That's going to be a part of the story, too."

"Emily, I don't think this is a good idea." My stomach had gone gymnastic on me and was doing Olympian flip-flops.

"It's a *great* idea."

"Dr. Reynolds won't hear of it, you know. He's not a supporter of my profession—or anything that 'crowds' his birthing rooms."

"He doesn't have the last word at the hospital."

"I'm not so sure about that," I said, thinking of the way everyone tiptoed around him. Until I'd seen the tender side of him, I'd tiptoed, too.

"His grandfather Everett has the final say, and he thinks it's a wonderful idea."

I felt my knees buckle.

"Charles called Everett with the idea and got his

full support. Like I said, this is on the fast track. The video company wants to interview the three of us, Charles, you and me, and if they can get permission from your client, follow her through her delivery day."

I thought about my client Penny Higgins and her husband, Pete, and my heart sank. Penny and Pete are both grade-school teachers—good ones. They believe in education with a fervent passion. What's more, they are the kind of people who are game for new adventures. Of course they'd agree to being filmed. It would be just up their alley—fun, educational, different—they'd love it.

And Clay will kill me. Everyone who is anyone will have ganged up against him, and it will be entirely my fault. My rosy bubble burst and I landed with a thud.

"I can't be involved, Emily. There are circumstances you don't know about."

"Of course you can. Everett wants you involved. He loves the story. Besides, if he throws his support behind the idea it will be big, not just for you but for all doulas. Isn't that what you've always wanted?"

I sat down on the floor right where I was, unable to negotiate myself to a chair. Now I had to choose between pleasing Everett Bradshaw and his grandson? There was no good way out of this except, perhaps, a long trip to Portugal.

"I've got to go, Molly, the baby is hungry. I just had to let you know the exciting news. The video team is on top of everything so they will be contacting you shortly. In fact, they've already got a name for the documentary. *Doula Day,* isn't that cute? The day they film, Bradshaw Medical will be swarming with doulas. They're planning to set up interviews in the boardroom."

I heard Emily's baby making small noises in the background. "I have to go. I just wanted to give you the good news myself. Bye."

I held the phone long after the line went dead. *Doula Day.*

I touched my finger to my lips where Clay's kiss still burned. Emily might as well have taken a hammer to a pane of glass and shattered it with a single stroke. Regrettably, that thin pane of glass is my life.

"*Doula Day?* Couldn't they have thought of something snappier than that?" Lissy complained as she sat at my table eating sardines out of a can. "How about Molly's Mothers?"

"Or Delightful Doulas Dance to Dr. Reynolds's Tune," Tony added sarcastically. "What does he think of this?"

Frankly, I haven't dared to ask.

"I haven't seen you at the hospital all week, Molly," Tony continued. He slathered mustard on little smoky sausages and popped them into his mouth.

"My client hasn't gone into labor yet. Frankly, I'm beginning to hope that when she does, she gives birth in an ambulance on the way to the hospital. Then I'd never have to show my face there again."

"Everybody is excited by this except you," Lissy said. "It's going to be great."

"Everybody but me and Dr. Reynolds."

Tony winced. "He has been a little…on edge… lately."

"Did he call you after the night of your family's party?" Lissy asked. "I was sure he would."

"He didn't have time before hearing about the *Doula Day* fiasco. Any slight interest he might have had in me no doubt went out the window." To be replaced by fear and loathing.

"Too bad. Your family loved him." Lissy slid a sardine onto a cracker.

I think I was starting to, as well.

Not that it mattered now. Whatever it is that drives Clay is far stronger than any warm feelings he might develop for me. Even Noah, who had called me a time or two on the phone to tell me about his day at school and to discuss Hildy, hasn't contacted me. His father has no doubt put me on the do-not-call list. I am being shunned.

"He just makes me so mad!" I blurted. "He's so stubborn and pigheaded…."

Geranium, who was acting as Tony's footrest, lifted her head.

"Sorry, girl."

"It will be over soon," Tony consoled. "Then we can all get on with our lives." He put his hand over mine. "You can marry me and we'll live happily ever after."

"How *is* Wanda these days?" I asked with saccharine sweetness.

"She's eased up, and it scares me."

"Why? You should be glad."

"I think she's changing her strategy, and I'm getting worried. A silent Wanda is far more sinister than a noisy one. Now, if you and I were to get engaged…"

"Then I'd have to be scared of Wanda."

"If you won't marry me, I'll have to come up with another escape plan," Tony warned. He eyed our friend. "Maybe Lissy would marry me."

Lissy nearly choked on her fish.

"If she weren't in love with your brother Hugh, that is."

"We are not…"

"Are, too. And you both know it and are just too afraid to admit it."

Lissy's jaw set stubbornly. "I'm not going first. Hugh has to tell me he loves me before I'll tell him anything of the sort."

"And Hugh's been hurt too many times to go first."

"Unrequited love," Tony said. "'And never the twain shall meet.' Rudyard Kipling."

"Eat your sausages," Lissy ordered. "If Hugh actually cared for me he'd leap tall buildings for me."

"In a single bound," Tony added.

"He's got a lot to overcome," I said. "He's very vulnerable right now. You have to understand."

"You and Clay have a lot to overcome, too," Lissy said slyly.

"That's different. Hugh's been hurt. Clay is just inflexible, obstinate, mulish…"

"There you go, insulting animals again."

"How do you know he hasn't been hurt?" Tony asked. "His strong feelings had to have come from somewhere."

"Ego," I shot back. "He wants to be king of the hill. It's about power with him."

"I'm not so sure of that," Tony said softly.

The phone rang just as I was going to bed. It was Emily. I could hear the baby making small sounds in the background.

"Hi. Is everything okay?"

"It is so 'okay' that I can hardly stand it, Molly. I love motherhood."

"I'm glad you aren't calling with a crisis."

"Just the opposite, in fact. Charles would like to talk to you."

Before I could ask her why, she handed the phone to her husband. Charles and I had not spent a lot of time together prior to the birth. What could he want to say to me?

He didn't waste any time on small talk. "I haven't been able to get you out of my mind. I've been thinking of you ever since our baby was born, about what you did for my wife and for the peace of mind it gave me knowing you were available to her."

"Thank you, I—"

"Emily's talked about your idea of a doula

program and I just wanted you to know that if you go ahead with it, I'll support you one hundred percent."

I felt a door opening. Granted, it was only a tiny crack, but now I know that one member of Bradshaw's board is willing to disagree with Clay about Doula Central.

Chapter Twenty-Seven

No matter how much I'd hoped Penny and Pete Higgins's baby would be born anywhere but at the hospital, far from the eyes of Clay Reynolds, it was not to be.

Worse yet, Pete called the documentary people before he called me to tell me his wife was in labor.

"Molly, this is Pete. Penny's contractions have started."

"How far are they apart?"

"We have plenty of time. Dr. Reynolds said it could go on for a while. Good thing, too."

I didn't think I'd heard him right. Most people can't wait for labor to be done.

"I've already called the documentary crew to tell them the baby is coming and they're on their way over here to follow us to the hospital. They want to make sure you're here when they start filming. The show is about you, after all."

"About doulas," I said, "not me in particular."

"Don't be modest, Molly, this *is* all about you. Penny and I are elated that we get to be a part of it."

Why me? I'm the last person who wants to call attention to herself, particularly when the act will infuriate Clay. Doomed. That one beautiful evening we had together has become the single jewel in a very tarnished crown.

"Molly?" Pete sounded concerned.

I pulled myself together. "I'll be right over."

"Great. You should get here at the same time as the video guys."

There was still the chance that this would be a very quick labor and delivery, I told myself as I gathered what I needed, fed my pets and drove away from my house. That dream was dashed when I arrived at the Higginses' home. Penny answered the door looking exceedingly pregnant but in no distress.

"I thought you were in labor," I said as I entered.

"Pete's a little trigger-happy. I'm having an occasional pain, but if these guys don't quit taping for a while, they'll run out of film." She looked at me sympathetically. "It's you they're after, of course, so be prepared for questions."

I walked into the living room and straight into the lens of a camera that was not to leave me until long after Pete and Penny's baby was born.

"The doula is here," someone yelled.

"My name is Molly."

"Okay, whatever," a man with a clipboard said.

"Just go about your business but occasionally turn to the camera and explain what you're doing."

"But I am totally focused on my client," I protested. "I'm not going to take time out to turn to the camera and…"

"Oh, please do, Molly," Penny said. "This will be such an awesome record for our family. Pete has relatives in Australia. They'll go wild when they see this."

I'm planning to go wild myself.

"I'll be asking you questions," the man continued as if I hadn't responded at all. "I'll toss them out and you answer the best you can. When we talk about massage, just start rubbing Penny's foot or something, okay?"

"I normally rub a mother's back."

"Okay. Feet, legs, back, whatever trips their trigger."

"Women have *back* labor," I said testily. "They don't have *foot* labor."

"Okay, cool. Rub her back. Just make it look realistic."

"Whatever I do will be realistic. There will be a baby born here shortly, you know."

Fortunately, Penny's labor began to progress rapidly and it wasn't long until Penny, Pete, strangers with cumbersome video cameras and I drove to Bradshaw Medical.

If the documentary makers had hoped to record the birthing event as it would normally play out, they were foiled at the outset. Someone had put the staff on alert that we were about to arrive. Even the woman at the registration desk had redone her makeup and hair and was as gushingly sweet as I'd ever seen her. She brought out a wheelchair with a flourish and proceeded to take Penny to her room to negotiate a little more camera time. Everyone on staff who had ever dreamed of being on television managed to make a cameo appearance as we made our way to the birthing room by popping through doors or leaning forward into the camera as we passed. Even Tony succumbed to the lure of momentary stardom and intentionally sauntered in front of the camera to smile at Penny when they arrived on the obstetrics floor.

I, on the other hand, made sure that I was as inconsequential and innocuous as possible. I'd even slipped into my plainest pale blue clothing so as not to stand out in the crowd. How was I to know that on film, that choice only made my hair look redder and wilder than ever and that I was like a candle with a bright, out-of-control flame at its tip?

While everyone else acted like the video crew was a group of visiting rock stars, Dr. Reynolds approached them as if they were lice on a dog. And I was the most offensive louse of all.

"I'm sorry, sir." I began to apologize. "I know this is upsetting to you but…"

The look he gave me could have frozen molten

lava. I've never known blue eyes to be as frigid as the ones he had for me.

I opened my mouth to say something but shut it again. There was no use trying to defend myself to this man, none whatsoever. My only job is to be the best doula and birthing coach I can be to Penny. No scathing looks from Clay Reynolds are going to stop me from that.

"Molly," Penny beckoned me over once we were in the room. "What's wrong with Dr. Reynolds? Isn't he feeling well? He looks very pale."

It is an odd turn of events when the patient worries about the doctor's well-being. Penny, however, was justified in her observation. Clay *was* pasty and his eyes had taken on a haunted expression that seemed vastly out of proportion to what was happening around him.

"What are you doing now, Molly?" one of the camera crew asked. Every move I made was of interest to them. I live in fear of needing to go to the bathroom.

"Rubbing Penny's shoulders. She finds it relaxing." I looked into the camera, trying to appear happy rather than miserable. "I try ahead of time to discover which things are comforting to a mother. She also likes ice packs on the back of her neck, grape Popsicles and Elvis music, particularly 'All Shook Up.'"

At that moment Clay walked in and strode toward the bed. "Penny, I just want to check…"

"Hey, Doc, give us another minute with the doula, okay?" the cameraman said. "I've got another question—"

Clay rounded on the man and I thought he was going to say or do something that we'd all regret later but managed to pull it together just in time. "Sorry, friend, but my patient and this baby come first in my book. If you don't mind…"

Reluctantly the man backed away.

"Into the hall," Clay snapped. "Take the three-ring circus into the hallway, please."

"Go ahead, Molly, answer the man's questions," Penny encouraged. "I don't need you right now."

"But I'm not here to—"

"Go," Clay ordered sharply. "This is not the time or place for a crowd."

So we went.

Unfortunately, the more unobtrusive I tried to become, the more interested in me the video crew seemed to be. If things could get worse, I didn't know how. The only ones who seemed to be enjoying this were Penny and Pete, who were thrilled with the idea of a professional videotape of their baby's birth.

James Peter Higgins was born at 2:15 a.m. The crew interviewed the proud papa while I made sure Penny didn't need me any longer and managed to exit the room unobserved. By using hidden stair-wells I escaped the hospital unnoticed. The film crew would have to find me tomorrow if they wanted to debrief me.

Unfortunately one person *had* noticed me leave and he was lying in wait beside my car.

Clay leaned against the driver's door looking ominous.

"Clay, I…"

"I realize that you weren't responsible for this, Molly." His voice was low and dangerous, but he was imperturbably calm. That was even more alarming than his fury. "It doesn't change the fact that we had a fiasco on our hands in there tonight."

"It wasn't a fiasco!" I was exhausted and my fuse short. "Penny and Peter are ecstatic. Their baby is perfect and beautiful. The crew was not terribly intrusive, and I believe it will be a good documentary. Just because you don't believe in the subject matter, doesn't mean it's unimportant. Maybe this is more about your ego than anything else. You want everyone to believe that the doctor always knows best, right?"

His expression darkened but he didn't lash out. "It will promote a dangerous practice. Birthing rooms should not have a carnival atmosphere."

"I do not promote a 'carnival atmosphere.' That's just insulting!" My distress turned to fury. "You are so unfair!"

"And you are innocent and naive. You have no idea what can happen—"

"But you do?" The pilot light on my Irish temper began to heat. "I know you're well educated and have a medical degree but sometime you've got to realize that birth is natural. Women have assisted other women with the miracle for hundreds of years, all around the world. Maybe it's you who is out of touch, have you ever thought of that?"

He looked at me pityingly.

Pity rubs me the wrong way, like petting a cat from tail to head rather than the other way around.

"Just stay out of my way, Molly. That's all I ask." He pushed himself away from my car, rolled the knots from his shoulders and rubbed his neck. Then he walked away, leaving me sputtering furiously.

Not only was I angry, but worse, I was hurt. I stared at his retreating back knowing that something that could have been quite wonderful had slipped through my hands. Then I got into my car and drove two blocks before pulling over to have a good, hard cry.

I'd gotten Clay's message loud and clear. He wants me out of his way and his life. What will make him happiest is to never see me again.

I hiccuped, blew my nose and was grateful for the darkness. If a filming crew turned up now to ask me what the doula was doing, I'd have frightened them all away.

I was thankful, for the moment at least, that Clay didn't know what was happening behind the scenes concerning Doula Central. Charles, in his enthusiasm, had encouraged several other obstetricians to call me with their questions. I was beginning to get the feeling that the center was coming together without me, like bees swarming everywhere to become a cloud. I hope I don't get stung.

What adds insult to the injury of falling in love with Clay and knowing he wants nothing to do with me is being forced to tolerate Hugh and Lissy's sappy courtship. It is, unfortunately, happening right under my nose.

Hugh: "Get me some lemonade, will you, sweetie?"

Lissy: "Of course, darling. Can I share yours or should I get my own?"

Hugh: "My lips are yours, lovie."

Lissy: "Hughy, you are so cute."

Hugh: "You're the cute one…."

Molly: "Stop it! My teeth are rotting from all the sugary drivel! If you're going to act like lovebirds, do it somewhere that I can't hear it. I'm getting nauseous."

"Temper, temper, sis," Hugh chided. "We can't help it if you're disenchanted with love. You don't want a man like Clay Reynolds, anyway. You deserve better."

"Who said I 'wanted' him at all?"

"'My only love sprang from my only hate! Too early seen unknown, and known too late.'" Tony stopped eating Hägen-Daz out of a carton long enough to quote a little Shakespeare.

I turned on him. "How can you stand this mushy, lovey-dovey talk?"

"I'm a poet at heart, remember? I've started

writing love sonnets just for the fun of it. I like the form. I'm hoping these two will inspire me."

I flung myself onto the couch, and Hildy came over to investigate my distress. She stuck her cold, wet nose into my neck, then licked away the errant tear that had escaped and run down my cheek. "I'm surrounded by dysfunction and no one else sees it."

"You're the one who has been wearing the same sweats for three days," Hugh pointed out. "And eating nothing but tapioca pudding and pepper jack cheese."

"I'm not hungry for anything else, thank you very much."

"I've known you a long time, Molly. That's all you ever eat when you're depressed or in love."

"Tapioca pudding?" Tony sounded horrified. "Maybe we aren't suited for each other after all. I don't like tapioca pudding."

"You mean there is a food you don't like?" Lissy came at Tony with a spoon and took a bite of his ice cream.

"Stop it, all of you!"

Hugh put a finger to his lips. "We'll go outside and leave you to mope, Molly. Let us know when you're done." And they all trooped cheerfully out the back door to my patio. Even Hildy and Geranium followed them, leaving me to stew in my own juices.

"Lord," I murmured when they'd gone, "forgive me for this mood I'm in. If Clay isn't the man for me—and it's become perfectly clear that he isn't—

help me to accept that and move forward. I don't want a war on Bradshaw turf. My life's in Your hands. I forget that sometimes. Fortunately You never fail to remember me."

I sighed and sat up. I needed to apologize to my friends for my grumpy, petulant behavior. Then I'll figure out what to do, now that I've given my heart to someone who doesn't want it.

Chapter Twenty-Eight

I quit making tapioca on day six, the day in the meeting room at Bradshaw Medical that I saw some raw footage of the documentary video and a few snippets of rough cut from the first day's filming. Clay lurked in the background, hovering near the door in order to escape quickly if he couldn't tolerate what he saw.

"It's amazing!" I blurted before remembering that I was one of only a few laypeople viewing the video. The rest were Bradshaw's elite—the board and the heads of several departments.

Charles Hancock and Emily, who'd been invited as a guest, nodded in agreement. Emily wiped a tear from her eye as the room erupted in applause.

"I wasn't sure they could actually capture what happens between a mother and her doula," I admitted, "but it's there already. The film will be beautiful."

One of the older doctors on staff, Dr. Francis, turned to me. "Why haven't we seen more of you, Molly? Mothers should be clamoring for your services. It makes perfect sense to me."

"That's something I wanted to mention." Charles Hancock stood to take the floor. Much to my chagrin, he told the entire group about our conversation, the ideas I had for implementing Doula Central, and he forcefully endorsed the idea.

"According to Molly, this could be up and running in no time. She knows practically every doula in the city already, or knows someone who does. Office space, a database, a few flyers in the Obstetrics Department and Molly's expertise in implementing her vision, why—"

"It's not quite that easy, sir." I tried to stop him, but Charles began waxing eloquent about the birth of his son.

"It also makes our job a little easier," Dr. Wickler, a pediatrician, commented agreeably. "The fewer C-sections the better, I say." He glanced up as a woman with a coffee cart entered the room. Several people got up to head for the pastries, still discussing the film. Emily and I worked our way toward a quiet corner of the room. Clay was no longer present, but I had no idea when he'd chosen to leave.

"It's a hit!" Emily tented her fingers and put them under her chin. "Isn't it wonderful?"

"I had no idea they'd make sense of all that footage, but they managed. Clay didn't make it easy for them."

"How are things going?" Emily asked. "Better?"

"If you're referring to Clay, no. Everything else is great."

"Have you seen him since…you know?"

Emily's husband had brought home the word that Clay Bradshaw had put up a fierce argument over the documentary and had indicated that he would have nothing to do with encouraging doulas for his patients. He'd been so adamant that Charles had warned her that if the documentary wasn't "something really special" it was likely that Clay's attitude would douse any keenness there'd been for the idea.

Fortunately—or unfortunately, depending on one's perspective—the video is remarkably good.

I didn't want to discuss Clay, so I asked the question most sure to divert Emily's attention. "How's the baby?"

"Adorable, of course. Perfect. Brilliant. Amazing." Emily grinned. "Did you expect anything less?"

"You're glowing."

"I didn't know I could be this happy, Molly. I feel so…complete." She looked me over with a keen eye. "And you feel very *in*complete right now. All the sparkle and zest you usually exude has dimmed."

"Just a disappointment or two, that's all. I'll get over it."

I put my hand on Emily's arm. "The last thing you need to do is worry about me. I'll be fine. I made the mistake of building up my hopes over someone who wasn't as interested in me as I was in him, that's all. It doesn't matter. It was over before it even started."

What I didn't add was that her husband had probably put the final nail in the coffin of any relationship with Clay. Because of Charles, I can probably get what I want—a doula clearinghouse at Bradshaw—but it will be at Clay's expense and over his protests.

I left the hospital not feeling any better than I had when I'd arrived. Even the wonderful reception to the film hadn't cheered me as much as I'd hoped. Clay's disapproval of the whole process had tarnished my enthusiasm more than I cared to admit.

I suppose that's why I didn't greet them with much eagerness when Lissy and my brother Hugh arrived at my house, holding hands and acting gooey as caramel on a hot day. It didn't seem to matter, however. They were too giddy to notice my gloom.

Hugh looks happier than I've seen him in months and Lissy positively radiates joy.

"What's up?" I untangled myself from Hildy, who'd been lying beside me on the couch.

"We wanted to tell you first. Hugh and I are getting married!"

I looked from my brother to my friend, thunderstruck. "But you've barely started to date! How can you know…"

They hung on to each other like Velcro as Hugh spoke. "Sis, Lissy and I have dated everyone who is *wrong* for us. After all that experience, it's easy to tell when someone is right. Besides, it's not like we just met. We've both hung out at your house for years."

"I'll give you that. You've been eating my food and commandeering my television remote longer than I care to think about. Maybe you are slow learners. Why didn't you figure it out earlier? You could have avoided that whole tree incident which, by the way, you may never live down."

"A small price to pay for love." Hugh kissed Lissy on the tip of the nose.

"When's the big day?"

"Soon," Lissy said. "Will you be my bridesmaid?" She flung her arms around me. "Now you'll be my sister-in-law as well as my best friend!"

Hugh then embraced both of us at once, engaging us in an emotional group hug. That's when Tony walked in.

"A lovefest without me? What's going on?" Without asking the reason for this outpouring of affection, he congenially slapped my brother on the back. Hugh lost his footing and the lump of us toppled over and sprawled onto the couch.

"That was fun," Tony commented. "What are we celebrating?"

"Hugh and Lissy are getting married."

"'In time the savage bull doth bear the yoke,'" Tony recited. "Congratulations."

Lissy gave him a dirty look. "You could have picked a better quote, Tony. I'm hardly a yoke to be borne."

He grinned at her. "'All that glisters is not gold.'"

Lissy ignored him. "Isn't it wonderful?"

"It couldn't have happened to a nicer, more gullible person."

Lissy swatted at him. "Behave."

"I can't. I'm in a pretty good mood myself." He turned to look at me. "My sister thinks she's pregnant." His dark brown eyes sparkled. "I'm going to be an uncle."

I felt tears come to my eyes. "Oh, Tony, I'm so happy for her."

"She told me to tell you that you were right about that 'deferred hope' thing."

"I thought she didn't believe it."

"She looked the verse up in the Bible because she wanted to read it in context."

"And?"

"I'm not quite sure. Gina said that one verse just led to another until she'd read several chapters. She told me it was time she got reacquainted with her faith. Gina has always depended on herself and she's beginning to realize that it's not enough." Tony looked thoughtful. "So God used this barren time to bring my sister around to Him again.

"You were right, Molly. God's timing is different than ours but He's working for us all the time."

God's timing. He's working fast on the doula center, that's for sure. I'd notified a few doulas of the potential opportunity at Bradshaw and it had taken off like wildfire. The board had agreed to provide a room, rent free, for three months so we could test the idea. Doula Central was going to happen whether I was involved or not. There were enough volunteers eager to help get the place up and running, work on the doula directory and promote the concept so that, had I wanted, I could have sat in the background eating bonbons.

Instead, I sat on the couch half listening to Hugh, Lissy and Tony babble about all the good news in their lives. My brother is going to be a husband; my best friend, a wife; and Tony, an uncle. And me? If I look at the trend, I'm going to be a lonesome old maid with a pig, a dog and a hundred children that aren't my own.

"This is such amazing news!" Lissy burbled. "Molly, have you got any food in the refrigerator? We need to have a party."

"There are almonds, peanut butter, celery, mayonnaise, bread and cheddar cheese. Help yourself, make a cake."

Lissy ignored my snide comment and pulled a bucket of ice cream out of the freezer. "So much has happened that I can hardly take it all in!"

"There's more," Tony said, "if you'd quit chattering so I can get a word in edgewise."

Lissy stopped dishing ice cream; Hugh closed his mouth and I watched Tony expectantly.

"I'm going back to college."

Of all the things he could have said, that was the last I'd expected.

"Why?" Hugh asked. "You've got a great job, a new promotion and everything a fellow works to achieve."

Tony sat down at the kitchen table and thrummed his fingers on the top. "I'm not quitting my job. Not now, at least."

"What brought this on?" I asked suspiciously.

"Remember that bet we made and the date I went on?"

"The woman in the library stacks?"

"She's a college professor. She talked me into taking a night class on Shakespeare. I might take an English literature class, too. Since I'm charge nurse now, I have a defined schedule and I know I can fit it in."

"With a little help from the professor?" Lissy inquired slyly.

"She's a friend," Tony corrected her but looked far too happy about it for that status to last long.

"What about Wanda? You're going to break her heart."

"I don't think so. She's interested in someone else." Tony looked smug. Too smug.

"It must be someone outside the hospital," Lissy commented. "Everyone there is wise to Wanda."

"I introduced her to someone, and she took to him like a duck to water."

"Where'd you find this lucky guy?" I asked. It takes a lot of manliness and diplomacy to handle Wanda.

"At the Cassidy bash."

"One of our relatives?" Hugh blurted. "But who…"

"Your brother Liam asked me if I was interested in selling my bike. I'd been thinking of upgrading to something with a little more power so I told him he was welcome to look at it and shoot me an offer. He met me at the hospital after work yesterday to check it out and…"

"…Wanda spied him and claimed him for her own," Lissy finished the sentence.

"She thinks his red hair is cute." Tony rubbed his hands together with naughty glee. "She really fell for him and has decided to put all her energy in Liam's direction. Apparently, I'm off her list entirely. She feels I'm 'elusive and distant.'"

Hugh and I stared at each other, wide smiles spreading across our faces. Liam and Wanda? This was better than any prank either of us could have thought to play on our brother. Besides, it might do Liam some good to meet a woman who is tough-minded like my mother and his sisters, someone who won't give up on him too easily.

Serves him right, too. He's been relentless in teasing Hugh about that tree incident. Liam needs something else to think about.

Heh, heh, heh.

Chapter Twenty-Nine

The silence has been deafening from the Reynolds camp.

I understand, but I still unrealistically harbor a faint hope that Noah might be permitted to call me. Tomorrow is his birthday, after all. I'd like nothing better than to watch him open his packages—especially the ant farm.

Maybe I'll just pull the covers over my head and go back to sleep.

I might have, too, if Hildy and Geranium hadn't been standing in the doorway of the bedroom staring at me.

"Quit looking at me," I mumbled. "Go away. I enjoy being depressed."

They didn't budge.

I threw a pillow over my head but Hildy jumped onto the bed and nosed it away.

"Can't anyone leave me alone?"

Not only was I being tormented by my dog and my pig, Lissy, Tony and several of my siblings had called to check up on me. None of them bought in to the message I'd left on my answering machine.

"Hi, this is Molly. I'm unavailable right now. I've heard rumors that *Doula Day* has Oscar potential and I'm out buying a dress. Don't call me, I'll call you."

I should have just said "leave me alone" since subtleties are rarely acknowledged in my family.

I need time to work through the roller coaster of emotions that have flooded my system lately. *Doula Day,* though *not* Oscar material, pleased everyone involved. Everyone but Clay, that is. It only deepened the chasm between us, as has Doula Central, which blossomed in front of Clay's eyes with him having no graceful way to stop it. The first women and doulas would be matched soon.

Hugh, Lissy and Tony are a little too euphoric for me most of the time, and the rest of the family is just plain annoying.

"Okay, Molly," I told myself. "Quit pouting and get up. Clay and Noah are history. Deal with it."

I rolled out of bed, and my feet hit the floor just as the telephone rang. I almost let the answering machine pick up, but impulsively I reached for the receiver. "Hello, I'm fine, thanks," I said, hoping to beat whoever it was to the punch. "I'm busy right now but…"

"Molly?" a small voice said. "It's me, Noah."

"Hi, Noah. I didn't expect it to be you."

"You sound weird," he said bluntly.

"Thanks. You aren't the first to say that. What can I do for you?"

"Are you coming to my birthday party?"

"I don't think so, buddy, I…"

"Daddy said your invitation came back 'cause we had your address wrong on the envelope and he thought it was probably too late now but—" he took a deep breath "—you can come, can't you?"

That's clever, I thought. Clay likely wrote the wrong address on the envelope in order to keep me away. That's illegal. Maybe I could report him for tampering with the U.S. Mail.

"Thanks, sweetie, but…"

"Please?"

Hard-hearted as I wanted to be, I couldn't resist the tremulous voice on the other end of the line. It isn't Noah's fault his father is impossible.

He caught my hesitation. "It's at our house tomorrow. It starts at two o'clock. Dad says 'be there or be square.'"

Now I wonder where he'd heard that. Surely his father wasn't quoting me—or was he?

It took me all morning to look appropriately casual for my first meeting with Clay since the board had gone over his head to make the Doula Center happen. By the time I'd settled on black pants, white shirt and a cinnamon-colored jacket that echoed the color of my hair, it was nearly one o'clock. I studied myself in the mirror, pirouetting, looking for obvious defects. None visible. Apparently the only holes and snags were in my heart.

I picked out Clay's home the moment I turned onto his street. Two-story, traditional, classy, expensive and pristine. The yard looked like an ad for a garden shop. His constrained black Mercedes was parked in the driveway. Only a small blue ball and a yellow plastic bat abandoned on the lawn hinted that a child resided within. I hoped that sushi wasn't on Noah's birthday menu.

There were several cars already parked along the street, Mercedeses, BMWs, one Porsche and a Jaguar. And here I am, a VW kind of girl.

If it weren't for the memory of Noah's small voice on the phone yesterday, I might not have walked up the sidewalk and rung the bell. I clutched Noah's gift, a set of face and body paints to use in the bathtub and a crazy Dr. Seuss–type hat I'd knitted with him in mind. I wasn't quite sure if I'd chosen the paints more for Noah's own enjoyment or the idea that it might drive his meticulous father crazy.

Lord, what's gotten into me? Forgive me for being petty, and give me grace for this occasion.

Then the door flung open and Noah erupted out of the house and flung himself at my legs. "You came! You came!"

"I couldn't miss your birthday, now, could I? Not

a special guy like you." My heart warmed at the small, delighted face. The difficult decision had been the right decision after all.

Only then did I notice an older gentleman standing in the doorway behind Noah. He was a round, pleasant man with a faint air of Santa Claus about him. "You must be Molly. Noah's talked about you nonstop. The rest of his guests are getting a complex. Please come in."

I warmed to the man immediately; his affable charm was irresistible.

Noah took my hand to lead me toward the festivities, but the older gentleman put his hand on my arm. "Sometimes storm clouds hide the sun," he said cryptically. Then he winked and walked away.

Maybe Clay's family was as loony as mine after all.

The kitchen and attached family room were full of people, mostly grown-ups. Noah pointed through the patio doors to the outside where the play yard sat in all its glory. "My dad got it for me."

"Excellent."

He crooked his finger so that I would lean down to let him whisper in my ear. "Come to my room later to see my ant farm. It's not a puppy, but maybe next year."

Ah, yes, hope deferred.

The older gentleman appeared again at my side, this time with a crystal goblet full of strawberry punch.

"My grandson seems to be hiding somewhere.

Don't worry, he'll come around. This is always a difficult day for him."

Grandson?

"Excuse me, but I'm afraid I don't know your name even though you seem to know mine." I stuck out my hand. "Nice to meet you..."

"Everett. Everett Bradshaw." He twinkled at me genially. "And you are the famous Molly Cassidy, the doula who put Bradshaw Medical on the map."

"Dr. Bradshaw!" I felt my throat constrict. "*The* Dr. Bradshaw?"

"One of the many." He chuckled. "My family is swarming with them, actually." He crooked his finger much like Noah had and beckoned me deeper into the room. "There's someone here who is anxious to see you."

I followed him feeling numb, like Alice must have felt when she stumbled into Wonderland.

I drew to a halt when I saw who it was who'd been waiting for me to arrive.

"Mattie? What are you doing here?"

The delightful woman from the nursing home, Hildy's favorite and mine, was ensconced in a richly padded leather recliner. She had an afghan over her legs and her hands folded serenely in her lap. "Hello, Molly, so good to see you. I don't suppose you brought Hildy with you?"

All I could do was dumbly shake my head.

"I didn't realize for a long time that you knew my great-nephew Clay," Mattie continued. "Noah kept talking about this wonderful 'Molly' but I didn't make the connection until recently."

Nephew? Clay? Mattie B. Olson. Mattie Bradshaw Olson!

This was the aunt that Noah went to visit? The aunt who'd taught Clay how to shop?

"I had no idea."

"My great-nephew is too closemouthed for his own good. He wasn't always that way, of course, but after Katherine…"

I must have looked like a blank slate because Mattie frowned. "You do know about Katherine, don't you?"

At that moment Emily Hancock walked into my line of vision. She was carrying her baby in her arms.

"I don't think she knows, Mattie. You know how Clay is. He clams up just about the time he should be talking."

Mattie gave a snort of disapproval. "Where is that boy's head? He's got to quit living his life in fear and old memories." She waved a hand in my direction. "Tell the poor girl what we're talking about."

"Emily," I began, "why…"

"Charles has been friends with both Clay and Everett as long as any of us can remember. Everett is responsible for bringing my husband onto the board."

No wonder she dared to talk back to Clay when no one else did.

"There's a lot more to Clay's story than he admits. It's time he began to talk about his past,

Molly. You've been a victim of it without even realizing it."

A victim of what?

"Clay's wife, Katherine, died in childbirth when
Noah was born."

I closed my eyes as a wave of sorrow flooded
through me. *Overprotective of his patients, fanatical about protocol, no distractions during delivery,
the birthing room is no place for a crowd.*

So Clay's motivation isn't to ruin me. It is to
prevent what happened to him from ever happening again. Everett had said that today was always a
difficult day for Clay. Not only is it his son's birthday, it marks the greatest loss of his life.

Mattie patted the seat of the chair next to hers.
"Sit down before you fall down, dear."

I did as I was told.

Emily continued to fill me in on the mystery
that was Clay.

"He wasn't the attending physician, of course.
And Katherine's death was due to an aneurysm
which none of them knew about. It wasn't connected
to the pregnancy and could have happened at any
time, but because it happened just after delivery…"

"They are forever connected in his mind,"
Mattie concluded.

Poor, poor Clay. My heart ached for him. And for
Noah. "I had no idea."

"Of course you didn't. Clay never speaks of it."
Mattie's eyes grew sad. "But he lives his life trying

to make up for her unexpected death. He blames himself for not seeing what was happening to her. He thinks that if he hadn't gotten swept up in the activity in the birthing room, he might have noticed something that might have saved her."

"But how could he?"

"He couldn't, of course. He knows very well that aneurysms can happen without warning. That still doesn't prevent him from attempting to control everything during every birth he is a part of. He's leading with his heart on these issues, Molly, not his logical mind."

Chapter Thirty

"This is the first 'real' party that Noah has ever had," Emily said. "Clay has always insisted that Noah's birthday be celebrated in a restaurant."

"Nothing too cozy or homey," Mattie added sadly. "It needed to be somewhere that kept the memories at bay."

"I had no idea."

"We're a family of Christians," Mattie said. "It's been hard to see Clay struggle with his faith. I'd like to thank you, Molly, for showing him that faith and adversity can cohabit."

"I don't understand."

"After Katherine died, Clay decided… Maybe you'd better have him tell you."

I turned to see what Mattie was looking at. Clay filled the doorway looking tired but not unhappy. He strode across the floor and took my hand. "I'm glad you came. I told Noah I didn't think you would."

"It's hard to keep a good woman down."

"You are definitely a good woman, Molly."

He tipped his head toward a door on the far side of the room. "Come."

I trailed him into his study, which is dark and woody, with a fireplace flanked by leather wing-backed chairs. The shelves were filled with books, the spines marching in a perfect row. Clay didn't take chances with anything, even his bookshelves.

He pointed toward a chair. "Sit."

"Is this a business meeting?"

"You could call it that." He opened his hands and splayed his fingers in a gesture of acquiescence. "Now you know the truth about me. You deserve honesty. I've resisted you at every turn without ever allowing you to know why. You took the brunt of my frustration. It wasn't fair, Molly, and I'm sorry."

His voice faltered. "It's been a difficult few years for me, but you, with your energy and persever-ance, made me see that life is not just about trying to 'fix' the past but also about improving the future. I'll tell you whatever you need to know about me. I want you to understand where I've come from. You warrant that much. Ask me anything."

The great Dr. Clay Bradshaw Reynolds was giving me carte blanche into his life and only one question came to my mind.

"Did you keep your promise? About the faith thing, I mean."

He shook his head as if utterly baffled. "You are

something else, Molly. I'm not sure what, but definitely something else."

"It's important to me, Clay."

"Let's just say God and I are in discussion. I'm beginning to see things that I couldn't have six months ago. Then I didn't think it did me any good to believe. Katherine was gone. I had a child without a mother and the profession I loved now only reminded me of what I'd lost."

He shifted in his chair. "At least, that's what I thought until you came along."

"I don't understand."

"I've never experienced an opponent quite like you before, Molly. Stubborn and opinionated as I can be about my position on birthing-room protocol, you're even more so. I set out to change how births are done at Bradshaw, not knowing what a persistent foe I'd find in you. Frankly, I was as difficult as I could be in the hospital because I wanted to scare you off."

"I don't scare easily."

"No, but you did 'fire' me if you recall."

I thought of our time together—at Al and Bess's restaurant, the St. Croix, even the Ax. "Why were you so nice to me outside the hospital when you felt so strongly about having me gone?"

"Because I liked you. Every time we were together I grew to like you even more. You have no idea what a challenge you posed for me. How could I run you off and yet keep you in my life?"

"How does this tie together with faith?"

"God is your jet fuel, Molly. He's what you run on. He makes it possible for you to keep forgiving and going forward." Clay pulled a chair close to me and picked up my hand and couched it gently in his own.

"You had Noah wrapped around your pinkie from the day you met. He kept pestering about the Noah-and-the-Ark business so I told him what I knew of it. Then he wanted more. It's pretty hard to tell your son Bible stories when your own information is rusty, so I thought I'd read a little…."

"And God dragged you in through the back door?"

"You told me once that you couldn't be un-equally yoked with someone. I knew that if faith wasn't palatable to me anymore, there would never be more between us. So I tested the waters."

"And?" My heart was attempting to pound its way out of my chest and my ears were full of thrumming.

"I found them warm and soothing. When I lost my wife, I also relinquished my faith. I shouldn't have. Now even if you tell me you aren't interested in a relationship with me, I'll still continue to dip into that particular pool."

Pursue a relationship with me?

"I need to restart my life. Today's party is a step. Until now I've never felt it was right to be happy on Noah's birthday. That was unfair of me. I have a wonderful little boy to celebrate."

My tongue went missing. When I found it again,

I stammered, "There's lots to celebrate these days. Hugh and Lissy are in love and planning to marry. And Tony's found the girl of his dreams, a college professor."

Clay looked at me with tenderness—and a twinkle in his eye. "Remember when you said Tony thought you might be susceptible to my 'latent charm'?"

I nodded dumbly, not sure where he was going with this but eaten with curiosity.

The smile grew wider. "Are you still? Susceptible, I mean."

"I could be, possibly, under the right circumstances," I managed to say, already thoroughly hypnotized by that charm.

"Even if we don't agree on something as important as our view of doulas?"

"You're a smart man, Clay. You'll see the light sometime. I'm a patient woman. The real question is, why would you *want* to get tangled up with me? I'm trouble. You say it yourself. My family is a nest of jokers and pranksters. I live with a pig and I paint pictures the size of Volkswagens."

"Those *are* the reasons I want to get 'tangled up' with you. You're full of life and forgiveness and pigheadedness and joy...."

For once, I thought, as Clay moved toward me and his lips met mine, I'd take pigheadedness as a compliment.

Geranium would be so proud.

Epilogue

Hugh and Lissy got married under the old elm tree in my parents' backyard, right beneath the limb they'd been caught on just weeks earlier.

Tony brought his professor—Janna—to the wedding. She seems lovely. Even if Tony doesn't get straight As at school, I think he'll receive them in his personal life.

Clay and I are next to be married, as soon as we can completely settle on the place, attendants, food and honeymoon location. I'm campaigning for a traditional ceremony at my home church, the same food we serve at our family get-togethers and a month in Ireland. Oh, yes, and Lissy, Tony, Hildy and Geranium as bridesmaids. My sister Krissy, offered to make Geranium a bridesmaid's dress. It's hard to turn down an offer like that.

Noah can hardly wait for the ceremony because

he feels it will then be official that Hildy is "his" dog as well as mine.

Clay, for some odd reason, thinks we should be married beneath the Ax at the mall. He's promoting a formal dinner at some spendy restaurant and wants his only attendants to be Noah and his grandfather Everett. He's good with the honeymoon in Ireland.

We're getting better at negotiation and compromise every day. God's fingerprints are all over our lives, that's apparent. Tentatively we've agreed on my home church as the site for the wedding. It will be catered by Al and Bess with my aunt Siobhan's input on family favorites. I've okayed Noah and Everett as groomsmen and Clay has said yes to Lissy and Tony. Hildy and Geranium will have to get over it.

We'll live in Clay's house because there's room for a studio for my art. The pet door and fence for the yard are already installed. The first thing I did was go into his library and make the books on his shelves less tidy.

That's another thing Clay will have to get used to. I love him more than words can say but his world needs a little shaking up.

I'm just the woman to do it.

QUESTIONS FOR DISCUSSION

1. Molly is a doula. Were you familiar with doulas before reading the book? Would you consider hiring a doula or encourage a friend to do so?

2. Emily is expecting her first child at forty-five. Another of Molly's clients is still a teenager. What would you consider the ideal age to start a family? How old is "too old"?

3. The trend now is to have a lot of family around during labor. How do you feel about having family or friends present at this time? Do you like the idea or would you prefer the "old-fashioned" way—with only medical staff present?

4. Geranium is Molly's pride and joy. Would you consider having a potbelly pig as a pet? Why or why not?

5. Sometimes doulas have to spend time managing the people around the laboring mother. Would you consider hiring a doula for your husband? Why or why not?

6. Molly has a boisterous, playful family. They take pleasure in meddling in one another's

business. Is your family like that? If not, would you enjoy that kind of relationship with your family? If not, why not?

7. Molly loves babies and the elderly. Do you have any elderly friends and relatives with whom you enjoy spending time? What kinds of things do you do together?

8. What is the best thing about having a friend who is much older than you?

9. Tony, Lissy and Molly have a conversation about "hope deferred." Was there a time in your life when you wanted something desperately and even prayed for it and the answer was "no"? What did you learn from this experience? Do you agree with Molly that sometimes hope deferred can lead to bigger blessings?

10. Lissy and Hugh are afraid to show their affection for each other because they have both been hurt so many times. Do you ever hold back your emotions for that reason?

11. Do you know anyone like Tony—a person who is equally comfortable with men and women and can so easily make and keep friends? What are their secrets? Would you like to be more

like that? If so, what is one step you could take to make this happen?

12. Clay is a conundrum. He wants to be with Molly anywhere but in the birthing room. Do you know anyone who is so determined to keep his or her personal and business life separate? What does this do for/to a relationship?